Charming the Spy

Scandals and Spies, Book 4

Leighann Dobbs
Harmony Williams

This is a work of fiction.

None of it is real. All names, places, and events are products of the author's imagination. Any resemblance to real names, places, or events are purely coincidental, and should not be construed as being real.

Chapter One

Tenwick Abbey
January, 1807

Edgar Catterson III, Catt to his friends, paused in the threshold to the Duke of Tenwick's office. Gideon Graylocke, the duke's younger brother and Catt's closest friend, leaned against the mahogany sideboard beneath a rectangular painting of a centuries-old fox hunt. Whatever the duke was saying to him, he didn't look happy about it.

"That's hardly her fault. Felicia and I did what you assigned us to do."

With a sigh, the duke ducked his head and fingered the white streak in his black hair. Already several inches shorter than Giddy—though who wasn't—Morgan Graylocke's slumped posture made him look even shorter. He pinched the bridge of his nose.

"I know. I'm not accusing you of wrongdoing. I'm just...frustrated. This spy has been operating beneath our noses for over seven months now. We're locked in a losing battle with Napoleon and finding this spy could be instrumental to turning the tide. We *need* this."

Spy? Catt narrowed his eyes. About three months ago, Giddy had revealed the secret of Tenwick Abbey. The ducal estate served as the training grounds for new British spies, trained by none other than the duke himself, who happened to be second-in-command to the Lord Commander of Spies. More than half of the fifty-odd servants at Tenwick Abbey were spies—new, retired, or between assignments. For a brief time last October, Gideon—also in service to the Crown—had feared that one of them was not loyal to Britain.

Thankfully, the matter had been resolved, but that day had opened an entirely new world to Catt. A world of danger and intrigue, a world he was now enmeshed in, having recently completed his training to become an official spy of the Crown. When his best friend begged for his help, Catt hadn't been able to deny him. After that, there had been no chance of turning back.

The fact that the Duke of Tenwick was here, at the ancestral estate instead of in London with his very pregnant wife, was troublesome. What had Giddy accomplished—or not—that had led to this visit?

Glancing up, Morgan noticed Catt idling in the doorway. He beckoned Catt forward. "Good, you're here. We can begin."

Begin what?

The duke retreated to the far wall of the office, behind a desk piled high with papers. His broad-shouldered figure cut off the cold winter light streaming in through the frosted panes of the window. Motioning for Catt to take one of the two chairs on the other side of the desk, Morgan sat.

"It's about bloody time."

Catt faltered as he crossed the Oriental rug. He caught his balance and kept from falling flat on his face as the occupant of the armchair leaned around the high back to glare at him.

Joy Rockwood, Gideon's other close friend and the lead gardener of Tenwick Abbey, crossed her arms across her bosom and leaned back into the chair, disappearing from sight. Catt swallowed against his suddenly dry mouth. He should have known that if he'd been called in, Rocky would have been as well. She'd been brought into the spying fold at the same time as Catt.

Unfortunately, she hated him. The feeling was mutual. Rocky was belligerent, accusatory, loudmouthed, and quite frankly, a brilliant botanist. Just because she was the equal of Catt or Giddy didn't mean that Catt cared to stomach her presence. They'd worked together in the past out of necessity. For the sake of everyone's sanity, it was best they avoid each other as much as possible.

Since turning on his heel and leaving the room was not an option when the Duke of Tenwick called an official meeting of spies, Catt adjusted his cravat and lowered himself into the seat next to Rocky.

He didn't look at her, but he could feel the glower she leveled in his direction. It raised the hairs on the back of his neck. He balled his fists, willing himself not to give her a reaction. It would only encourage her.

A flash of the ducal colors of azure and silver caught his eye. Reflexively, he glanced at the woman next to him. She patted down her trousers, snug against the womanly shape of her legs and hips. When she adjusted her shirt to better show the ducal crest of a stag rampant sewn onto the breast, the fabric pulled tight across the ample swell of her chest. She adjusted her spectacles and folded her hands in her lap. Her brown hair, hastily secured in a bun, escaped her coif to frame her cheeks.

Catt forced himself to look at the duke once more, if only to avoid staring at the prickly woman next to him. This wasn't the first time he'd seen her in men's clothes and he doubted it would be the last.

Straightening from his position near the mantle, Giddy crossed to perch on the corner of Morgan's desk. He crossed his long legs as he answered Catt's inquiry.

"I hope you recall the project Felicia and I were tasked to complete last October."

Catt nodded. A rustle to his left hailed movement from Rocky. He forced himself not to react, even though the awareness of her raised an uncomfortable prickle along his left arm.

The project in question had cost Giddy his orangery in a dangerous accident, including the exotic orchid he and Catt were attempting to coax to bloom. Without that project, Catt had been at a bit of a loss in the convening months. If not for his training as a spy, he would have been aimless. He tried not to think of it. That accident had been the catalyst which had convinced Giddy to reveal the secret of Tenwick Abbey to Catt and Rocky.

Although neither had been granted the details of the assignment which Giddy and his new wife had been tasked to complete, their lives hadn't been the same since.

When neither party spoke, Gideon glanced at his brother. The duke nodded. Running his fingers through his hair, Giddy faced forward again.

"Felicia and I created the truth serum."

Catt raised his eyebrows. "The research that she published in *Chemists Quarterly*?"

Giddy nodded.

"The reason that you called her a crackpot?"

A muscle in Giddy's clean-shaven jaw twitched. "I might remind you that you are speaking of my wife."

Rocky sniggered.

Catt glared at her before turning back to his friend. "Obviously you don't feel that way anymore."

Morgan leaned back in his chair and raised an eyebrow, as if to say, *Are you quite done?*

Clearing his throat, Catt adjusted his cravat once more. He swallowed before speaking. "It works? The serum, that is." A year ago, Giddy had been adamant that it wouldn't. In fact, he had been adamant that F. Albright was a fool.

Of course, that had been before the two had met in person and he'd been captivated by her beauty. Catt had seen the attraction between them from the moment he'd been introduced to Felicia, not that Giddy had been willing to admit it at the time. Somehow, they'd managed to put their differences aside and complete the impossible.

Gideon nodded. "It works."

"It does." Morgan rubbed at the white streak by his temple. "Unfortunately, it hasn't brought the answers we'd hoped."

Catt pinched his lips together and sat back. What did he mean?

Fortunately, the information was vital enough that the duke didn't keep it to himself. "Last May, we captured a high-level French spy."

Rocky frowned. "That's a good thing, isn't it? You don't seem enthused by the notion."

Morgan grimaced. "It was a stroke of luck for Britain, or so I thought. We couldn't convince her to talk and give up the ringleader of the French spy network here in England. Monsieur V remained at large."

Crossing his arms, Giddy piped up. "That's why Felicia and I were tasked with creating the truth serum."

Morgan nodded. "It was. And the serum worked—she told us everything she knows. Ciphers to French codes I hadn't cracked yet, details of the assignments she'd been given, and of course all the information she knew about Monsieur V."

"So what's the problem?" Catt and Rocky both made a face as they spouted the same sentence. Catt hated to admit that he shared any commonalities with...her.

Ignoring their twin expressions, the duke informed, "I thought she'd been withholding information out of loyalty or fear. And she had been, what little she knew. She is our only link to Monsieur V, and she wasn't able to give us a better description of the man other than the fact that he is near six feet tall with an athletic build and usually clean-shaven with brown hair. No name, not even a possible age or a better description of his face. He could be one of thousands of men in London."

Catt shifted his position, suddenly uncomfortable. How was he supposed to help? Were he and Rocky destined to be sent on a wild goose chase, now that they'd been trained?

With a sigh, Morgan leaned back in his chair. He drummed his fingers on the desk top. "In the months since we've learned this information, we've managed to use her descriptions of the places where they've met and exchanged information to pinpoint the household we believe he is operating from."

Catt leaned forward. "That's encouraging, then. You've nearly found him."

Rocky scoffed. Catt gritted his teeth and ignored her.

Morgan shook his head. "All we suspect is that he's operating from within Lady Belhaven's household. I assume you've heard of her?"

"The genius behind the nursery that caters to everyone with even a lick of sense in *le bon ton?*" Catt raised his eyebrows. His family might not be of the same caliber as the Graylockes, but he'd been around them long enough to have learned the trappings of High Society. "I don't think men with titles accept proposals for their daughters anymore unless they come with a posy from Lady Belhaven."

"Exactly so." The drumming of Morgan's fingers increased in pace. "The deliveries provide the perfect excuse for her servants to be in any household in Mayfair."

Catt pressed his lips together as Morgan turned his attention to Rocky. She straightened, as though her spine had been affixed to a lamppost.

"I've had to field off multiple inquiries of buying your services over the years, Rocky. Your work around the estate is unparalleled."

Something sharp unfurled in Catt's chest. He clutched the arms of the chair to keep from crossing his arms defensively. He knew that Rocky was a talented botanist; she, Giddy, and he exchanged ideas and information all the time. It shouldn't come as a surprise that someone other than the Graylockes wanted her services. If she was poached from the Tenwick estate, Catt wouldn't have to face her or her sharp tongue day in and day out. Not that he believed for a second that Morgan would relent to one of these requests. More likely, if someone offered more money for Rocky's services, he would match the amount. She might only be twenty-two, three years younger than Catt, but she had been working for the Graylocke family for years and the Graylockes were nothing if not loyal to their servants.

The duke continued. "With the orangery out of commission until the spring, I'm getting more offers than ever. Including, ironically, one from Lady Belhaven. Her eyesight and health aren't what they once were and she's offered to give Rocky temporary employment over the winter until the orangery is fixed. She's planning a big masquerade ball and the extra duties are just too much." His piercing gray eyes rested squarely on Rocky. "This is the opportunity we need to gain access. I'd like you to take the offer and work from inside the house to uncover Monsieur V's identity. Word on the street is that Monsieur V plans to meet with a powerful spy at the ball to pass along vital intelligence on England's war strategy, information so important that if Napoleon gets his hands on it, it could lose us the war. He must be stopped from relaying this information, but be aware, this is a fact-gathering assignment only. You are not to confront him. Once we know who he is, we can decide how best to deal with him."

Rocky's expression was fierce and determined as she nodded. "Of course. I won't let you down, Your Grace."

Morgan's mouth twisted at the formality—he'd long requested that she, as his brother's personal friend, address him familiarly—but he didn't comment. He looked content.

Clearing his throat, Catt caught the duke's attention. "Forgive me, but where do I come in?" It sounded as though they could have held this meeting without him.

His expression like granite, Morgan said, "I don't feel comfortable sending one of our spies into a dangerous assignment without backup. I've arranged to send both her and an assistant to work in Lady Belhaven's hothouse."

Catt nodded slowly. He still didn't see how this affected him. Were any of the gardeners Rocky oversaw a part of the spy network?

The duke added, "You will be that assistant, Catt."

Catt's mouth dropped open. He shot a bewildered glance toward Rocky—a mistake. She all but radiated smugness and superiority. He held her brown gaze for a moment before looking away. What a nightmare.

Weakly, he protested, "We've only just been trained. Wouldn't you prefer to match her with a more seasoned spy?" Not that he wanted to back out of the mission. To the contrary, hunting down a slippery French spy sounded like just the purpose Catt needed in his life.

But with Rocky?

With an impassive expression, Morgan answered. "You both will have duties from Lady Belhaven that you'll need to complete. I need someone with equal botanical expertise to Rocky. I need you, Catt."

Damn and blast. It made sense. Catt clenched his teeth to keep from saying another word and sounding ungrateful or worse, provoking an argument from the woman next to him.

Smug, she leaned forward to ask, "Does this mean that I'll be taking the lead in the investigation?"

Please say no.

Morgan shook his head. The muscles in Catt's body relaxed marginally. He still couldn't forget Rocky's presence next to him.

"You are equals in the investigation, but for the sake of appearances, Catt, you will have to play her subordinate."

In other words, the duke of Tenwick had just taken their positions—a friend of the Graylocke family and the servant of said family—and reversed them. Rocky needed no encouragement to pretend as though she was his superior.

"Can you do it?" Morgan asked, even though his tone warned that it was an order. "The only other person I could possibly send in is Giddy. He'd have to be undercover as a servant and I'm afraid Lady Belhaven would recognize him."

Not to mention the poor man would be separated from his new wife for Lord-only-knew how long. Catt couldn't do that to his best friend, not when he'd finally found such happiness. He swallowed hard.

"It won't be a problem. I can do this assignment."

"Good. Then I'll see you both to London and into your new positions at once."

Catt risked a glance toward Rocky, now his partner. Her gaze crackled with satisfaction. That looked promised that working with her would not be easy.

No, if anything, this assignment was going to be a living hell.

Chapter Two

There was a time when Rocky was young when she'd dreamed of marrying Lord Gideon Graylocke, never mind that she was only his gardener. Never, *ever*, had she dreamed of marrying his pigheaded best friend, Mr. Catterson. In fact, she'd rather eat belladonna than spend time with him.

Three days after the fact, her ears still rang with the revelation that she'd agreed to spend time with Catt, to work with him—alone—as they hunted the French spymaster in London. Even so, the look of gratitude on Gideon's face as she'd spared him the dangerous mission that would separate him from his new wife had warmed the cockles of her cold heart.

Enduring the long journey to London in a closed coach with Catt had frozen that particular organ again. By the time the coach pulled to a stop in a modest neighborhood just outside Mayfair, every muscle in Rocky's body suffered spasms from the prolonged tension. She bolted from the carriage first, letting the fur in her lap drop to the floor.

Unfortunately, her skirts hampered her and she all but tripped out the door.

A footman caught her. His heavy greatcoat was trimmed in green and gold and had a flower embroidered next to the lapel. "Whoa there, little lady. Are you all right?" He gave her a warm smile as she straightened and pushed away.

She adjusted her spectacles. "Perfectly fine, thank you." If only she wasn't forced to wear skirts. When it came to movement, trousers were ever more practical. However, all her shirts and trousers were in the Tenwick colors. For the duration of this assignment, she no longer worked for the Graylockes. She worked for Lady Belhaven. Since the lady was not a peer despite the moniker, there were no family colors to match.

The footman gave her a crooked grin and took her hand. Despite her gloves, his touch was warm. He must have come from inside the house, not someplace as cold as the carriage.

"You must be the new gardener Lady Belhaven's brought on."

Rocky nodded stiffly, wanting to reclaim her hand. She was here to root out an enemy spymaster, not to make friends. Could this stranger be Monsieur V? A fur hat obscured his hair, but he had the height the Duke of Tenwick had described.

Mostly clean-shaven, too; a few whiskers poked out the bottom of his chin, where he'd missed shaving.

"Botanist," Catt corrected as he exited the carriage. Disdain tinged his voice as he pulled his greatcoat closer around his shoulders.

Rocky reclaimed her hand and adjusted her hood to better shield against the winter chill. Did Catt think that her job was somehow lesser than his? They both worked with plants. Why quibble over what name they were called?

The footman didn't seem perturbed by Catt's clipped tone. His smile never wavered as he held out his hand. "I'm David. David Joyce, hostler 'round here. You must be Rocky."

Rocky bristled. "I am, actually. Joy Rockwood, taking on the botanist position in the hothouse. This is my assistant, Mr. Catterson."

Catt hunched his shoulders at the word 'assistant.' Rocky lifted her chin. He couldn't contradict her, but he would do well to at least attempt to appear subservient.

David the hostler wasn't at all upset by Rocky's correction. His convivial expression remained in place as he shook Catt's hand. "Forgive the mix up, Miss Rockwood. Mr. Catterson."

He still looked more at Catt than he did at her. Rocky gritted her teeth. She was spoiled at Tenwick Abbey, accustomed to servants who accepted her position of leadership despite her gender. It hadn't always been that way, but she'd worked with the same people for so long that even the new arrivals soon learned that, when it came to the plants around the abbey, she was in charge.

Here, she would have to eke out a place of respect while juggling the assignment the duke had given her. She didn't relish the challenge.

"I prefer to be called Rocky," she corrected. The less people who referred to her as "Miss," the better.

David tipped his head and turned to the driver, still seated ramrod straight on his perch. Perhaps he'd frozen that way. "Will you be staying a spell to warm up?"

The driver shook his head, proving that he had not, in fact, frozen in place despite the prolonged travel. "I've got orders to return the carriage to Tenwick straight after we unload."

With a shrug, David turned. "Seems I'm not needed, then. Shall I show you inside?"

Hesitating, Rocky turned to the boot. The footmen at Tenwick Abbey had helped her to load, since her trunk was too big for her to handle. Would she be expected to carry it herself?

David waved his hand, chasing her away from the coach. "I'll help Stefan unload them trunks once you're inside and warmed. Come now, both of you."

When she exchanged a tense glance with Catt, he swept out his hand to indicate that she should precede him. How nice of him to give her permission. They locked gazes, Catt's eyes as cool a blue as the overhead sky. Despite his calm demeanor, Rocky got the impression that he was just as uncomfortable as she was at their reception. The signs were subtle—the stiffening of his upper lip and the way he flicked a strand of his reddish-blond hair beneath his cap once more—but Rocky had been subjected to his presence for years. She knew him. She gave him a tiny, surreptitious nod. They would complete their assignment and return to their respective lives.

Which, come to think of it, intersected far too often.

She followed David to the manor. Although the neighborhood was less affluent than Mayfair, where the Duke of Tenwick resided, this house didn't match its modest surroundings. The grounds seemed to consist of two houses that had been strung together with a new wing built at least ten years ago. The manor soared in the air four stories tall. To the right, a short drive led to a stable big enough to lodge six horses. The hothouse couldn't be seen from the street.

The painted green door swung open at their approach. A bland-faced butler with short, bushy sideburns and an air of disapproval around him held the door wide as Rocky entered. He wore a black coat trimmed with the same green-and-gold braid as the hostler's greatcoat. Although he must be seventy if he was a day, his hair hadn't gone completely to gray. There was enough color left in it for Rocky to know that it had once been brown.

"Thank ye kindly, Lewis," David said, his voice chipper as he knocked the snow from his boots before he entered. "It might be a good idea to let Lady Belhaven know her new gardeners have arrived—or, botanists, I should say." He tipped his hat to Catt as the lanky man stepped in after Rocky.

The butler, Lewis, shut the door after them. Rocky shivered as she waited for the warmer air to thaw her.

Without waiting for a response from the butler, David strolled into the house. His boots left wet prints as he stepped off the rug and onto the wet floor.

"Abby, get off your pretty arse and fetch Lady Belhaven, will you?"

The square foyer of the home was framed by four doors, two of them shut. A woman with dark brown hair loose around her face emerged from one open door. She had a feather duster in her hand. Her gaze skated from David, who stood closest to her, in order to rest on Rocky and Catt in the doorway.

Unlike David, she neither broke into a friendly smile nor introduced herself. "You're the new staff?"

Rocky nodded.

"I'll fetch Lady Belhaven." After setting down the duster just inside the other room, she stepped through another archway into what appeared to be a corridor, given the echo of her steps. Her hips swayed as she passed David. He followed her with his gaze, his attention likely on her rear.

Rocky turned away, happy she wasn't under his inspection. She didn't need to be ogled. In fact, it undermined her authority. Better people thought of her as genderless, not that that was possible when she wore skirts.

With a shake of the head, David turned in the opposite direction, hollering for Stefan.

"May I take your winter clothes?"

Rocky bit the inside of her cheek to keep from jumping at the butler's voice. It was just as stiff as he was. His eyes were a piercing blue and seemed to cut her almost as deep as the Duke of Tenwick's. Hopefully, he was not as astute, or Rocky and Catt would have their work cut out for them in hiding their true purpose while in the manor.

With a soft, "Thank you," Rocky removed her pelisse, hat, and gloves. She wiped her feet on the rug as best she could, not wanting to track water into the spotless house the way David had. As Catt bestowed his outerwear upon the butler as well, the maid, Abby, returned.

"Lady Belhaven is this way," she informed.

Rocky squared her shoulders and followed without bothering to see if Catt did the same.

Instead of walking with purpose, Abby strolled as though she was out for a walk on a warm summer's day. Her hips swayed with every sashay. Rocky gritted her teeth and tried to find some other way to occupy herself other than envisioning pushing Abby into motion. The woman was young enough to be able to walk faster—not yet forty at Rocky's estimate. She seemed in no hurry.

Rocky took a deep breath so as not to snap at her. "Have you worked for Lady Belhaven long?"

Abby cast a glance over her shoulder, her expression guarded. "Most of us have been with the household for years."

Why was she avoiding the question? Rocky's skin prickled with instinct.

The duke had informed them of his suspicions about Monsieur V operating out of the household, but he'd given precious little information about the staff members. According to the French spy the

Crown had captured, Monsieur V was a man. Abby, with her curvaceous figure and decidedly feminine strut, most certainly was not. But could she be working with him?

Rocky opened her mouth to ask another question, if only to discover if the maid would evade that one as well, when the woman stopped outside a closed door. She rapped twice, then informed, "The gardeners are here." Opening the door, she stepped aside in order for Rocky and Catt to enter.

The room was a spacious one. Dressed in shades of red and burgundy, it had a warm glow to it that made her feel as though wrapped in a blanket. The roaring fire in the hearth helped. The sitting room contained just as many plants as furniture, each in an expensive patterned pot.

An old woman rested in a wing-backed armchair close to the fire. A wool blanket covered her lap. A pair of spectacles perched on her nose, but they didn't appear to make much difference, for as she hunched over to prune a miniature rosebush, she squinted and jutted out her lower lip. Her gray hair looked thin and was cut short. A green turban covered all but a few wisps escaping the front to frame her lined face. Her skin was so pale that even from across the room, Rocky could pick out some of the purple veins transecting the flesh beneath.

A young man in his twenties with dark, burnished gold hair by the light of the fire lounged in a second armchair. He had a book open on his lap, but he didn't appear to be engaged with its contents. He drummed his fingers against the arm of the chair instead.

As Rocky stepped inside, Catt close behind her, Lady Belhaven glanced up. The grooves around her mouth deepened as she smiled.

As she started to stand, only to have the color drain from her face and force her to sit again, the young man jumped to his feet.

She waved him off. "I'm fine, Stanley."

She grimaced, then slowly got to her feet again. Stanley helped, his hand on her elbow and concern written across his face.

"I was only dizzy for a moment. I'm fine now. I'm not an invalid."

Rocky wanted to agree with the lady, considering that she had too often been assumed weaker by men. However, Lady Belhaven must be eighty if she was a day. Her back was bowed. Her arms were thin. She likely *was* frail and weak, whether she wanted to admit it or not.

Shaking off the young man's hold, she beamed at Rocky and Catt. "Come closer, let me see you."

Rocky exchanged a glance with her partner. Had Lady Belhaven confused them for someone else? They were employees, not long lost grandchildren. Hesitantly, Rocky shuffled forward.

"Pay no mind to Stanley. He's one of my grandsons and a bit overprotective," the old lady told them. "I'm as fit as I ever was."

Rocky doubted that very much.

"It's only my eyes that have gotten a bit weaker with age and there's the extra work for the masquerade ball. That's why you're here, of course."

She reached out to clasp Rocky's hand. Having given her gloves to the butler, Rocky's hands were bare. Even after being outdoors, they were warmer than Lady Belhaven's. Her palm was clammy and her fingers might as well have been of ice. She clutched Rocky in an iron grip.

"You're Miss Rockwood, of course."

"Rocky, yes." She tried not to show how much she hated being referred to formally. While she was here, she might have to grow accustomed to it.

Lady Belhaven turned her attention to Catt, who loomed over Rocky's shoulder. "And you'll be Mr. Catterson, then."

He gave her a shallow bow. Although with her bowed back she wasn't as tall as Rocky, the movement brought him within range of her hands.

She clutched his chin, keeping him in a half-bent position.

Rocky bit the inside of her cheek to keep from laughing at the alarmed expression on his face.

After a moment's scrutiny, Lady Belhaven released him. She beamed and leaned forward, her voice lowering to a confidential murmur as she spoke to Rocky. "A handsome companion, you have."

Catt, handsome? Rocky glanced sideways at him in time to watch a blush climb up from beneath his collar. He'd heard, even if he pretended he hadn't.

No one refuted that the Graylockes were handsome. They all shared the same chiseled jaws, dark colorings, and devil-may-care smiles. In comparison, Catt was like a pale shadow. But, now that he wasn't standing next to one of the ducal sons, Rocky noticed him more. His hair swept over a narrow forehead in the same haphazard way Gideon's often did. He had a straight nose, and his mouth was softer-looking than any of the Graylocke brothers. Odd how she'd never noticed that detail before. He was nearly as tall as them and carried himself with a straight manner of bearing that drew the eye to the cut of his tailcoat. And his eyes... Not even Tristan, with eyes like molasses, had a gaze as inviting as Catt's. It reminded Rocky of a summer sky. He was handsome.

At least, before he opened his mouth. Rocky had far too much experience with his particular faults to be able to see him with any degree of admiration. She straightened her spine and turned back to Lady Belhaven, hoping the old woman hadn't noticed Rocky's lengthy perusal.

From the twinkle in her eye, she had. Though maybe that was a reflection of the fire on her spectacles.

"You make a handsome pair," the old woman pronounced, louder.

Pair? Oh, no... "We are not..." What? Married? Romantically inclined?

"A pair," Catt completed for her, his voice clipped. He offered a thin smile to their employer. "I am her...assistant." His mouth twisted with the word.

Rocky glared. *You could look more pleased about it.* Or, at the very least, he could pretend as though he hadn't just sucked on a lemon.

"Nothing more," he added. As if his statement hadn't been clear enough.

Lady Belhaven's lips curled in a knowing smile, as if she didn't quite believe him and had her own ideas about what was going on between Catt and

Rocky. "Very well then. If you'll lend me your arm, I'll show you where you'll be sleeping."

Trepidation crossed Catt's face, but he did as she asked and held out his arm.

As Lady Belhaven stepped past Rocky to take it, she winked. "I might be old, but I'm not dead."

Rocky pressed her lips together to keep from giggling.

For such a large manor, there weren't nearly as many staff members as Rocky assumed. They passed David and Stefan, a brawny man in his thirties with brown hair, as they joked while carrying Catt and Rocky's belongings. Both fell quiet as Lady Belhaven approached. Stefan tugged on his forelock, whereas David only grinned.

Aside from that pair, Rocky glimpsed Abby from afar once more, and no one else. Lady Belhaven gave a cursory tour of the manor as they crossed from the servant quarters—where Rocky was relieved to note she would have a room in a separate wing from Catt, housed next to the men— to the hothouse.

The hothouse jutted out from the back of the manor. The walls were glassed in on two sides, the roof also made of glass. The wall along the right hand side was shared with the kitchen, the back of the brick oven used to heat the vacuous space. The left side of the hothouse faced the stables, though with all the frost and fog clouding the glass, Rocky couldn't discern more than the silhouette.

The hothouse itself was like a jungle. The floor was made of marble tile. Rows of wooden tables with levels similar to shelves circled the perimeter and cut down the center of the room. On and beneath these were potted plants, all of them in various stages of flowering. The air smelled sweet with the fragrance of so many flowers. As Rocky breathed it in, the tension in her shoulders dissipated. Even if this was her first official mission as a British spy, she felt better knowing that at least some of her time would be spent putting her skills to good use.

"This room is my pride and joy," Lady Belhaven confessed. "All the plants are in the pink of health, but that doesn't mean you'll be without work. I get many orders for flowers in a given week, more now that the Season has begun again. There are few in London who can deliver their product in the winter months and I pride myself on being one of them. So, you'll have to tend the plants, coax them to bloom, and fill those orders as well as put together the ornamental plants and arrangements for the ball."

"A tall task, I'm sure."

Rocky jumped at the man's voice. Mr. Stanley Belhaven stood in the open doorway, looking aggrieved. He strode forward to reclaim his grandmother's arm. "Cook's sent up some coffee and seedcake, Gram. I know how you like your seedcake. You can inform them of the particulars of their duties after you sit for a spell."

"I'm not an invalid," Lady Belhaven snapped, though even Rocky could see that her strength was beginning to fail. Throughout the arduously slow tour, she'd leaned more and more heavily on Catt's arm.

"The seedcake has the iced glaze you like."

"Maybe just a thin slice," the old lady agreed as she let herself be steered out of the hothouse. "To keep up my strength."

Rocky shut the door behind them to keep in the heat and humidity of the hothouse. She and Catt met each other's gazes, then looked away. The silence stretched between them.

They had work to do.

Steeling her spine, Rocky lifted her gaze to meet Catt's. He leaned against one corner of the nearest table. He nearly toppled a potted plant before he leaped to catch it.

Rocky crossed her arms. "Watch what you're doing. We can't afford to earn Lady Belhaven's enmity. We need to stay in the household."

He made a face. "I'm not an imbecile. I know that."

That remained to be seen.

She lifted her chin as she approached nearer. Given the remote location of the hothouse and the thick brick walls that separated them from the kitchen and corridor, she didn't think it likely that someone could overhear them, but it couldn't hurt to lower their voices, just in case.

She took charge of the investigation. "The first thing we must do is find a way to insinuate ourselves into the household. We are newcomers right now, strangers. They have no affinity to us."

He raised an eyebrow. "Are you speaking from the many years of experience you have fitting in to a large household?"

Rocky balled her fists. Was he trying to insinuate that she was somehow less capable than he was, simply because she worked as a servant? She only did that to give her sister the best life she could—and a Season, if possible.

No, that wasn't completely true. She'd searched for work as a gardener because she hoped to give her younger sister, currently residing with a distant aunt, those things. But once she'd been brought into the Tenwick household, she'd realized how much she loved and thrived on the work. She lived and breathed plants.

As did Catt. Simply because he lived off a family stipend instead of relying on the fruits of his labors to maintain his lifestyle did not mean he was better than her. If anything, it made him worse.

"Yes," she spat. "I am speaking from experience, something you can't do. So perhaps, for once in your life, it might behoove you to follow my lead."

His other eyebrow lifted to join the first. Hostility crossed his face. "Why don't I? With that attitude, you'll seduce all the servants into your confidence."

Balling her fists, she took a deep breath. Along with the heady fragrance of flowers was a deeper undertone, Catt's scent. It made her head spin. She gritted her teeth. He couldn't be wearing one of Felicia's perfumes, could he?

The notion was preposterous. Felicia Graylocke, Gideon's new wife, created and sold perfumes that muddled the senses of the opposite sex and induced lust. Rocky would never feel anything approaching lust for Catt, not even if he would lower himself to wearing such a perfume.

Which she doubted he would. He was much too stubborn and seemed to think he had charm aplenty all on his own.

"You think you can do better without me?" she hissed. "Then go ahead."

A smile played around his mouth. It didn't match the glittering expression in his eyes.

"Is that a challenge?"

"You bet," she snapped. "The first person to find a viable suspect in the household—with reasonable proof for suspicion—wins."

He leaned closer. For a moment, her breath caught. They'd never been this close, not even in the carriage.

"And what do I win?"

Bragging rights. But no, he did that enough already.

"If you find a better suspect than I do, I'll give you first look at the plants." It would have been sufficient lure for her.

He glanced at the hothouse and the plants piled within. "I get to choose my workspace?"

In a roundabout way. "Yes."

The grin he flashed her was almost wicked. "Then you have a wager. Be prepared to lose, Rockwood."

"Not on your life."

Chapter Three

Years of working as a servant had taught Rocky that the best gossips resided in the kitchen. At some point in the day, everyone traveled through the kitchen, whether it was to fetch something for the master or mistress of the house or if they'd come in search of a hot drink or vittles for themselves. The cooks were on the best of terms with the entire household. In Tenwick Abbey, the lifeblood of the gossip mill originated in the kitchen.

And Rocky didn't even have far to travel in order to make it there. As she arrived, she paused to analyze who to approach.

She didn't have much choice. The large room was crammed with stoves, the oven, counter space, a basin for washing, and a tall table in the corner ringed with stools. Only two people resided in the room. Even in the quietest times of day, at least a half dozen men and women worked in the kitchens of Tenwick Abbey. But the ducal estate also had a much larger staff population to feed.

On a pockmarked wooden table stained with the evidence of food leavings, a woman busily punched dough. She sprinkled the heap with flour, folded it over, and punched some more. From the pinched look on her thin face, she wished that she was punching something else.

Behind her, a pimple-faced boy scrubbed at a pot in the basin of steaming water. Both the woman and boy wore white, stained aprons over their clothes. The boy, not quite as boney as the woman, looked to be no older than thirteen or fourteen. The younger members of a household saw more than they let on. People rarely paid them much mind, and they were much more astute than they were given credit for. Rocky knew—she'd first joined the Tenwick household at age fifteen.

As the angular, sour-faced woman vigorously kneaded the dough, Rocky rounded the perimeter of the room to approach the scullery boy.

"Hello, there."

He turned his back on her, hunching his shoulders and ducking his head as he finished his work.

Rocky frowned. "Hello?"

Stopping her efforts, the cook scraped dough off her boney knuckles and tucked the dough into a round bowl. She covered it with a cloth. Wiping her hands on her apron, she turned to face Rocky.

"Hello. You must be the new arrival."

For all her tart expression, she greeted Rocky with a friendly enough tone. Rocky switched targets. She approached the table.

"I am. I'm Rocky, the lead botanist." She held out her hand. "I don't mean to bother you if you're hard at work."

The woman shook it firmly. "Eliza Dowden, assistant cook. Don't worry about the intrusion. I'm due for a break, in any case. It's nice to see a woman in charge."

Rocky narrowed her eyes. "Assistant cook? Shouldn't the head cook be in the kitchen at this time of day?"

The woman's mouth twisted in disgust. She batted away the single wisp of brown hair that escaped her tight bun. "He should be, but my father had other business to attend, it seems."

Other business such as sabotaging the British spy network?

Rocky offered a commiserating smile. "Men. I have an assistant who is always taking breaks in the middle of the day to run personal errands."

For all she knew, it might even be true. She and Catt hadn't had the opportunity to work together yet in order for her to find out.

"Tea?" Eliza asked. "I have a fresh seedcake still warm from the oven."

Triumph surged through her. It was gratifying to know that cooks behaved the same way in all kitchens, always ready for a word or two of gossip, a friendly exchange of stories.

Rocky nodded. "Please." She retreated to the corner table and hopped onto a stool while the assistant cook sliced the cake and put the kettle on to boil. She carried two plates to Rocky and set them down side by side.

"This isn't nearly as big a household as the one I just left," Rocky said, keeping her voice conversational. She picked at the corner of her cake, not wanting to eat it in full until after she had tea to wash it down. "You must be much closer than what I'm used to."

Eliza's expression blanked. In a neutral tone of voice, she said, "I've worked here all my life, since my father was one of Lady Belhaven's first servants. I've never known any different."

Had Rocky offended her in some way? "It seems nice, like much more of a family than what I'm accustomed to." When Eliza's expression didn't soften, Rocky uttered a little self-deprecating laugh. "Then again, families can be tedious, can't they? Always squabbles going on and everyone knows everyone else's secrets."

The woman's nostrils flared. The kettle whistled and the scullery boy jumped to pour the hot water into the teapot. He carried the ceramic pot and two cups over to the table, then moved a dish of sugar lumps and some milk.

Eliza didn't speak. Her lips thinned as she ate her cake.

Why was she suddenly so cold? Did she know about Monsieur V—did she support him?

Rocky tried for a confidential smile as she whispered, "I saw David and Stefan when I came in. Are there any other handsome men around the manor?"

"No one in particular."

Without looking at Rocky, the woman poured the tea. She set a cup in front of Rocky and pushed the sugar and milk closer for Rocky to help herself. She did so, trying to maintain a warm air of familiarity that was quickly withered by Eliza's non-responsiveness. She had a bet to win! At this rate, Catt would probably put her at the smallest, most uncomfortable corner of the hothouse.

When she tried to flash the scullery boy a smile, he whirled and jogged out of the room. Did she have something in her teeth?

Turning her attention to Eliza once more, she tried to probe deeper. "Are you...close with any of the men on staff?"

Eliza's eyebrow twitched. Her mouth pursed. "Not especially."

"Do you know if they happen to be close with anyone else?"

The question made Rocky sound as though she were hunting for a husband. She most certainly was not doing that, not even if she hadn't been on the hunt for a French spy. She did perfectly well on her own, thank you very much. Not to mention, she didn't even know what her life would look like if she were married.

Rocky spent her days working. In her spare time, she read books, most of them botanical treatises that improved the skills she used while working. Her best friends were botanists—yes, for all that she and Catt never got along, she included him in that number. She woke up and went to bed with the sun, and worked during the time in between. She honestly didn't know where a husband would fit.

Let alone what such a man would expect from her. Would he demand she leave her job? Unlikely. Not only did it provide for her and her sister, but she enjoyed what she did. She wouldn't be happy living Catt's lifestyle, without a sense of purpose even if he did get to pick and choose the projects he devoted himself to. She liked the challenge of running her staff and ensuring that not a leaf was out of place on the Tenwick estate. Occasionally, she even consulted for the stewards of some of the other estates held by the Graylocke family, in particular when there was an agricultural problem. She felt needed where she was.

Whether or not she would marry was moot; she'd yet to find a man who appealed to her enough to give up her independence for even one hour, let alone a lifetime. She was happy on her own.

Eliza made one aloof, non-committal response after another. Rocky kicked herself for not being more subtle as she had most certainly done something to aggravate the woman. But no matter how she tried to open up and connect with Eliza, she couldn't manage to break past the cook's exterior. By the time the tea and seedcake was finished between them, Eliza stood and informed that she had to return to work.

In other words, Rocky was no longer welcome. Dejected, Rocky returned to the hothouse to await Catt's results. Unless he had as little luck getting his choice of suspect to open up, she was about to forfeit her position in the hothouse, where she would be forced to work for the foreseeable future.

Rocky left the kitchen with more questions than she had answers. Was Eliza hiding something? Could she be in league with Monsieur V? Did she suspect that Rocky was looking for him?

None of these questions boded well for the investigation to come.

Chapter Four

The bite of winter lessened as Catt stepped into the shelter of the stables. His breath still fogged in front of his face, but the air was less cutting.

The building was long and narrow, with two rows of stalls. Horses resided in four of them, snorting and nipping at mounds of hay. David worked in an empty stall, mucking it out and tossing the contents into a wheelbarrow. When he glanced up, wiping the sweat from his brow, a broad grin spread across his face like spilled ink. He set his pitchfork next to a brazier giving off waves of inviting heat.

"Catterson! Good to see you."

A second man came out of another empty stall, a bridle dangling from his fingertips and a rag held in the other. This man was a bit older, perhaps in his mid-forties, though he hadn't gone soft. Even his expression was hard as stone.

"Hollander," David crowed. "Come here and meet Mr. Catterson. He's one of the new gardeners."

"Botanist," Catt muttered under his breath, not that either man seemed to pay him any mind.

He shook hands with the other hostler, Hollander. When he dropped his hand, he turned back to David, the friendlier of the two by far. If Catt was going to win this bet with Rocky—he couldn't let her win and lord it over him, after all— he would take whatever advantage he could find. David seemed like an easy nut to crack.

Rolling his shoulders, David said, "What brings you out this way?"

Why hadn't he prepared an answer for that question? Catt smiled, hoping to match David's friendliness. For all that Catt was often invited to the Graylockes' events to fill out numbers, he wasn't the most sociable under normal circumstances. He didn't make friends easily.

"My..." Catt refused to call Rocky his superior. "My associate is setting up in the hothouse, so I thought I might get the lay of the land before we start work."

"Right you are." David thumped him on the back.

Catt was right about...what, exactly?

With a grin, David said, "Why don't you come with me and get the lay of a pint? Ol' Snaggletooth's is just down the lane."

Old...what? Catt frowned. "I beg your pardon?"

"Ol' Snaggletooth's. The local pub." He snagged his greatcoat from over the stall door and shrugged it on. "It must be near noon, wouldn't you say?"

Catt would guess that the time was closer to ten of the morning. But if David wanted to invite him off Lady Belhaven's property, where Catt might ply him with something to loosen his tongue, who was Catt to argue?

He nodded. "It can't hurt to go for a pint." Even if he suspected a place called *Snaggletooth's* would have questionable ale.

Grinning, David turned to the other hostler. "Will you be joining us, Hollander?"

"Thank you, no." His tone was final.

He accepted David's ribbing over the refusal with the same cold aplomb as he did the rest of the conversation. Perhaps that was simply the sort of person he was, not prone to socializing much. Catt could respect that. Given his druthers, he wouldn't be going for a pint, either.

But he was no longer Catt, the man who visited Tenwick Abbey daily when Gideon was in attendance and who tended the orangery plants while his friend was away. Never mind that Rocky was perfectly capable of adding the orangery to the rest of her duties. It was one of the few times Catt felt useful. Without the plants, he wouldn't know what to do with himself.

Now he knew what he had to do, even if he didn't like it. Here, he was a stranger. He had to invent a character for himself—one more outgoing than his usual demeanor. He had to be the kind of man others would confide in. So he tried to mimic David's posture and demeanor as they strolled along the cobblestone street toward this infamous pub. Since he'd left his hat, gloves, and greatcoat with the butler, by the time they reached the quaint, two-story edifice, he was chilled to the bone. He should have insisted on stopping for his outer clothes, even if he hadn't wanted to give David the chance to change his mind. They were, after all, indulging in a pint when they should be working. That must be frowned upon even in Lady Belhaven's household, and even though it was risky for Catt the reward of learning something about M. V was worth it.

As they stepped through the door, warmth swirled around Catt's body and he relaxed somewhat. He rubbed his hands together to promote circulation as David doffed his greatcoat and flung it at the rack.

Not surprisingly, the establishment was empty at this hour of the morning. Catt was astounded it was even open. The door, unlocked, led to a large room with windows that let in little light. Worn, round wooden tables were clustered together along with spindly chairs. David led Catt to one such and flagged the matron working behind the counter.

She didn't seem surprised to see him here so early in the day. Batting her hair out of her face, she asked him, "What'll it be, David? We just put on a stew, if you're hungry."

"Just a pint," he answered smoothly. "For me and my friend Catterson, here."

Catt doubted the moniker of friend, but he dug into his pocket for the requisite coins nonetheless. Before long, the matron returned with two tall mugs of frothy ale. David clinked his with Catt's.

"To your recent arrival!"

At the mouthful of ale that followed, Catt fought not to make a face. It was cruder than what he usually drank, if he imbibed at all. Giddy only indulged in spirits with his brothers in the evenings, and Catt rarely joined them.

"So, Catterson, do you have yourself a ladylove?"

Catt opened his mouth to tell him no, but David didn't seem interested in hearing the answer.

The hostler winked. "That Rocky seems like a feisty gal."

Horror washed through Catt. He chased it with another gulp of ale. "You're welcome to her." He couldn't imagine the sort of man who might court

Rocky. She was brash, sharp-tongued, belittling. She would emasculate the poor fellow who tried.

In fact, he couldn't picture her romantic or married at all. She always seemed like such a solitary woman, a lone rock in an ocean lapping at her heels, aloof from it all. She didn't have soft moments like he saw between Felicia and Gideon, when they appeared to be in a world all their own making. Secret smiles, stolen kisses—that didn't seem to be in Rocky's repertoire, something for which Catt was happy. Knowing her, she would find a way to turn her wedded bliss into yet another reason he was lacking.

He gritted his teeth. He would win this bet between them, but it was only a small chip in her exterior. It would take a lot more for him to erode the hostility between them.

David laughed off the suggestion that he pursue Rocky romantically. "She's not for me."

Was she for anyone? For some reason, thinking of a man touching Rocky, kissing her brought on an odd hollow feeling in the pit of his stomach.

David winked. "I have a lady of my own, you see."

That wasn't the sort of secret Catt hoped to uncover, but he didn't want to make an enemy of David so he forced a smile. "Do you, then? Congratulations."

The other man chuckled. "No congratulations necessary...yet."

Catt didn't know how to respond to that, so he took another swig of the ale instead. The more he drank, the better it tasted to him. Or perhaps he had drowned his taste buds by now.

David leaned forward and winked. "We're in it for a bit of fun right now."

Something else Catt did not need to know. However, muttering something non-committal under his breath didn't get David to stop. If anything, it encouraged him. Catt felt himself flush from his neck to the tips of his ears as David described his ladylove in exquisite detail. Every inch of her but her face, that was. Catt did not need that mental picture.

"She sounds...lovely."

"Oh, she is. And she makes this little squeal when we..."

Lawks! Catt, in general, abstained from such activity, not wanting to find himself trapped in an undesirable situation one day. He couldn't promise a woman the kind of lifestyle Gideon could, and most women he interacted with in the company of his best friend, so it hadn't seemed worth the trouble to try courting someone. Certainly not...indulging in more. It seemed irresponsible when, with Catt's financial situation, he was uncertain of his ability to provide for a wife and child. For the time being, he received a stipend from his uncle, but he didn't know how long that would last. One day, his uncle might turn his back on Catt the way the rest of his family had. Even if his uncle had been the one to encourage his scholarly pursuits when his parents had tried to steer him in the opposite path. Though, now that Catt was a Crown spy, he had an income all his own.

After learning far, far too much about David's romantic life, Catt tried to steer the conversation toward other people at the manor. Somehow, it always returned to David's affair in excruciating detail. The moment Catt finished the ale, he used the excuse to cut the conversation short.

"We should return to the manor. Rocky will be missing me, no doubt."

David winked and elbowed him in the ribs. "Ah, so there is something between you two."

"What?" Catt's heart stopped beating for a moment. "No. Of course not. I'm—" Her enemy, given the way she treated him. "—her assistant." He didn't like that word any better.

"At work, sure, but after..." David cast him a sly look.

"Nothing comes after." Catt tugged on his cravat as they approached the door to leave. Even the frigid outdoor weather was preferable to this line of questioning. Shouldn't he be the one questioning David?

"Of course it doesn't." David chuckled. "Nothing comes after for me, either."

Oh, Lud. What had Catt done? If David bandied about that particular rumor and Rocky heard of it, she would eviscerate him.

Catt shoved his hands in the pocket of his tailcoat. "Honestly, you're welcome to her, if you decide you aren't happy with your arrangement. There is nothing, not a single emotion, between Rocky and I."

Unless that emotion was hatred.

By the time he they reached Lady Belhaven's manor or not, he still wasn't sure if he'd convinced the hostler there were no romantic feelings between them. At the very least, he hoped the man would keep the suspicion to himself. Though, given the way he'd spilled his every sordid secret, Catt highly doubted as much.

He scrubbed the back of his neck with a hand that felt like ice as he navigated the manor to find the hothouse once more. It was easy to find. He paused at the door, steeling himself for the woman who awaited him inside.

He had nothing. The only thing he had adequately ascertained was that David was most likely not Monsieur V. With the amount of liaisons he purportedly indulged in with his ladylove, he wouldn't have the time.

Which meant, if Rocky had found a better suspect, he had lost the bet. She would never let him live it down, not while they remained under Lady Belhaven's roof. Their already tense association would only get worse.

He squared his shoulders, opened the door, and stepped inside. The warm humidity wrapped around him, a welcome respite from the cold that had seeped into his bones. He shut the door and faced Rocky.

She was already waiting for him, of course. Given the slight disarray of the pots, she must have started working as she awaited his return. She crossed her arms beneath her breasts. The movement tugged her fawn-brown dress tight against her. She tapped her toe, raising one eyebrow as she met his gaze. She didn't seem to notice the wisps of hair falling from her coif into her face. One clung to the corner of her pursed mouth.

"What took you so long?"

He gritted his teeth at the waspish greeting. "I didn't know gathering suspects was supposed to be a speedy endeavor."

Her body stiffened. She dropped her arms to her sides, balling her fists. As usual, she couldn't seem to stand still. "Then you found someone?"

No.

He crossed his arms, refusing to be intimidated. "You first. You did return before me."

She made a face. For a moment, his hopes buoyed. Had she found as little information as he had?

"The cook's daughter is hiding something."

"She can't be our man. Seeing as she isn't a man." He gave Rocky a pointed look.

Her eyes narrowed. "I know that. But she might be in league with Monsieur V. He could be her father or maybe her lover."

He shook his head. "You're reaching." He was *not* going to forfeit a prime working location simply because she refused to admit defeat.

Her mouth tightened. The movement drew his gaze. The wisp of hair still clung to the side of her plump lower lip. His fingers itched to brush it aside.

"I am not," she snapped.

He struggled to recall the conversation. Or rather, the argument. Hadn't he been winning?

"Did you meet her father?"

"No," Rocky admitted.

"Then you can't count him as a suspect."

She stepped closer, bristling with hostility. "You can't discount him, either."

"No." He gritted his teeth. "But he doesn't count against our bet, because you've found nothing on him."

"I've found that he was away from the kitchen in the middle of the day while there were chores to be done."

The way she held her shoulders thrust her chest out. Did she do that on purpose, just to boggle his mind? Simply because he was a man and she was a woman did *not* mean he would be susceptible to her charms. In fact, before this moment, he'd never even considered that she might even have charms much less employ them. Wasn't she always nattering on about how she was the equal of any man? A man wouldn't thrust out his chest in order to win an argument.

At least, Catt wouldn't.

"That is circumstantial," he insisted. "The cook might have gone to the privy or to the market."

She crossed her arms, pushing her breasts even higher. Why did she have to stand so bloody close? He couldn't help but look down her bodice, from this angle. Even when he tried to focus on her face instead.

"And what did you find?" she asked. The look on her face was anything but seductive. Her mouth was a hard pucker, not at all enticing a kiss.

And yet, kissing her would probably soften that mouth. And her expression. And her stiff posture...

What was he thinking?

He shook his head. "David spilled most of his secrets to me."

She looked dismayed. She shouldn't—not one of those secrets was the fact that he worked for the French.

Although he doubted his words, he insisted, "His openness could be to hide his true secret. I certainly didn't dig any deeper after he started to describe his latest liaison."

The look on her face spread to a smirk. It would have been pleasant if not for the smugness that radiated from her. "You didn't find a viable suspect, either."

"I did so." He took a step back so he didn't have to look at her from quite that angle. It was muddling his brain. "We can't rule him out, yet."

"Just as we can't rule out Eliza's association with our spy."

Then it appeared they were at a standoff. Given the look in Rocky's eyes, she was not going to back down. If Catt let her win, she would stick him in the furthest, coldest corner of the hothouse—or worse, the fetidly hot section next to the brick oven. Unlike when he worked with Gideon, Catt wouldn't be at the luxury to remove some of his clothing if he got too hot. He would suffer if he had to work there.

And Rocky, vindictive as she was, would probably enjoy every second.

"I have a better suspect than you do," he insisted. "Mine is at least a man."

"A man who doesn't appear to be hiding anything, if he confessed his secrets to you in such detail." The look in her eye made it abundantly clear that she thought he was lying.

Let her try speaking with David. Catt would eat his left boot to be a fly on the wall for that conversation. If he spilled his secrets to the first stranger who came along, Catt suspected that he wouldn't hold back simply because Rocky was a woman. Especially not with the demeanor she usually enacted, as though she was the same as any other man. She would be scandalized.

He opened his mouth to counter her accusation, but she held up her finger. She looked almost accusing. "Neither of us found a suspect."

That much was true.

"The bet isn't over."

He was willing to accede that, as well. He nodded, jerkily. "Agreed. We will keep looking.

More importantly, who gets which side of the hothouse in the meantime?"

They couldn't agree on that, either.

Chapter Five

If an argument were a living being, theirs would have grown roots and flowered overnight. As Catt encountered Rocky on his way to the breakfast room, the tension in the air redoubled. Sometime in the night, she'd grown even angrier at him. How, he didn't know. Once Lady Belhaven had recovered her strength, she'd spent the afternoon teaching them their duties and ensuring they would treat her plants correctly. By evening, the manor had become like a ghost. Lady Belhaven had retired early making a cryptic comment about "her man" bringing her tea, which made Catt wonder about her sanity. Perhaps she referred to Stanley or maybe some other servant he had yet to meet. But when one of the maids prepared and delivered the tea it made him wonder all the more. The quiet house was not what Catt expected.

Wasn't there some degree of socializing after work? But no, everyone had seemed so bone-weary from the day that they had eaten supper in near silence and slinked off to bed just as disgruntled.

Their attitude had apparently worn off on Rocky, because when he nodded cordially to her in greeting, she glowered at him. The infuriating woman probably blamed him for something that had happened in a dream or something equally absurd. He tried to ignore her hostility as he entered the breakfast room with her on his heels.

It didn't bode well for the day.

The other staff members, except for those who worked in the kitchen, milled in the breakfast room. Six, in addition to Catt and Rocky, who appeared to be near the last to arrive. He didn't spot Abby, though she might be tending to Lady Belhaven this morning. The sun hadn't yet fully separated from the horizon, necessitating a branch of candles to light the room.

Steam rose from a row of covered trays on the sideboard. Catt found a plate and stood in line behind a pretty blond woman he'd been introduced to last night at supper, Miss Towney, another maid. She tipped her face up to his with a smile as he stepped beside her.

"Mr. Catterson, you look well-rested."

Did he? He'd tossed for what must have been near an hour, worrying about the lack of progress on his assignment and the fact that he and Rocky couldn't get along. Eventually, he'd fallen asleep, only to wake once he heard movement in the corridor.

"I slept well, thank you. I hope you did the same?"

She scooped eggs from the tray and set them on his plate, not hers. "I did. I had a lovely dream."

Did she mean to imply that she'd dreamt about him? Her thick eyelashes fluttered in front of her eyes as she helped herself to some kippers. She put nothing more on his plate, for which he was glad. Even without turning around, he felt Rocky's glower.

"Do you prefer coffee or tea, Mr. Catterson?" Miss Towney asked as they reached the end of the table. A carafe rested next to a teapot, with four empty cups left beside them.

"Coffee," he answered. His brain was still muddled from sleep and he needed all the help he could in waking up. "But I can serve myself."

"Nonsense," Miss Towney said with a giggle. "I also love a strong cup of coffee in the morning. I'll get some for us both."

The way she emphasized the word *strong* made him question whether or not she spoke the truth. Given the sour look on the footman, Stefan's face, he was usually greeted with Miss Towney's sunny flirtation.

You can have her. Catt bit the inside of his cheek to keep from saying the words aloud. He needed to get closer to the staff if he was to determine who among them was a traitor. If Miss Towney plied him with enough attention, he might be able to use her to learn what he needed. Or at least find himself pointed in the right direction.

Hesitantly, he sat at the table. Rocky stomped after him and chose the seat at an angle from him, as far as she could place herself, given the choice of seats. Her expression was black with a scowl.

He caught her gaze. *I didn't ask for her to flirt.*

Not that it should matter whether or not he was the magnet for a woman's affections. He wouldn't allow himself to be distracted from the mission. Rocky should trust him that much, at least.

It appeared she didn't. She speared a kipper with her fork in a violent action. David, chuckling, nudged Stefan and jerked his chin down the table toward them. Catt didn't know what was said, but he didn't think he would like it much.

Miss Towney deposited her plate in front of the open seat next to him, bypassing the empty seat at the end, and returned to the sideboard in search of coffee. When she returned, she slipped it in front of him.

"I can sweeten it up for you, if you'd like." She leaned closer.

Lud, she was going to get him eviscerated. Rocky was in a bad enough mood as it was this morning.

He smiled, trying to keep the expression neutral. Not encouraging, but not discouraging, either. "Only one lump," he answered, making it clear that he meant sugar, not any other sort of sweetening she might be contemplating.

She sashayed to the sideboard and returned with the sugar and cream. As she added both to his cup for him, Rocky seemed to be trying to do her best to murder Miss Towney with her eyes.

Catt caught her gaze. *What are you doing?* She didn't appear to understand the pointed look he gave her. Down the table, Stefan, who seemed in a much better mood, was sniggering with David over something Catt didn't quite catch.

David had already insinuated once that there was more going on between Catt and Rocky than botanist and assistant. He was right, but not in the way he thought. Catt didn't want to let it on that they were, in truth, close friends.

Although "friend" had never aptly described his relationship with Rocky, it was a sight more accurate than "associate" or even "enemy." They rarely got along, but they were brought together by their mutual friend, Giddy. They knew each other better than a botanist and assistant might normally. Despite the fact that Catt was trying his best to fit his new role, he knew that someone would be able to discern that their relationship was not what it seemed.

If Monsieur V dug too deep into their relationship, he might accurately deduce that they were not botanist and assistant but partners. Partners who rarely got along, but partners nonetheless. It wouldn't be a leap to realize that, if not romantic, they must be partners in some other way. Such as spying.

Catt hardened his expression, trying to impress on her the danger of her reaction toward him. If they were discovered to be spies—and considering the hasty change in staff, it must have crossed Monsieur V's mind—they would not only be at a disadvantage when trying to find him, but they would also be in danger. Morgan had sent them both into Lady Belhaven's manor for good reason. While here, they had no other support but each other.

Despite his pointed looks, Rocky didn't seem to understand the situation. Or perhaps she just didn't care. Every time Miss Towney brushed his arm or giggled at something he said, Rocky's expression grew tighter. The moment she stood, bringing her plate jerkily to the section of the sideboard reserved for dishes that needed to be washed, he finished his meal and followed her out.

He extracted himself from Miss Towney's hold with a smile and the ready excuse of work.

Stefan gave him a glare as he left. David waggled his brows suggestively. Catt tried to ignore them both, as the other members of the household were doing—he hoped.

In the corridor, he loped to catch up to Rocky. Although her legs were shorter, she moved at a fast, furious clip. He caught her by the arm, tugging her into the doorway of an unlit, unused parlor.

"What do you think you're doing?"

"Me?" She pulled her arm free and thrust out her chin. "I'm not the one who just yanked me into this doorway."

He gritted his teeth. "Not here. Back there, in the breakfast room. You were acting peculiar."

"I was not."

She crossed her arms, brushing them against his chest as she did. He ignored the contact. He didn't move away. He wanted to keep this conversation private.

Catching her gaze, he held it for a moment, trying to stress with his eyes how serious he was. This wasn't a petty argument. She might have caused them a real problem just now.

"Do I really have to remind you that looking peculiar at this moment will draw a certain man's eye?"

"We've already drawn his eye—or you have. Miss Towney is in league with him."

"What?" He shut his eyes and pinched the bridge of his nose. "How do you figure that?"

She didn't have a cogent reason to offer him, of course. That didn't mean she didn't try.

"Isn't it obvious, with the way she suddenly latched onto you this morning? She didn't have a second glance for you at supper last night."

He glared at her. With the way she held her head, her lower lip jutted out slightly. The soft pout was completely at odds with her hostile expression and the way her eyes glinted behind her spectacles.

"That is indicative of nothing and you know it." His temple throbbed. He resisted the urge to rub it. "You're only jealous that someone was flirting with me, while no one thought to flirt with you."

Her mouth dropped open. "That is not true! I'm glad no one in the staff has flirted with me. I don't need to be treated like a—"

"Like what, a woman? I don't know if you've noticed, Rocky, but it's potently obvious that you are female." He gestured at her dress. "You do nothing to hide it."

She clenched her jaw so hard he almost heard her bones creak. "I can't wear breeches here."

Even when she wore breeches, she never concealed her chest. Her figure was always on full display in scandalous detail. The men at Tenwick Abbey probably dreamed about it whenever they closed their eyes, even if she was too waspish to romance. Catt had even had a disturbing dream or two about the rare instances when she let her hair down and didn't try to eviscerate him.

If she wasn't jealous of the attention Miss Towney had been lavishing on him, then why had she behaved so absurdly? Unless...

"You aren't jealous that she noticed I'm an attractive man, are you?" He didn't share the Graylockes' dark coloring, but he'd turned a few heads from time to time. Granted, they soon turned back when they learned he had no fortune, title, or connections.

"Of course not," she snapped, but her voice was unusually high.

Had she been jealous? A hot, tight sensation gripped his chest and for a moment, he couldn't breathe as he considered it. In order for her to be jealous, *she* would have had to have noticed that he was an attractive man. Until that moment, he hadn't realized that he wanted her to think of him that way.

He dropped his gaze to her mouth, admiring the plump curve.

Had she had dreams about him? That hot feeling overtook him and he lowered his head.

Footsteps echoed off the floor, coming closer. Catt jumped away. What was he doing? He met Rocky's bewildered gaze for a moment before they both looked away. They strode in silence to the hothouse. Rocky took two clipped steps for every one of his. As he held the door open for her, she breezed into the humid room. He hesitated by the door.

What madness had overcome him just now? Had he almost kissed Rocky? That would have been a disaster. She would have gutted him for treating her that way. Truthfully, he would have deserved it. At the end of the day, she was his friend, wasn't she? She deserved...respect.

Not that he didn't respect her. She demanded it and accepted no less. But for a moment, he'd forgotten that she was always jockeying to prove she was superior. Would her lips soften beneath his? Would she turn pliant in his arms?

Unlikely. There wasn't a pliant bone in Rocky's body. More likely, she would seek to take control. But that thought didn't disturb him nearly as much as he expected it to.

He couldn't step into the hothouse with her, essentially alone. When she rounded on him, her eyes glinting with an emotion he dared not name, he grabbed a small watering can and stepped back.

"I'll further our search for V." They'd agreed last night to use a shortening of the French spymaster's moniker, in case someone overheard them.

She matched his curt, clipped tone. "We were hired to do a job. We have orders to fill."

He tried for a grin and a joking demeanor but it fell short. Did she not realize what he'd almost done? "Have you forgotten? We have only days to figure out who V is or the results could be disastrous. Besides, I'm sure you'll be able to charm the plants into blooming all on your own."

She bristled.

He stepped back and shut the door before she started another argument. If only one door was enough to bar him from his agonized thoughts. What had he almost done?

He couldn't begin to understand it, so he prowled the manor in search of suspects. He used the watering can as an excuse, pausing in each room to find and tend the plants along the way.

On the second floor, an argument met his ears. A man's hostile voice cut through the air, making the silence afterward ring. Catt couldn't decipher the words, but he crept closer to the source in the hope that he could discover the nature of the argument. Could Monsieur V be ridiculing one of his spies? Morgan had said that the French spy he'd captured had refused to reveal French secrets out of fear.

The door to Lady Belhaven's upstairs parlor was ajar. Catt crept closer, adjusting his hold on the watering can in his hand as he did so. He peeked through the gap between door and wall.

The glow of the fire cast an orange light across Lady Belhaven's face. Her expression was hard, the grooves in her skin deep as she stood to face a much larger man. Lady Belhaven was perhaps five and a half feet tall, but the man loomed at a foot taller. He had a stiff manor of bearing and his clothes were askew, as if hastily pulled on. He looked to be in his late fifties, with gray liberally threading his receding brown hair. Who was he?

"No, Kenneth," Lady Belhaven said, her voice hard. "I will not facilitate your carousing. You've been gone for days and now you show up like this." Lady Belhaven waved a pale hand down the man's person.

Kenneth scowled. He used his size to advantage, looming over the old lady with a monstrous expression on his face. Would he strike her? Lady Belhaven looked so frail that she wouldn't survive such a blow.

As Catt reached for the door handle, Kenneth spat, "You won't help your own son, but you'll house that degenerate, Stanley?"

"That *degenerate* is your son, in case you've forgotten. It isn't his fault that he's following in his father's footsteps." Her chin quivered, as if the words cost her dearly. "Besides, he's a sweet boy. He helps me. There's hope for him yet."

"But no hope for me?" Kenneth snarled.

"I don't give Stanley money. I only let him stay under my roof, in return for the help he provides."

Where was Stanley now? Catt hoped the man would have put an end to this argument, if only for his own preservation.

"You've gone senile. You give him money all the time. You don't remember!"

Her soft-looking cheek quivered as she clenched her jaw. "I'm not senile. I remember what I do and don't do."

Kenneth sneered. "You forget things all the time. Apparently, one of those things is how to be a good mother."

The handle of the watering can dug into Catt's palm. He'd witnessed his father accuse his mother of some variation of that before. Every time, it cut her so much deeper than the surface.

Lady Belhaven insisted, "I've given you money before. You always gamble it away."

The big man scoffed. "Now, it's 'gambling' not 'carousing.'"

"It's always gambling."

"It is not." The big man puffed himself up, as if he wasn't large enough already. "There is an element of chance, but more of it is skill."

"Then why don't you win? All I ever hear is how you come this close." She held her fingers half an inch apart.

Kenneth's expression contorted in mixed disgust and rage. "You don't complain when I win and bring home more blunt."

Her face hardened. "It should all go into repaying your debts."

With a dismissive shrug, Kenneth said, "If the shops are stupid enough to keep offering me more credit, why should I?"

How daft was this man?

"They offer you credit because of my good reputation," Lady Belhaven snapped. "A reputation you're dragging through the mud."

"If you care so much about it, then you settle my accounts."

The old lady quivered. Catt couldn't tell if it was from rage or fear or some other emotion. "I have, far too often. It ends now. You're a grown man and must take care of yourself."

His upper lip curled. "You don't care about the well-being of your own flesh and blood?" He gripped her arm—hard, judging by the way she flinched. He spat, "You're a horrible mother."

Tears filled her eyes, whether from the pain of his hold or of his words. Catt shoved the door open. Mission or no mission, he was not going to let any man treat his mother that way. Not even a man a few inches taller and several stone heavier than Catt.

Catt had always had a great affinity for his mother—a kind, loving woman he had no contact with since his father had cut ties with him. He wasn't able to protect his own mother, but he could damn well stop Lady Belhaven from being victimized in this manner.

The moment Kenneth noticed he was no longer alone, he dropped Lady Belhaven's arm and stormed from the room. Catt pressed himself against the door to avoid being trampled. The man's shoulder slammed into his on the way out. It stung, but Catt fought not to show it.

Lady Belhaven dissolved into tears. She swayed as though her legs no longer wanted to hold her. Catt dropped the watering can and leaped across the room, catching her by the elbow and easing her down into the nearest chair. How could she weigh so little?

"Are you hurt?" he asked, crouching beside the chair.

She pulled a handkerchief out of her sleeve and dabbed at her eyes. "I feel so shaky inside." She pressed her palm to her chest.

"Rest a moment," Catt said. He stroked the hand clenched around her handkerchief, hoping to offer comfort. Her skin was as silky and thin as a spider's web. Purple veins pulsed over the back of her hand. She grabbed him and clutched him, her strength surprising for such a frail old woman.

"I'll fetch you something from the kitchen to make you feel better. A tonic, perhaps."

She dabbed at the moisture on her cheeks again and nodded. Catt slipped away to perform the task he'd promised. He gathered the all-but-empty watering can on the way. As he stepped into the corridor, he burned with rage.

Any man who made his mother cry was a heinous creature. If there was any justice in this world, Kenneth would be revealed to be Monsieur V, if only so Catt would have the satisfaction of seeing that he got his due.

Chapter Six

"What is wrong with you?" Rocky mumbled under her breath as she angrily deadheaded a rosebush. Even though Catt had long since abandoned her in the hothouse to do both their jobs while he explored the manor, her body still prickled with awareness. When he'd leaned closer to her in the heat of their argument, she had nearly surrendered to the urge to press her mouth to his. It was a good thing he was so blasted tall, or she might have kissed him.

The notion should appall her. She and Catt were always at odds. He was pigheaded, sarcastic, infuriating.

And handsome. She gritted her teeth. She'd always been able to ignore his good looks in favor of focusing on his less amiable qualities. But despite the fact that he'd been displaying nearly all of them in the corridor, she couldn't keep her eyes off his mouth. She'd never had to battle that strong an urge to kiss someone before. If she hadn't thought it would cause more trouble between them, she might consider doing it. It would buy her a moment or two of respite while his mouth was occupied doing something other than arguing.

No, that was madness. She couldn't possibly share such intimacy with...Catt. Anyone but him.

The door opened, drawing her attention. She hunched her shoulders and tended to another plant, a fickle orchid. It required a delicate touch. Catt... She didn't want to face him just yet.

"What an unremarkable day."

The new arrival wasn't Catt at all. Rocky shouldn't be surprised; the day before, all manner of servants had entered and exited the hothouse in some routine task, most to collect one of the bouquets left on the front table for delivery. The place was nothing if not busy.

The man had stooped to admire a lily that had just bloomed, his entrance as unremarkable as everyone else's. Rocky noticed he was tall and broad with brown hair. Monsier V? Then again most of the men in the house fit that description.

She wiped her hand on her skirt, then leaned over the table and held her hand toward him. "I'm Joy Rockwood."

He shook her hand and gave a slight not. "Benjamin Faulker. I tend to Lady Belhaven, and some of her special flower deliveries."

"Of course," Rocky said.

"I'm here for Lady Hastings' bouquet. She likes a plain posy that will fade in among her décor." He lifted his head to speak over his shoulder. "You didn't overlook such a one?"

"No." Rocky finished trimming the far-from-plain orchid and readjusted the pot so it wouldn't fall. "On the far left."

"Ah. Easy to miss. You'd think I had my eyes shut."

He scooped up the bouquet in question—a few yellow and white tulips—and exited. Rocky replaced the bunch with a less forgettable mixed bouquet of peonies and baby's breath. As she tied a ribbon around the stem to hold the posy together, Catt stepped inside.

He didn't overlook her presence. The plain expression in his eyes faded, replaced by something not as easy to miss. Resisting the urge to shut her eyes and thereby deny what she feared was the same reflected desire she battled, Rocky looked away. She finished her task as she said, "Did you learn anything?"

"Perhaps."

One terse word. He said nothing more. She dropped the posy and turned to look at him. Their moment together in the corridor...she feared it wouldn't be as easy to forget as she'd hoped. Was she imagining that he'd felt the same for her?

She must be. If he'd wanted to kiss her as well...

No. It was unfathomable.

"Then perhaps we ought to work. Since you decided your task was more important, you forfeited your spot in the hothouse." She crossed her arms, jerking her chin toward the brick wall radiating heat along that side of the room. "You can work over there."

Irritation crossed his face, something she found much easier to overlook. With nothing more than a curt nod, he strode to that side of the room, far away from her.

It didn't take him long to start clawing at the cravat at his throat, loosening it and the collar beneath. He rolled his shoulders while he worked, clearly uncomfortable. Would he doff his jacket like he did while working with Gideon? He still had his shirt and waistcoat on beneath, more formal than many men of Rocky's acquaintance. She'd seen men in less.

Not that Catt, unerringly the gentleman, seemed to realize. She sighed. His constant fiddling made it impossible to overlook him. Unless she shut her eyes, her gaze was constantly drawn to his lean form. As he glanced up, meeting her gaze, a shiver of awareness coursed through her.

She cleared her throat. "You can remove your jacket. I won't faint at the sight of you in your shirtsleeves."

He frowned. "I didn't think you would."

He made no move to doff his clothing. She shrugged. If he wanted to ignore her offer, then he could suffer. She'd made herself plain.

As Catt pushed up the sleeves of his jacket for perhaps the tenth time, Lady Belhaven entered the room. She looked flustered. "Can you send a posy off to Lady Hastings posthaste? She must receive it this morning. I forgot…"

"Of course, Lady Belhaven," Catt said, his voice low and soothing as though he spoke to a child, not a grown woman. "We'll see to it."

"Actually, it's already been seen to," Rocky interrupted. "Benjamin came in not an hour ago and collected it."

Although she'd expected the news to bolster Lady Belhaven's obvious distress and put her mind at ease, the old woman only looked more distraught. In fact, she looked near tears.

"Oh, is he back already? Forgive me for being so stupid. I must have asked him." She turned away, her face contorted with mixed pain and self-loathing.

Catt stepped forward. His shoulders were bent, making him seem less imposing than his height would suggest. "Think nothing of it, Lady Belhaven. It is always good to double check."

She rubbed beneath her eye with an impatient movement. "I don't mean to be so stupid lately…"

"Not stupid," Rocky interjected. "It's an easy thing to miss. We're happy you stopped by."

"Do you need a cup of coffee or some seedcake?" Catt offered.

He encircled the old lady with his arm as though it was the most natural thing in the world. Had Rocky ever seen him act so nurturing toward someone? Lady Belhaven seemed to take comfort in him.

She shook her head. "Thank you, no. I believe I'll lie down for a spell." As she left the room, she waved off his offer to escort him. "My man will help me."

Her man? Did she mean Faulker? She did seem confused. Although she touched the walls for balance, she didn't seem terribly unsteady on her feet.

When Catt turned, he found Rocky staring at him. He frowned. "You aren't going to criticize me for being kind to an old lady, are you?"

"No. Why would I?" She balled her fists. The fact that he even thought her capable…

He shrugged. "Good. I found her son yelling at her earlier today. She could use a bit of kindness."

His posture turned surly, putting the conversation to an end as he resumed his post. Rocky bit her lip as she continued to work. Somehow, she doubted that seeing him so attentive was something that she would forget.

Chapter Seven

How did Morgan expect them to find any spies in the household when they barely had a moment to breathe? In the two days since Catt had arrived, he and Rocky had spent ninety-eight percent of their time in the hothouse, tending the plants around the house or preparing arrangements to be placed in the ballroom and around the house for the masquerade ball. Although tending the plants afforded them a moment away from each other's company and the excuse to snoop, it always left the person in the hothouse with a larger work load.

Catt now understood how Lady Belhaven had amassed her fortune. Bouquets were in demand for nearly everyone with any remote connection to High Society. Fortunately, her hothouse was even larger than the orangery at Tenwick Abbey, which allowed for enough plants in various stages of their cycles for Catt and Rocky to be able to harvest the blooms without running short. Every morning was a mad scramble to prepare the bouquets and deliver them before fashionable Society awoke. Every afternoon consisted of tending the remainder of the plants and ensuring they were in good health. It was exhausting work and even together, Catt and Rocky never seemed to be able to tend more than a quarter of the hothouse before they fell into bed, exhausted. He had no idea how Lady Belhaven had handled the work on her own, even if she had purportedly employed a servant without botanical expertise to help.

Somehow, Catt and Rocky had to find the time to hunt Monsieur V. Morgan—not to mention the rest of Britain—was counting on them. Catt darted a look across the hothouse toward Rocky, who worked in the corner today. The only way they could make progress without devolving into an argument about plant care and who had done what was if they chose opposite ends of the hothouse. After working in the heat next to the oven yesterday, he'd wolfed down his breakfast in order to choose first.

Since the hour approached eleven of the morning, this should be the last batch of deliveries. Every member of the staff had entered the room at one point or another to fetch bouquets for the driver, Hollander. Even David had stopped by, though in his case it had been more to brag about his conquest the night before. Catt had been happy for the excuse of work, and for Rocky's glower chasing the hostler away.

As Catt affixed ribbons to the last order of bouquets, he frowned. The leaves of this lily...were they perforated? Catt ran his fingers lightly over the oblong leaf. Could they have a pest in the hothouse that he and Rocky were unaware of? It could be disastrous to the plants.

No, these holes couldn't have been made by vermin eating the leaves. They were too regular, each the same size and shape, a tiny pinprick in the membrane as if made with a needle. Had someone pierced the leaves on this plant on purpose? He checked the other bouquets, but found nothing telling on the other plants. An ominous feeling tightened his stomach.

"Rocky."

"I'm nearly finished," she said, her voice a grumble. She used her teeth to tie the ribbon around a bunch of tulips. When she lowered the bouquet to notice his rigid posture, she faltered in mid-step.

"Did you prepare the lilies?" Try as he might, he couldn't recall if he had.

"Yes. Why?"

"Were the leaves like this when you harvested them?"

With a dubious frown, she trudged toward the table to examine the leaves he indicated. Her posture stiffened as she saw them. "Pests?"

"I don't think so. Look closer."

She did nothing of the sort. As she straightened, worry was written on her face. "If the hothouse is infested, it could endanger the rest of the plants."

Did she think he'd taken up botany yesterday? He knew that.

"The holes are manmade. I think it's a code."

Rocky made a face. "You must be mistaken. We weren't taught any code involving plants. I would have remembered."

So would he. He rubbed his temple. "I know we weren't taught the code, but I'm certain that's what it is. What other reason could someone have for poking holes in a plant leaf?"

"Such a code wouldn't be sustainable," Rocky argued. "Every leaf is individual. There would be no uniformity. If V poked a pattern of holes in this leaf, the next one might have an imperfection that could interfere with reading it."

He gritted his teeth. "I considered that. That's why he'd have to pick and choose the flowers he uses carefully, and possibly why we haven't seen the code until now."

Rocky shook her head and crossed her arms. "You're jumping to conclusions. It's more likely to be a pestilence."

Under normal circumstances, he might agree with her. But they were hunting a French spymaster who had eluded capture for almost a year. The Crown had little to no knowledge about him, which considering the scope of spies in London and abroad, was astounding in itself. They had just as little knowledge about the methods Monsieur V used to pass information to his spies. *This* could be the key to solving that lingering question.

But, if Rocky was determined to be stubborn, there was no use arguing about it. It would only waste valuable time. Turning to the table, Catt ran his fingers over the lily bouquet inch by inch, searching out anything else suspicious.

"What are you doing?" Rocky asked, exasperated.

"Proving my point," he gritted out.

She walked away.

In less than a minute, he felt something on the flower itself. Was there something stuck in the throat? He beckoned Rocky closer as he tipped the flower to try to see inside.

"There's something in here." He tried to reach it, but the stigma was too delicate and his fingers too clumsy. If he tried, he would crush the stigma and alert someone to the fact it had been tampered with.

"Let me." Rocky nudged him aside. For once, she didn't seem belligerent or accusing. She was focused, her eyebrows set and her lower lip held between her teeth as she used a pair of forceps to painstakingly remove a small slip of paper.

When she unrolled it, he positioned himself next to her to read over her shoulder. Not that either one of them could decipher the script.

"It's definitely a code," Rocky pronounced.

Not one he recognized by sight alone. Although he'd packed a few books to help deciphering known French and British codes, he had a feeling that they would be of no help in this case. This, like the holes poked into the leaf, was a new code.

Rocky tilted her face up to meet his. Her eyes were fearful. "What do we do?"

He wished he knew the right answer. Rocky was usually the first to reach a conclusion and offer an appropriate solution. In fact, her quick mind was one of the things he admired most about her. At least, when she didn't oppose his ideas on principle. His life was a lot simpler if he went along with her suggestions. That she was now looking to him for a solution made his stomach cramp. What if he chose the wrong course of action?

She asked, "Do we stop the code from going out?"

He could tell from the tight look on her face that she wanted to, if only to thwart the French in some small way. But this was different than thumbing their noses at the enemy. Lives might rest on their decision.

He had to make one. "No. V will know we're onto him."

He braced himself, waiting for her to argue against the notion. She didn't. Trepidation was written across her face. Her lips were pursed.

"Do you have any paper? We'll take a tracing of the leaf and copy out the code to send to Morgan. Maybe he can puzzle out its meaning."

If anyone could, it was Morgan Graylocke. Not only was he in charge of training new recruits like Catt and Rocky, but he was also their mastermind at coding and could decipher a new code faster, even, than the Lord Commander of Spies.

Rocky had to tear a page out of a journal they used to monitor the changes in the plants. Catt used a graphite pencil to gently rub out an etching of the leaf, replete with the holes, in order to send to Morgan. He scrawled the message beneath the etching and carefully folded the page while Rocky replaced the slip of paper.

As he tucked it into his pocket for safekeeping, she paused. "Are we certain we want to let this message go out? By the time the duke deciphers the code, it will be too late."

His chest tightened. He should have known that she would question his choice. Surprisingly, when she turned to look at him, her gaze was questioning, not accusatory.

He answered slowly, carefully choosing his words. "Morgan assigned us to watch, not to intercept. If the message never gets to the recipient, V will know we're on to his game. He could switch households or even corner us. It's better if we play this out. These ones have no cards, but maybe we can find out to whom these will be delivered. The recipient must also be a spy. We can pass that on to Morgan as well."

Rocky hesitated. Catt heard movement in the corridor, muffled by the thick walls.

"Someone's coming," he hissed. "Replace the code, quickly."

Rocky used the forceps to position the scrap of paper in the throat of the lily once more. Catt retreated across the hothouse and pretended to tend to one of the plants near the hot brick wall. The heat slid over him, an uncomfortable sensation when combined with the ominous prickle on the back of his neck.

The door opened and Eliza, the cook's daughter, stepped through. "Don't mind me, I'm coming to fetch some garnish."

It wasn't the first time she'd done so today. Catt and Rocky stiffly pretended to go about their tasks as the assistant cook claimed a sprig of leaves and left the room. She didn't so much as glance at the bouquet of lilies. Once the door shut behind her, they exchanged a glance. Catt crossed to Rocky.

"It could be her," Rocky whispered.

Catt frowned. "What do you mean?"

"One of the people who came in this morning must have tampered with the lilies. It could have been her."

Catt glanced at the door, still firmly shut. It offered no answers. "She's a woman," he pointed out.

Rocky scowled. "Thank you for pointing that out. I hadn't noticed."

He raised an eyebrow as he met her gaze again. Sarcasm did not become her. "V is a man. Even with a disguise, I doubt Eliza could be mistaken for one."

Though she was a good deal thinner and more gangly than Rocky. Side by side, dressed in men's clothes, Catt's attention would be much more drawn to Rocky. If it was dark...

No. It was preposterous. V couldn't be a woman. How would she disguise her voice?

Leaning close enough to him that Catt caught a whiff of flowers—perfume or a byproduct of time spent in the hothouse—Rocky whispered. "Consider the facts. She was outright cold to me when I searched for gossip the other day. She has had the opportunity when she entered the hothouse earlier. She might not be V, but she could be working for him."

Catt took and released a deep breath.

Rocky added, "She could be assisting her father."

A man Catt had yet to personally meet because he was so often away from the kitchen. Tightly, Catt nodded. "It bears investigation, at least."

Rocky looked smug.

Chapter Eight

Rocky peeked into the kitchen and quickly retracted her head. Next to her, out of sight from the room beyond, Catt lifted his eyebrows in askance.

"They're both in there," Rocky hissed.

After the afternoon they'd had yesterday trying to pin both Eliza and her father down in the same room, the fact that they'd finally succeeded was a minor miracle in itself.

She caught Catt's gaze and held it. "Are you ready?"

He made a face. "Ready to flirt with a sour-faced woman who will likely try to sharpen her tongue on me? Why not. I've had practice."

Rocky glared at him. Was he trying to imply that he'd practiced with her? She couldn't tell from his casual stance, so she turned her back. "Let's do this."

The cook and his daughter were currently the only two people in the kitchen. Rocky took advantage of that fact, approaching the tall, wide man who stirred a savory pot of broth over the stove while Catt advanced toward Eliza, who monitored the baking bread. As he reached her, he leaned against the counter, offering her a warm smile.

A tight, unpleasant sensation crawled up Rocky's spine. He couldn't have been referring to her as his practice—after all, he'd never smiled at her that way. In her presence, he was composed, occasionally joking, but he never wore quite that wicked a grin. So who had he been flirting with?

It doesn't signify. She tried to push it from her mind as she reached the cook, Mr. Dowden. He hummed off-key under his breath as he stirred.

Trying to match Catt's smile, Rocky said, "I don't mean to bother you. I don't suppose you have a minute to help me find something to tide me over until dinner?"

A broad smile broke across his face. He set down the spoon and fished a handkerchief out of the pocket on his apron. Patting the sweat dotting his wide forehead and receding hairline, he said, "Of course. We have some mincemeat pastries that should be about ready to come out of the oven." As he stepped away from the stove, he hollered, "Eliza, how are those pastries doing?"

Rocky winced. The kitchen wasn't that big. He didn't need to shout. Not to mention, it drew Eliza's attention to Rocky once more. Rocky met the woman's gaze as trepidation filled her. Did she suspect why Rocky sought to talk to her father?

The assistant cook made a pinched face. "Those pastries are for supper. If you go handing them out, we won't have any left."

"Nonsense," Mr. Dowden said, his voice booming as he crossed to the oven to check on the contents. "What are they for, if not for eating?"

Eliza glared. Balling her fists, she muttered under her breath. It sounded something uncannily close to, *You didn't slave over them.*

Coupled with her murderous expression, Rocky expected the barb to hit home. Instead, Mr. Dowden shrugged it off. His smile didn't waver as he bent to check on the tray of pastries. He shut the oven door without pulling them out.

"They still need a few minutes more," he said, his tone jovial. "Why don't you sit and I'll put on a pot of tea."

When Rocky accepted, Eliza's mouth thinned. Anxiety flashed across Catt's face before he smoothed it. No doubt he lamented having alluded that it was Rocky's demeanor that had driven Eliza's friendliness away, not her questions.

Rocky met Catt's gaze and lifted one eyebrow, smug. *Go ahead, lover boy. Show me how to charm a woman.*

He didn't get the opportunity. No sooner had Mr. Dowden filled the kettle with water than Lady Belhaven entered the kitchen. Relief crossed her face.

"Rocky, Mr. Catterson, thank heavens you're here."

She exchanged a look with Catt. They both straightened and approached their employer.

"Forgive us," Catt said. "We were only out of the hothouse for a moment."

Lady Belhaven waved her hand through the air, dismissing the notion. "I'm glad I've found you. I need a delivery made posthaste."

Rocky and Catt followed her into the corridor as she led the way toward the hothouse. When she reached out to touch the walls to steady herself, Catt offered his arm. The progress was slow, but Rocky tried to stifle her impatience.

"Which flowers do you need?" she asked.

"I'll need six bouquets. They were made up this morning. The ones without the cards. You'll need to deliver them yourselves, though. I can't spare anyone else."

That was unusual. Rocky exchanged a glance with Catt, he seemed just as confused as she was, but neither of them were about to question it. Lady Belhaven was about to give them the exact address that the lily with the code would be delivered to.

The recipient was a Lady Montrose who lived a brisk ten-minute walk away in Mayfair. Rocky and Catt hastened to the hothouse and wrapped the bouquets in oiled cloth to shield the flowers from the elements, then bundled themselves just as tightly.

Rocky was surprised to discover that the air was almost balmy, certainly more than it had been over the past several weeks. Fat snowflakes drifted from the sky to collect on the townhouses and the street. Tracks through the snow indicated the routes of carriages. Rocky and Catt trudged along the gutter of the road, allowing room for the vehicles to pass them.

"Do you suppose anyone is tampering with the plants while we're away?"

A shudder crawled down Rocky's spine at the notion. "It's afternoon. This is the last of the deliveries. They would have no reason…"

She pressed her lips together. She shouldn't discount that the French spymaster might seek to prepare another code to go out in the morning.

Squaring her shoulders, she said, "We'll check the plants when we return."

It would take hours. But if they managed to intercept another message from Monsieur V and copy the information for the Duke of Tenwick, that would make the endeavor worthwhile, wouldn't it?

"Do you think this lady Montrose is a spy?" Rocky asked.

"Hard to know," Catt said. "There are six bouquets. Perhaps its someone else in her household. We'll have to keep an eye out and see if anyone seeks the lily bouquet in particular."

Rocky didn't say anything more. She was too preoccupied with the fact that they were carrying a secret code to an enemy spy to worry about it. The fact that they were, indeed, delivering the code irritated her, but Morgan's instructions had been clear. They were not to interfere.

By the time they reached the address in question, Rocky's shoulders were taught with tension. She and Catt stepped up to the narrow, stucco-sided building and knocked on the door.

After a moment, it was opened from within by a plump, middle-aged woman with graying hair. She wore a warm pink gown that looked too expensive to belong to a servant.

Hesitantly, Rocky said, "We're to deliver these flowers to Lady Montrose? They're from Lady Belhaven."

A broad smile broke across her face. "Oh, yes, of course. Please, do come in."

She stepped back, revealing a long, dark corridor with closed doors punctuating the length. When she shut the door behind them, Rocky blinked as she waited for her eyes to adjust. One door along the hallway was ajar, letting in a sliver of daylight from the room beyond.

The woman beckoned to them. "I am Lady Montrose. Right this way, please."

Since there was no place to set down the flowers in the narrow entryway, Rocky followed the woman down the corridor and into that room.

It was a cozy sitting room with one sofa opposite a chair, a table in between with a silver tea service on it, and a chuckling fire in the corner. A painting on the wall depicted a man and woman staring soulfully into each other's eyes.

"You can set the flowers on the table," the lady said. She claimed the armchair, wiggling as she found the most comfortable spot. As Rocky trudged to the table and set down her burden on the end opposite the tea service, Lady Montrose gestured toward the sofa. "Please, sit down."

Rocky frowned. "We aren't at liberty to stay, my lady. We have work to be about."

"Nonsense," the woman exclaimed. Her welcoming smile didn't waver. "Lady Belhaven won't be expecting you back for an hour at least. Please, do sit."

When Rocky hesitated again, a bullish expression crossed the woman's face. She pointed to the sofa. It was an order, not a request. Besides, Rocky wanted to hang around so she could see who would get the lily bouquet.

Reluctantly, Rocky lowered herself to sit on the edge. Her snowy outerwear probably wet the upholstery. Catt shucked his greatcoat, hat, and gloves before sitting on the opposite end of the sofa. He laid the articles in his lap. He appeared every bit as uncomfortable as Rocky.

Lady Montrose frowned. "What, are you strangers? Sit closer together!"

Catt and Rocky exchanged a glance. They sat slightly closer. At the woman's insistence, they moved closer still, until Catt's thigh pressed against Rocky's and the heat of his body seeped into her side.

Pleased, Lady Montrose murmured, "Now, let's see what's in these bouquets." She hummed cheerfully under her breath as she unwrapped the first to display the carnations, baby's breath, and coneflowers inside. Without looking at Catt and Rocky, she pronounced, "Lovely. I like to give out a few flowers to each of my clients."

Clients? This woman lived in Mayfair. Wasn't she a peer like the others who lived in this neighborhood?

"You can have one, if you'd like," Lady Montrose said as she unwrapped another bouquet.

"No, thank you," Rocky said, gritting her teeth. How were they supposed to figure out who the flowers were intended to go to now? "Do you have particular clients in mind for each bouquet?"

"I let the clients choose which ones speak to them." Lady Montrose unwrapped the bouquet with the lily in it and frowned. "This one isn't up to your usual standards."

Rocky shot a look at Catt. Apparently Lady Montrose didn't know about the code, but one of her clients must. The question was, which one.

Lady Montrose set the bouquet aside. "Would you care for some tea? I just put on a pot."

"Thank you, but we can't possibly stay so long."

At this protest, Lady Montrose appeared to ignore them. She unwrapped another bouquet. "Oh, daisies! My favorite. Such a simple flower, but often the simplest things are the most splendid." She plucked one long-stemmed daisy from the bunch and laid it on her lap, claiming it. Without looking at them, she asked, "How long have you two known each other?"

"Not long," Rocky answered.

At the same time, Catt said, "Years."

They glared at each other. *We're supposed to be botanist and assistant, remember?* Apparently, it had escaped his mind.

Lady Montrose frowned. "Oh, dear. You two aren't on the same page at all, are you? I understand why Lady Belhaven sent you to me."

"I believe she sent us to deliver the flowers," Catt put in. His voice was even, but his posture was stiff. The tension in his body seeped into Rocky's, knotting her muscles. She shifted in place.

"That, too," Lady Montrose agreed as she uncovered the last bouquet of flowers. "But if you don't start compromising and communicating, this union won't last long at all."

Oh, dear. Had the tension between Catt and Rocky been that obvious? She'd known it wouldn't be easy to work with him so closely, but if Lady Belhaven had picked up on the fact that they were so often at odds, their position might be more dire than she'd assumed.

"To what union are you referring?" Catt asked, his voice tight.

Glancing up, the woman batted a strand of hair out of her eyes. "Why, your upcoming nuptials, of course."

Panic spiked through Rocky, the code all but forgotten. She exchanged a glance with Catt. He looked about as pleased at the notion as she felt.

Somehow, someone had come to a misunderstanding.

***

Upcoming nuptials? With Rocky? Catt's eyes widened as he glanced toward her reflexively. He braced himself for her inevitable outburst, sure to be a vehement denial. She said nothing.

Could she be considering it? Of course not. It was preposterous! He cleared his throat. "I believe there's been some mistake. We work together, nothing more."

Nothing? Only the other day, he'd almost given into temptation and kissed her.

Lady Montrose, seeming to guess his thoughts, nodded in sympathy. "Workplace romances can be difficult. That's likely why Lady Belhaven thought I could help. She's somewhat of a matchmaker, you know."

Catt and Rocky exchanged another confused glance. Had Lady Belhaven sent them there on purpose to try to push them together? Rocky tensed to stand, but he stopped her with a hand on her arm. If this was one of Lady Belhaven's regular clients, they couldn't afford to offend her and risk upsetting Lady Belhaven's business. At the moment, they were the face of her enterprise.

Perhaps she hadn't made the wisest choice.

Oblivious to Rocky's anger, though Catt was not, Lady Montrose added, "I'm a pre-marriage counselor, you see."

Lud.

"I help all sorts of peers in reaching equilibrium before they embark on the most exciting and frightening ventures of their lives." Leaning back in her chair, the woman laced her fingers together across her stomach. "Of course she could be sending one of those grandsons. About time one of them got married and produced a great-grandchild for her. Well, that Stanley isn't proper husband material but Lance has a nice position. A barrister I think. Then again, I've seen him lurking around some shady areas. Something sneaky about him. But anyway, back to the two of you. There's nothing to be ashamed of in admitting you're afraid. We can address it and go forward."

Rocky gritted her teeth. "I am not afraid..."

He coughed into his fist to cover her words. She would only encourage the vapid woman.

Lady Montrose, beaming, added, "You have the same indicators of poor cohesion that I see in many arranged marriages."

"We are not in an arranged marriage." Catt struggled to keep his voice cordial. He didn't know how well he succeeded.

"I see. Did you have a fight, then?"

When didn't they fight? The muscles in Rocky's forearm bunched beneath Catt's restraining hand. She jerked free.

"We are not romantically involved." Her voice was waspish.

Apparently, the thought of marrying him put her in a sour mood. He expected as much, but still wasn't prepared for the way his stomach dropped. He took a deep breath and added, "If Lady Belhaven asked for your assistance, it must be in relation to our professional cohesion, not our personal one."

Lady Montrose pursed her lips. She didn't seem convinced. "The personal bleeds into the professional. If you're having difficulty connecting in one aspect of your lives, it will affect the other."

Surely she didn't still think he and Rocky were a romantic couple?

Rocky stood. "Thank you for that advice. We will take it under consideration." Given the tone of her voice, she intended to do no such thing. After patting down her coat, she cast him a glare and turned toward the door.

Catt stood and started to don his coat.

Lady Montrose called after Rocky, "Just a moment, dear. If Lady Belhaven did send you to me to help your working relationship, I should think you ought to stay and hear what I have to say."

Frustration crossed Rocky's face. She didn't appear to be making any effort to hide it. With obvious reluctance, she trudged back to the sofa and perched on the edge.

Catt returned to his seat. He glanced at the bouquets. Maybe if they stayed long enough, they would run into the next client and discover who the code was meant for because surely it must be the next person Lady Montrose would council, otherwise it was too risky that one of the innocent couples would choose the lily bouquet.

Beaming, Lady Montrose said, "You say you have trouble working together. Why do you think that is?"

Catt exchanged a glance with Rocky.

"Because he's pigheaded," she answered without hesitation.

He rolled his eyes. "That was my answer."

She glared at him. "I'm your superior. You should be nicer to me."

He gritted his teeth. This assignment from Morgan couldn't be over quick enough. At least then he wouldn't have to put up with jibes like that one. As it was, he couldn't set the record straight. For the time being, she *was* his superior.

"Why don't you respect each other? Do you find the other under-qualified for their job?"

"No," they answered simultaneously. They exchanged another glance. Rocky pulled a face, no doubt realizing that she was in agreement with him.

"Do you think you might have trouble battling physical attraction while at work?"

Yes. Catt cleared his throat. "No."

He answered on the heels of Rocky's *no*. She glanced at him and he steeled himself for her usual venom. Instead, she looked guarded. His breath seized for a moment as their eyes locked. He couldn't read her expression behind her spectacles. Could she be lying as well?

It was ludicrous. Madness. They didn't get along and never had. If, after years, they suddenly developed a tendre for one another...

No. He hadn't kissed her, and he wouldn't. He couldn't. It would turn Catt's life upside down.

Though perhaps his life was too boring as it was.

If Lady Montrose noticed Catt's lie, she didn't call him on it. Instead, she said, "Communication is the key to getting rid of the tension between you. If you tell the truth, everyone's feelings will be out in the open and there will be less of a chance of a misunderstanding."

Catt was *not* going to admit that he'd thought of kissing Rocky recently. Several times. He didn't understand the urge as it was, and she would only use it as a means to attack him.

Fortunately, Lady Montrose seemed to sense that neither of them would be cooperative. She moved on.

"I'd like you to each say something good about the other person. Positivity, more so than negativity, will help to heal the rift between you two."

Did Catt really want it healed? Even if it might help with their pursuit of Monsieur V.

At this point, he would do whatever sped along this session and allowed them to return to the mission at hand.

"Decisions come easily to her. She always knows what to do and rarely has to think for long to find a solution."

Rocky, her mouth open to say something, shut it again and looked at him. Inwardly, he cringed. He half expected her to rub in her position of superiority in Lady Belhaven's townhouse, regardless of the fact that it was only a cover. However, she didn't speak.

"Good," Lady Montrose said. "And what of you? What do you admire about him?"

Given the way Rocky narrowed her eyes, he expected her not to answer or to give a negative trait instead. She took a moment to ponder her words before she answered.

"He's cool under pressure." Glancing to him, she added, "You never seem to agonize over what needs to be done in such a short time, you work and do what you can and always keep up a cheerful outlook throughout it."

"Brilliant." Lady Montrose beamed. "See? I feel as though we're making progress.

Catt certainly hoped so. Although something in his chest warmed over the fact that Rocky admired something about him, he was eager to be away from this conversation.

Even more so when Lady Montrose said, "When you two are working, what is the one thing you find most irritating about one another? Perhaps if we address that, we'll be able to put you on the path to a smooth relationship."

She meant working relationship, didn't she?

Catt didn't need to think in order to give the answer. "Rocky constantly talks to the plants."

"I do not!"

He raised an eyebrow. "You do. Nonsensical stuff mostly, about the weather or the latest book you've read. Oddly enough, it's never the same conversation. You have an inexhaustible number of topics. It's quite astounding, when you think of it."

She glowered. "I don't do that…"

She didn't realize that she chattered under her breath while she worked? Perhaps he shouldn't have brought it up.

"You're making it up so you could stop me from answering."

Why would he do that? Lady Montrose seemed bent on allowing them each an equal turn. To the older woman, he shrugged. He didn't rise to Rocky's bait and engage with her in yet another futile argument. If she wanted to believe she spent the work day silent, he would let her believe that.

Now and again, she voiced something that he actually found interesting.

"Instead of refuting his claim, perhaps you ought to offer something in return. What does he do while working that irks you?"

"He's pigheaded." Rocky crossed her arms, leaning back into the sofa.

Catt gritted his teeth. That, right there, was precisely why he couldn't entertain the notion of kissing her. He could only imagine how much worse his life would become should he befuddle what little common ground they had.

Gently, Lady Montrose pointed out, "That is not a habit in specific."

Rocky sucked in her cheeks. After a moment, she answered, "He discards my ideas based solely on the fact that I am a woman."

What? Was she touched in the head? "I do not do that. If anything, it's the other way around!" More likely than not, Rocky got her way.

She glared. "If you would only accept the fact that I am qualified—"

"I do! If anything, *you* need to learn that there are other methods of solving problems than only your own."

That was likely the most civilized moment of their ensuing argument. Rather than stopping them, Lady Montrose only encouraged the discourse in order for them to get their every emotion out in the open. When it was done, Rocky's eyes glimmered with passion. Her cheeks were rosy. Her lips were plump after she'd bitten them so many times. Her chest heaved as she balled her fists. She'd never looked more captivating.

And that, if anything, led Catt to believe their conversation with Lady Montrose was more dangerous than he'd originally believed.

Nearly an hour later, Catt and Rocky managed to part ways from the persistent Lady Montrose.

Rocky turned to him in the street and whispered. "Lady Montrose's next clients must be the spies the lily is intended for. We need to wait and see who it is."

"I thought of that too, but we have no idea when those clients are scheduled. It could be tomorrow. And if we don't get back soon it could raise suspicions and ruin the whole mission. V could be watching and if he thinks we're trying to figure out who the recipient we'll lose our chance."

At Rocky's sour look he added. "Morgan's instructions were clear. Our priority is to ferret out the identity of Monsieur V. We can't risk it. Best we can do is pass along the information that Lady Montrose's services are being used to pass along messages."

Rocky glared at him. "See, this is exactly what I was talking about in there. You're pigheaded and you don't value my input!"

"It's not that. We have to follow Morgan's instructions. He's the boss," Cat said softly, but it was no use.   Rocky had stormed off ahead of making Catt rush to catch up.

The return to Belhaven manor was made in silence. If anything, the atmosphere between them was more tense and charged than ever. Catt couldn't glance at her without remembering how her eyes sparkled when she fought with him, even if the words cleaved by her sharp tongue were a good deal less alluring. He was going mad. It was the only possibility.

Rocky stormed past him as they entered the manor. She shucked her outerwear brusquely, though she didn't snap at the butler, Lewis. Catt was more cordial as he relinquished his winter gear to the man. By the time he had delivered the items, Rocky was already storming off. He wiped his boots briskly and jogged to catch up.

Her strides were clipped. Her body hummed with tension. He reached her elbow just as they turned the corner into the corridor toward the hothouse. Ahead, the hothouse door opened and a man slipped out.

Stefan.

Both Catt and Rocky faltered for a moment. He clasped her elbow and hurried her along, nodding to the footman as they slipped back into the hothouse. What business did Stefan have there?

The deliveries had all been filled by this hour. He should have no reason to enter.

The moment Catt shut the hothouse door after them, the warm air enveloping him, Rocky rounded on him.

"Why did you let him walk away? We should have questioned him."

Catt gritted his teeth. "What if he is V? Better he not believe we're onto him. Besides, we have work to do if we're to find which plants he tampered with."

"He might have had a perfectly cogent reason to be in the hothouse, but now we're going to have to waste time going after him."

Had she developed some kind of tendre for the footman that he didn't know about? Something hot and painful stabbed at Catt at the thought but he shoved the notion aside.

"It isn't a waste. Everyone in the manor is suspect, until we learn otherwise." Obviously, Stefan had had no reason to be in the hothouse at that hour, especially while it was otherwise unoccupied.

"Then I'll go and see if I can discover why he was in here."

That sounded like a bad idea. "We have to check the plants for tampering." That alone would take the two of them hours. They might not finish in one afternoon.

"Then check them," she said with a falsely sweet smile. "I wouldn't want to irritate you with my incessant chatter."

Catt gritted his teeth as she stormed from the room.

Chapter Nine

Stefan was, quite possibly, the most boring footman Rocky had ever met. He polished the silverware in the dining room, begged sweets from Eliza who treated him with just as much frost as she did Rocky, and joked with Abby in the doorway of a room while she was dusting.

He delivered a sprig of baby's breath to Lady Belhaven who was in the sitting room. Rocky hovered just outside the door.

A look of delight spread on Lady Belhaven's face. "Oh, I do so love baby's breath." Then she frowned. "But you brought it. I thought I sent my grandson, Lance…or was it Benjamin. I do so get confused sometimes. Or did I send you?"

"No, Ma'am. You're not confused. I had my orders."

Rocky faded back into the hall. Orders or was he making up an excuse for being in the hot house? Monsieur V was clever. He'd likely figure out ways to give himself an alibi and bringing a sprig of flowers to Lady Belhaven gave him a reason to be in the hothouse. He could easily grab that while tampering with the leaves in case he needed a reason later on. And he knew he'd been seen by Rocky and Catt.

Stefan came out of the room and Rocky faded back into the dark end of the hallway. He'd done nothing suspicious. Did he know she was following him? Perhaps he was going out of his way to appear inconspicuous.

As he crossed the front hall toward the stairs, Rocky hung back, waiting for him to disappear before she trailed him. The moment his boot winked out of sight, she darted to the bottom of the staircase.

"Miss Rockwood."

She cringed at the moniker. She hated being formally called by her name instead of her nickname. Squaring her shoulders, she turned to greet the butler, Lewis. The older man stepped forward from the shadows of the coat closet. She hadn't realized that he'd been nearby.

"Mr. Welsh." If he wanted to hold on to formality, so would she.

He raised one eyebrow, still dark though his brown hair was thick with gray at his temples. "A word, if you please."

She bit the inside of her cheek to quell the urge to glance up the staircase after Stefan. Had he planned this, in order to make good on his escape?

Reluctantly, she approached Lewis, who led her into the corner where he'd been lingering in the shadows, unnoticed. They crossed his cheeks, making the planes look hard and obscuring some of the wrinkles.

Meeting her gaze, he said, "I know you're new to the household, but I feel I must inform you of the rules. Lady Belhaven does not tolerate romantic entanglements among the staff of her household. In fact, it is grounds for dismissal."

***

Since he resided in the hothouse alone for the moment, Catt shucked his tailcoat and rolled up his sleeves as he examined the plants nearest the oven. He and Rocky usually kept the most exotic plants, those whose natural habitats were hot, in this area. He bent as he ran his hands through the leaves and petals of the plants at the bottom of the shelving first, searching for pinholes. The work was methodical and humdrum. No wonder Rocky chattered.

The door to the hothouse opened to admit the click of heeled shoes and the swish of skirts. Stifling a sigh of relief, Catt took a breath to compose himself before he faced Rocky again. When he stood, however, he didn't find his partner.

Eliza Dowden hunched over an iris plant, stripping off the leaves. What possible use could she have for that? She couldn't cook with it; ingesting any part of that iris would cause gastrointestinal upset.

Frowning, he stepped into her path. "What are you doing?"

She jumped. Fear crossed her face as she turned to him, stuffing her hand behind her back. It was too late. He'd already seen.

"I just need a bit of garnish for the plates."

"No, you don't." Well, perhaps she did, but that couldn't be what she was about. She couldn't be so daft as to use a poisonous flower, out of all the options in the hothouse.

He stepped closer. He'd never had cause to use his height to intimidate, seeing as he was so often with Giddy, but he steeled himself and tried now. Could Rocky be right, and Eliza was up to something on behalf of Monsieur V?

He cornered her. "I'll have the truth now, or I'll go straight to Lady Belhaven."

Although Eliza was also tall, he still topped her by several inches. Her mouth quivered and she looked away from him. "Please don't." Her voice was a hush. She wasn't quite as good at shielding her emotions behind an icy mask when she was off balance.

He stared her down, trying his best to imitate Morgan. If anyone could get a person to spill their secrets with nothing more than an eerie stare, it was the Duke of Tenwick.

Eliza met his gaze for only the briefest moment before she crumbled. Tears gathered in her eyes. He willed himself not to react. Despite the discomfort a woman in pain cultivated in him, he couldn't afford to show mercy. Not when the woman in question might be a traitor to the Crown.

With a broken sob, she spilled her secret. "I put traces of iris in the food so Lady Belhaven will believe that my father is losing his touch. It's time for him to retire, to give me the job of head cook, but he refuses. I do all the work, in any case! He's so slow, there would never be any meals if he were left to cook alone. I deserve that position."

Catt sighed. He rubbed his forehead. He didn't care a whit about the machinations and jockeying going on inside the Belhaven household. His concern resided with Britain.

"Please," she begged. "Don't tell Lady Belhaven. She'll turn us both out if she knew."

"No more tampering with the food," he said, his voice hard. After all, he ate it, too. He wasn't certain if she only put the iris into Lady Belhaven's food or if she also dosed the servants. He didn't care to question the food he put into his mouth.

Her mouth turned mulish, but she didn't say a word to contradict him. He held out his hand for the iris leaves, which she relinquished to him.

When he stepped aside, allowing her to pass, he warned, "Don't let me catch you near the iris's again."

She hurried from the room without responding. Once she'd gone, he sighed and glanced up toward the frost-paned glass ceiling. Thin daylight drifted through the crusts of ice.

Was Eliza's story true or had she made that up to cover for the fact that she was really in the hothouse to pierce a code into the leaves of one of the plants? And if it was true, why was her father remiss in his duties? Was it because he was busy spying for France?

Catt wouldn't say a word. Not because he felt any loyalty but because if he did, it would upset the balance of the household and might drive Monsieur V underground. He couldn't risk that.

Eliza hadn't been piercing a code into the leaves. She'd been ripping them off, but her visit had brought up more questions, but at least now he had something to report to Rocky. Would she have something to share with him?

Rocky frowned. "Forgive me, but I'm not certain to what you're referring."

Lewis's mouth turned down into a scowl. The crescent lines around his mouth deepened, exaggerated by the shadows. "You know exactly to what I'm referring. Don't think I haven't noticed you trailing after Stefan like a lovesick calf."

That had not at all been what Rocky was doing. In fact, although Stefan was reasonably attractive, he didn't appeal to her at all. He didn't have that devil-may-care smile that emerged at inopportune moments. His hair didn't fall onto his forehead and his cravat wasn't perpetually askew. In fact, Stefan didn't even wear a cravat.

"I am not remotely interested in Stefan."

Lewis, unfortunately, didn't seem to believe her. He narrowed his eyes, looking shrewd. When he leaned closer, she caught the faint whiff of brandy or port. "Don't play daft with me. You must see the merit of the rule, given your past."

Rocky fought to keep her innocent expression in place. "My past?" What the devil could he be talking about?

"With Mr. Catterson. It's obvious that you two used to be lovers."

That they used to be *what?!*

"We were never—"

Lewis glared her into silence. "Don't deny it. It's obvious you had a falling out after some lover's quarrel or other. I don't care for the details. Obviously, you can see how it would be disruptive to the household if the staff were to fall in and out of each other's beds."

This was...potentially the most ludicrous conversation to which Rocky had ever contributed. Tenwick Abbey had no such rule. In fact, several of the staff were married. The duke preferred to keep families intact and the dowager actively encouraged romance in the house, especially now that three of her four sons were married.

Not that Rocky had ever indulged in that freedom herself. She preferred to focus on work, and the staff in the house kept well away from her. When not working, she often found herself in the orangery with Gideon and Catt, in any case.

The thought of her and Catt having been lovers...it was laughable, wasn't it? Unfortunately, the memory of their near kiss surged in her mind and a small part of her wondered what might happen if they became lovers.

Certainly, it would entail all the misery and chaos that Lewis envisioned. She was mad for considering it for even a moment. If she and Catt couldn't function adequately as friends, what made her believe there might be room in their relationship for something more intimate?

Not that she'd ever considered such a thing before, and she wouldn't again. She had her work to focus on, now more than ever, since she was now a spy for Britain. There was a war to be fought and won. Rocky would do her part—without being distracted by a tall, handsome, often maddening man.

She bit the tip of her tongue as she forced herself to focus on the matter at hand. "I've never heard of such a rule being enforced," she told Lewis. "You can't tell me there aren't any married couples in the house."

His expression hardened. "There are not."

"What of Eliza's mother?" Father and daughter worked at the Belhaven residence, after all. It would be heartbreaking to force the family apart and the mother to find other employment.

"*That* is precisely why marriage among the staff is forbidden."

Rocky frowned. "It is?" Since her arrival earlier that week, she hadn't heard a single word about Eliza's mother, not even her name. Who was she?

"Mrs. Dowden is dead. Although it was ruled an accident, I fear that Mr. Dowden was the man responsible and we certainly don't need anything like that happening here again."

Chapter Ten

When Rocky stepped into the hothouse, something about her manner told Catt that all was not right. Maybe it was the way she held herself, stiff-backed and chin raised as if she faced down Napoleon himself. Perhaps it was the flash of trepidation in her eyes as she checked the corridor before shutting the door behind her. She looked as though she could use some good news.

Unfortunately, for all that he'd learned about Eliza, he couldn't very well point to that as good news. All they'd done was rule her out as a suspect. They still had the rest of the household to actively pursue.

What had happened with Stefan? Had she found him—Monsieur V, that was? Catt took an instinctive step forward, raising his hands to shelter Rocky. When he realized what he was doing, he balled his fists and dropped them to his sides. They weren't lovers. They were barely friends. Even if he wanted to offer her comfort, she wouldn't accept it.

"What happened with Stefan?" he asked.

"Oh." She looked surprised by the question. "I didn't discover anything about him. But I may have unearthed something more troubling about someone else in the house."

He didn't say a word, waiting for her to collect herself. Belatedly, he realized that he still hadn't donned his jacket. He rolled down his sleeves and righted his appearance. There. At least now she couldn't pretend to be scandalized by his state of undress.

Not that she'd appeared to notice it at all. She dragged one of the stools in the room next to another and perched on one. Apparently, she meant for him to join her. Sitting, he braced his forearms on his thighs.

"What did you discover?" More importantly, had that person caught her doing so?

"Lewis told me that he suspects Mr. Dowden of killing his wife."

That explained why there was no Mrs. Dowden loitering in the building. Catt sat for a moment, absorbing the information. "He suspects? There hasn't been confirmation?"

Then again, if Mr. Dowden had been proven to kill his wife, Lady Belhaven wouldn't continue to employ him. He would have been hauled off to prison.

"It was ruled an accident. Lewis didn't give the details. When I tried to learn more, he responded to a call from Lady Belhaven."

"But *why* would Lewis blurt that out to you. Seems out of place."

Rocky shrugged. "He thought I was having a fling with Stefan and wanted me to know household romances were forbidden because of what happened to Mrs. Dowden."

Catt raised a brow and she added. "Because I was following him trying to see what he was up to."

"Okay, but still seems a bit drastic to blurt that out."

Rocky chewed her bottom lip. "It does doesn't it? Unless..."

"What?"

"Unless he was trying to throw me off track. Maybe Lewis is V and wants to cast suspicion on Mr. Dowden, so we don't look at him."

Catt pursed his lips. Could the cook be a murderer? He seemed like such a jolly man. It could be a front for something much more sinister. Were Catt and Rocky at risk, as well?

"Did Lewis mention any other mysterious deaths in the household?"

"No."

Catt drummed his fingers on his leg as he thought.

Rocky, clearly impatient, jumped to the conclusion for him. "V could be Mr. Dowden. If he's capable of killing his own wife, he's more than capable of turning on his king and country."

That, Catt believed wholeheartedly. Though they hadn't yet proven that Mr. Dowden had done either of those things.

"If he is V, he's not getting help from his daughter."

Rocky frowned. "Why do you say that?"

"She was in here earlier to steal irises to put in the food."

Rocky looked appalled. "But those will make you sick!"

He nodded. He knew that as well as she did. "She confessed that she hopes to make her father look incompetent so that he will be forced into retirement and she can take his place as lead cook."

Rocky still looked uncomfortable. "Perhaps we should devise a means of taking our meals outside the household for the time being."

"That would be suspicious. We don't want to draw attention to ourselves. At any rate, I've ensured that she won't be continuing her scheme."

Rocky met his gaze for a moment, her eyes narrowing as she studied him. Finally, she nodded. "Very well. But that doesn't mean that Mr. Dowden isn't working on his own."

"You're absolutely right."

She seemed to relax a bit at his agreement. Now wasn't the time to fall into an argument, not over something so dire.

"We'll have to investigate further."

Thrusting her shoulders back, she hopped off the stool. "Let's find a cold lunch from the kitchen, shall we?"

Apparently, she meant to investigate right at that moment. Catt hesitated, staring at the room full of plants he had yet to check for evidence of tampering. Rocky, on the other hand, exited the hothouse without paying him another thought. He couldn't let her face the cook alone. If Mr. Dowden *had* killed his wife and Rocky asked the wrong question, drawing suspicion to herself…

Catt didn't want to contemplate her suffering the same fate. He jogged to catch up, reaching her side moments before she entered the adjacent kitchen.

Eliza, for the moment, had vacated the kitchen. Perhaps he'd frightened her more than he'd thought. Squaring his shoulders, he tried to imitate that same unnerving stare. He didn't know how well he succeeded.

The cook had his back to the room as he hummed tunelessly under his breath and chopped vegetables. The scullery boy washed and skinned yet more root vegetables to prepare them for the same treatment.

As Rocky sauntered between the two men with a smile, the scullery boy seemed to pale three shades. He grabbed two handfuls of the vegetable skins and bolted out the back door in nothing more than his shirt sleeves, presumably to add them to a compost heap that wouldn't take effect until spring arrived.

Had Rocky frightened him? Catt slowly made his way across the room as she asked Mr. Dowden after a cold collation for their midday meal. The cook seemed more than happy to fetch something for her. Catt relaxed marginally when the man set down the wickedly sharp knife. The juices of the vegetables gleamed from the blade.

Catt lingered by the door, waiting for the scullery boy to return. Was there a reason he was avoiding Rocky? Perhaps if Catt befriended him, he might be able to find out.

As the boy re-entered the kitchen and found Catt loitering near the back door, he stopped short.

"Why don't you close the door?" Catt said gently. "It's quite frigid out there. You'll catch a chill."

Without saying a word, the boy did as he asked. "Is there something you need, sir?"

"I wouldn't mind a moment, if you have time to chat."

The boy danced on his feet, looking anxiously at the cook, who didn't appear to be paying either of them any mind. "I have work to be about."

Work that he did while under the cook's eye. Did he know about the man's past misdeeds? Could he be under Mr. Dowden's thumb, forced to do the bidding of Monsieur V? He was far too young to be the man himself.

"I know all about work," Catt said, trying to commiserate. "I'd much rather have a moment to myself to breathe. How is Mr. Dowden as a taskmaster?"

The boy shrugged but didn't meet his gaze. Instead, he stared across the room at the cook. Or perhaps at Rocky. When she glanced in their direction, the boy quickly turned his back on her.

"He's not bad. A better taskmaster than Lady Belhaven in the hothouse."

"Ah," Catt said. "You were her assistant then, I take it."

"Not by choice, sir. I've no inkling of plants aside from the ones I like to eat. She said she needed my young eyes."

Catt nodded. "It is thankless work, getting all those flowers ready for deliveries."

Could the boy be working for Monsieur V after all? With Lady Belhaven admittedly unable to see as well as she used to, the boy could have been hiding the code this entire time and no one would have noticed. Although Catt's gut swarmed at the thought, he tried to remain casual.

"You must have spent a lot of time with those plants."

The boy gave a noncommittal shrug. "No more than you, I'm sure, sir. If you'll excuse me, I have work to do or the cook will yell."

Did Mr. Dowden have a temper he kept well-hidden? The jovial man seemed in a delighted mood as he slowly put together a tray for Rocky to take back to the hothouse with her as they resumed work. The scullery boy turned his back on the entire kitchen, his shoulders hunched as if he hoped to turn invisible while he attended to his work.

Might Monsieur V be taking advantage of his youth and timid personality? It was a possibility Catt wanted to avoid mentioning to Rocky at all costs. She had a soft spot for young men and women taken advantage of in the work place. She had once been that young and forced to work at an unsavory job, too.

He met her gaze as he approached her and Mr. Dowden. He never wanted to have to remind her of that time in her past. Not if he could help it. He would investigate that particular lead on his own.

Chapter Eleven

Catt laid a restraining hand on Rocky's arm as he noticed her tense to start forward. Footsteps lingered, growing fainter and fainter as the last members of the household filed out on their way to Church. In the shadows of the stairwell, Rocky cast him a quizzical look. He shook his head, his mouth flat, as he cocked his ear to listen. He wanted to be sure before they started their search.

Sunday morning was perhaps the only time when the entire household, including Lady Belhaven and her relatives, would be out of the house. In truth, Catt was happy to see Kenneth, Stanley and another young man who he assumed was Lady Belhaven's other grandson Lance accompany her. Though he knew relationships were strained, they seemed happy together this morning.

Lady Belhaven had made a stop into the hot-house early in the morning acting coy and asking if they'd learned anything new from Lady Montrose. For a moment, Catt thought she might be referring to the code in the lily, but then he realized her question had deeper meaning. It was as if she were fishing about to see if Lady Montrose had counseled Catt and Rocky as a couple. But why would she do that if she had a rule against relationships within her staff?

It was clear Lady Belhaven's health was failing and possibly her memory. Her actions and words might not have any meaning. He didn't have time to ponder that, though. If they were to search through the possessions of the staff for anything that might point to Monsieur V, they had to do it quickly. The staff would notice their absence from Church if they didn't make an appearance, too.

When he was certain that the only sounds were those of the wind against the walls, he nodded to Rocky. "Let's make this quick."

"We should stay in the same room. If we split up, we'll spend more time wondering if the sounds we make are each other or someone returning."

He nodded. "Agreed."

If she was surprised that he agreed to her idea instantly, she didn't show it. She led the way down the corridor and back to the men's quarters.

They entered the first room and started to search, each taking separate corners of the room and systematically moving through it until they met in the middle. Just as they were about to give up this room as a lost cause and rule out its owner for the time being—Stefan—a noise sounded from the hall. Was that...a crash? Catt met Rocky's gaze. Her eyes were wide with alarm.

Someone had returned home.

His heartbeat quickened as panic overwhelmed him. Maybe they wouldn't come this way.

Footsteps sounded in the corridor. Two pairs, an irregular beat as if the couple jogged a few steps, paused, and then carried on.

They might not enter the room, but he couldn't take that chance. "Hide," he mouthed to Rocky. She nodded, turning as she searched the room.

The bed was narrow, built to fit only one person. Even if she could squeeze beneath, Catt wouldn't be able to fit.

The wardrobe was far too small for either of them.

That left only one option—the heavy curtains pulled away from the window. If Stefan was the person who returned, he might notice if they were suddenly drawn across again. In fact, he might notice Catt's feet sticking out of the bottom. As the intruders neared, Catt no longer had time to think. The curtain was the best option.

He grabbed Rocky by the arm. She opened her mouth, likely to protest, but he spun her and pressed her against the window. He fumbled with the ties. In a panicked thrust of his arm, he hauled the drapes across the window, enclosing him and Rocky in the heavy fabric.

In order to keep the drapes as flat as possible, he had to press against Rocky intimately. Her breasts were crushed against his ribs, his pelvis aligned with her stomach. He felt the beat of her heart acutely. The rapid pulse matched his own. She fit against him as if they'd been made to hold each other in this way.

Madness.

Rocky opened her mouth, but at that moment, the door to the room banged open against the wall. Catt clapped his hand across her mouth as a woman's giggles, then a low moan punctured the air. Rocky's eyes widened, her soft lips tickling his hand as she recognized the sounds of kissing. The mattress shifted as bodies fell onto it.

Lawks. He and Rocky were trapped and the very erotic scene unfolding behind them couldn't be ignored. He met her gaze. Light twinkled through the glass of the window, falling across her expression. He lowered his hand, exposing her mouth.

The woman moaned, "Stefan," confirming that the other party was, in fact, the owner of the room. Damn and blast! Why had they chosen his room first to search?

Catt had no good excuse to offer for being here, no means of escape without detection. He was trapped, pressed against Rocky and unable to deny that he would rather be doing with her what Stefan was doing with his ladylove. Ever since they'd taken on this assignment and been thrust into the perils of spying alongside one another, Catt had started to think of her differently.

At Tenwick Abbey, she spent so much of her energy ensuring that no one thought of her as a woman. She wore breeches, she took command, and she used her sharp tongue liberally. While they often found themselves in each other's company, they rarely found themselves alone together. Gideon was always around, working on an assignment of his own.

In Lady Belhaven's house there was no Giddy to serve as a buffer between them. They grated on each other's nerves. He couldn't stand to be in the same room with her sometimes, but there were other times, like now, when he didn't want to part from her. He only wanted to get closer.

Thinking about kissing her was lunacy. If he tried while they were anywhere else, she would slap him and berate him for treating her like a woman, as if that made her somehow lesser. He didn't know what sort of women she'd had cause to associate with, but all the women of his acquaintance were forged of steel. Felicia, Lady Graylocke, her daughter Lucy—none of them backed down in the face of something they wanted, and all remained poised under pressure, whether that pressure was the threat of an enemy spy or the machinations of High Society.

Rocky... She was stronger than all the other women of his acquaintance put together, but for some reason, she seemed to think that very fact made her weak. Aside from a flaying or two when he misspoke or she misinterpreted his words, her demeanor in regards to her gender had never bothered him. But now...

If a man wanted to kiss her, how would he do it without her thinking that he meant to disrespect her?

Perhaps the only way would be to corner her behind a curtain, when she couldn't make a sound without revealing their location.

The air charged between them as she met his gaze. Was she as impacted by the romantic interlude taking place behind him as he was? Maybe she wouldn't protest him kissing her at all. Licking his lips, he raised his hand to cup the side of her face. He bent, intending to meld his mouth to hers before she had the opportunity to make a sound.

She gasped, retreating an inch to press against the window.

The movement on the bed stilled. *Damn and blast!*

"Is someone there?" That was the woman's voice. He remembered it, but couldn't put his finger on the name of the person it belonged to.

Catt met Rocky's fearful gaze. He remained very still despite the fact that their mouths were mere inches apart. He didn't want to draw attention to the fact that they stood there.

A moment later after the rustle of clothing, the curtain was ripped aside. The wash of cool air crawled down his spine. He separated from Rocky, trying to use his body to shield her from sight. Not that she allowed him to do that. No, she was bent on exposing herself by stepping up to stand in front of him.

Miss Towney, on the other hand, flew her colors from behind Stefan's shoulder. Their clothes were a bit disheveled, their hair was mussed, and her mouth was as pink as her cheeks.

For a moment they stared at each other, not speaking. Catt hoped that Rocky's quick mind would jump into action with an excuse, because he drew a blank. If Stefan was Monsieur V he could now know with utmost certainty that Catt and Rocky suspected him.

To Catt's surprise, the first words out of Stefan's mouth weren't an accusation. "Please don't tell Lady Belhaven."

Catt exchanged a glance with Rocky. Her ominous expression turned into one of puzzlement. "Because romantic entanglements are discouraged in the household?"

"Exactly," the young blonde woman gushed. She fished a necklace out from beneath her chemise. A ring dangled on the end. "We're married. Have been for a couple weeks." She and Stefan exchanged a tight glance. He reached for her hand, squeezing it with a fond expression.

He added, "We hope to tell the staff—and Lady Belhaven, too—but we've been waiting for the right moment. We don't want to be turned out."

"This explains why you were in the hothouse when we left the manor."

It did? Catt glanced at Rocky with a frown.

Blushing, the blonde nodded. "It's so hard to find time alone with everyone watching. We try to keep up appearances as if there is nothing going on between us, but..." She glanced up at her husband, helpless and obviously in love. "Before you came, the hothouse was relatively empty most of the time since Lady Belhaven can only work in short spurts. When he's instructed to go there for flowers...well...we take what privacy we can."

Catt sighed. They'd been in the hothouse for a romantic interlude, much like now.

Donning a fearful sort of bravado, Stefan said, "You'd best keep our secret if you don't want us to spill the fact that you're up to the same thing."

A bullish expression overcame Rocky's face, though her cheeks flushed with color. "We aren't—"

Catt wrapped his arm around her shoulders and hauled her into his side, temporarily silencing her. "Going to spill your secret. Next time I'll have to make doubly sure I'm walking into the right room."

Catt was lucky his resided next to Stefan's.

Stefan laughed as Catt herded Rocky toward the door. Their search had been cut short, but at least their true secret was intact. Given the way Rocky bristled, however, this didn't bode well for their working relationship.

Apparently she liked the thought of people believing they were romantically involved even less than she liked the notion of being exposed for a spy. That, if nothing else, convinced Catt that he was wrong to ever have tried to kiss her.

There was no circumstance he could devise where she might welcome it.

Chapter Twelve

Pretending she hadn't felt something for Catt when she'd been pressed up against him yesterday worked much better when Rocky wasn't trying to fool herself. For all of Sunday, she'd tried to scour her brain of the memory of his body against hers, the feel of his breath near her lips. Every time, it returned, unbidden, to taunt her.

Had he tried to kiss her yesterday? Did she want him to? They'd known each other for years without feeling remotely attracted to one another. In fact, they fought constantly and often hated each other...didn't they? With jerky movements, she clipped several flowers and bundled them together in the bouquet she was preparing.

Did she want him to kiss her? With any other man, she wouldn't have thought twice about the question. Never had she found herself in a position where she'd craved a man's kiss. The few times men—be they another member of the staff or a guest at Tenwick Abbey—had sought to pursue her for a romantic tryst, turning them down had been a simple decision. But this wasn't any man. This was *Catt*... Rocky's temple throbbed as she tried to discover at what point she'd started thinking of Catt differently.

The ribbon tying the bouquet was askew. Gritting her teeth, she balanced the bouquet in her hands as she tried to redo it. It wasn't working. Reluctantly, she marched to the front of the hothouse to ask for Catt's help. She approached his tall, lanky form. She couldn't see his expression, but even so, she was acutely aware of the fit of his dove-gray tailcoat and the way his breeches hugged his thighs.

Stepping up beside him as he matched bouquets with cards from the senders, she mutely thrust the bouquet at him. He held it while she retied the ribbon. The matter was complete within seconds. She found the correct card and affixed it next to the ribbon. Catt placed it neatly in the line next to the other flowers to be delivered.

He met her gaze briefly before he looked away, saying nothing.

This is madness. Squaring her shoulders, she raised her chin and blurted, "Did you intend to kiss me yesterday?"

Fiddlesticks! She should have phrased that better.

His blue eyes seemed to turn darker as they fixed on her. Probably a trick of the shadows. His expression turned to stone as he surveyed her for an impossibly long moment.

She held her breath, waiting for an answer.

"No."

Only one word. He turned away immediately afterward, even though he had nothing with which to busy himself on that particular work bench.

Her stomach sank. He couldn't even look at her. How foolish was she to believe that he'd been attracted to her, even for a moment?

That aching feeling rippling through her was not disappointment. It couldn't be. After all, it was *Catt*. They hated each other. She slinked a step back to paw through the cards still left to fill. On each, they dictated which kind of flowers the buyer had ordered.

Catt turned to pierce her with his gaze. "I never want you to think I mean any disrespect."

Because he hadn't wanted to kiss her, whereas she'd been so consumed by the moment that she hadn't been able to stop thinking about it since? She shrugged, turning a cold shoulder to him. "It's forgotten."

If only she could promise herself that she *would* forget about it as easily.

Catt took a step closer. His body radiated heat and electricity. Her left side smoldered as if she was on the verge of igniting. She swallowed hard.

"We should turn our attention to work."

"Indeed." It was all they did, day in and day out. Work together. Sometimes cohesively, most of the time less so. Before this mission, she'd enjoyed revolving her life around work. Now...

No. She still enjoyed it. At least, that was what she told herself. She didn't need something more.

She hazarded a glance at him, but it didn't give her the answers she hoped for. "We'll focus our efforts," she muttered under her breath. "We'll get this done."

The sooner they found Monsieur V, the sooner she and Catt could part ways. They would no longer be forced into each other's company day in and day out. Even at Tenwick Abbey, she could avoid him and tend to her work. Even if, with the orangery out of commission, that work wasn't as affluent as she would like. She would volunteer to clean out one of the most remote, forgotten sections of Tenwick Abbey.

Maybe then she could forget the kiss that she didn't want to happen.

Chapter Thirteen

Of the male servants in Lady Belhaven's household, nearly all were tall with brown hair. This didn't make Catt and Rocky's lives any easier. Even if they'd cleared Stefan of suspicion for the time being—considering that he devoted his free time to sneaking private moments with his wife, Catt didn't believe he could find the time to perform the tasks of a French spy, let alone a spymaster—they still had a handful of other servants to investigate. Not to mention Lady Belhaven's grandsons. Discussing the possibility of pursuing David only led to an argument between Catt and Rocky, so they focused their attention on another man: Michael Hollander, the hostler and Lady Belhaven's driver.

Hollander, tall, fit, and with hair that might be considered brown or black depending on the light, constantly entered the hothouse when he retrieved bouquets to deliver to Lady Belhaven's clients. He had ample opportunity to hide a code in certain plants. At meals, he usually ate by himself, standoffish and rarely contributing to the conversation at large.

Since Catt had been able to approach David and get him to open up so easily, he opted to try cozying up to Hollander as well. Rocky argued with him, believing she could do it better, but Catt ultimately won out. If he didn't get any information from Hollander, Rocky was never going to let him hear the end of it.

In fact, she lingered at his heels as he crossed to the front closet to fetch his coat.

"You don't have to follow me. I won't forget what I'm supposed to be doing."

She grabbed her pelisse from the closet as well. "How do you plan to occupy David so you can speak with Hollander alone?"

He hadn't thought of that. The fellow was unlikely to loosen his tongue if there were others around to hear. He stifled a sigh. "You intend to engage with David?"

She flashed him a triumphant smile. "I will. Perhaps I'll glean something from him that you haven't."

Given that he had spilled all his secrets in sordid detail, Catt didn't believe so. But if she wanted to listen to his prattle, he wished her luck.

As they stepped out of the manor, the cold air wrapped around them. The day was still, the clamor of work and rattle of carriage wheels a distant sound. Small specks of snow danced in the air, making Catt feel as though he was inside a snow globe. The snow crunched beneath his boot as he strode toward the stables with Rocky at his side.

As they stepped into the interior, David hailed them from a stall. Rocky separated from Catt with a broad smile that might even be considered flirtatious. She never flirted. The fact that a stranger could bring that smile to her face, even in artifice, when Catt could not made him bristle.

You could have told her that you wanted to kiss her.

No. It hadn't been an option. With her chin and shoulders so set, she'd obviously been ready to do battle with him over the insult. She wouldn't welcome his advances. Logically, he knew she wouldn't welcome David's either, that she was only putting on an act to put the man at ease, but he couldn't help but feel defensive.

The unfortunate fact was that he did want to kiss her, desperately. If only he could find a way to steal a kiss without having her hate him afterward...

Turning away, he focused on the assignment, not on his personal feelings. He didn't have time to wrestle with that kind of inner turmoil. Britain needed him.

He approached Hollander, who finished rubbing down a gelding and led him into a nearby stall. The man spared him barely a glance as he checked on the water level in the trough in the stall.

Catt leaned against the post next to the stall, trying to look casual. "It's been quite the hectic week. Are you always so busy delivering flowers in the dead of winter?"

Hollander grunted. "Sometimes."

He didn't contribute anything else to the conversation.

Catt tried again. "It doesn't leave you with very much energy at the end of the day. I know I've been falling into bed at the first opportunity. Can't a man get a little time to himself?"

He tried for a friendly smile. It and his words went unanswered as Hollander inspected the buckles on the gelding's halter.

"I wonder how David finds the time to keep his ladylove happy."

Hollander didn't appear interested in that conversation, either. He patted the gelding's neck and moved to the next stall to check on the horse occupying it.

"Do you have time to pursue a lady?"

That sounded like an odd, prying question, but Catt couldn't very well take it back now that it had emerged into the open air. He tried not to grimace.

Hollander met the question with a peevish expression and a muttered, "No." His tone clearly indicated that he would prefer to end the conversation and return to work.

Perhaps that was the problem. When David had opened up to Catt last week, he'd done it at the pub, not in the stables. Catt tried for an air of camaraderie as he said, "Now that the deliveries are over for the day, I was going to head down to the local pub. Care to join me?"

The other man looked down the bridge of his nose at Catt. "I think David's the one you ought to ask for that."

Across the stables, David's laughter cut short as he heard his name. "What's this now?" He stepped closer, Rocky trailing him. She wore a look of distaste at being interrupted.

Had she managed to get David to open up more than Catt had? Lud, he almost hoped not. She would lord it over him for the rest of the assignment.

Hollander said, "Catterson here wants to go to the pub."

With a broad grin, David clapped Catt on the shoulder. "That's my man. You know I'm always up for a pint. Let's leave this stodgy old man to his own devices, eh?"

Hollander wasn't terribly older than David, ten years at most. He looked irritated as he got back to work.

Catt shot a look over his shoulder at Rocky. She wore a smirk as she said sweetly, "You boys have fun." She turned her attention to Hollander.

Blast her! She was going to usurp his suspect. And, now that he'd suggested visiting the pub, there was no way he could back down.

Leading him out of the stables, David started to babble about his escapade the night before. Catt suspected it was going to be a very long afternoon.

***

Hollander didn't seem in a talking sort of mood after his conversation with Catt, so Rocky bided her time. When Catt returned from the pub, irritated, he seemed surprised that she hadn't capitalized on her time alone with the hostler.

She frowned. "I'm not daft, you know. You obviously didn't make any headway with him. If anything, he seemed annoyed by your presence. Talking to him then would have been pointless." She'd tended to some of the plants instead, keeping an eye through the frosty glass wall of the hothouse as she tried to glimpse movement in the stables. It was how she'd been alerted to Catt's return.

They lingered in the hallway that ended with a closed door, the closest to the stables. If either David or Hollander were to enter the manor to warm themselves—despite the brazier in the stables, a chill clung to the building—the easiest way would be through this door. Catt shucked his outerwear and wiped his boots on the mat as they spoke.

He raised his eyebrows. "So when do you intend to speak with him? Assuming, of course, that you do."

She scowled. "I can do a sight better than you did. I'll wait for him to warm himself. He'll be more willing to linger in the warmth of the manor, especially so close to the kitchen."

"Do you plan to wait here with a pot of tea and a hot biscuit?"

She grimaced at his sarcasm. "Do you have a better idea?"

He offered none and had no new information about David that he was willing to impart. She stepped to the side, happy to let him pass in order to put away his winter wear. Her side prickled with awareness as he passed. She rubbed her arms, trying to banish the uncomfortable sensation, and found a position in the doorway of an empty parlor opposite the kitchen. If any of the servants ventured in this corner of the manse, she could duck into the parlor for a moment to remain unnoticed.

It wasn't long after David returned to the stables that Hollander thought to make an escape. The door leading outdoors let in a flurry of snow, a blast of cold air, and one impassive man. If he hadn't had such a stiff manner of bearing, he might have been handsome. He kept himself clean-shaven—unlike David, who perpetually missed some of his chin whiskers each morning—and maintained a tidy appearance. Normally, that was the sort of thing that Rocky might consider attractive. It was certainly better than portraying oneself as a disheveled slob.

And yet...with his neat appearance and manner of bearing, Hollander seemed to fade from the mind, almost as though he was a fixture of the décor. His appearance showed little personality and even less encouragement for someone to approach him.

Catt, while sometimes less than pristine with his appearance, drew the eye. The way his hair sometimes stuck out and his cravat sometimes hung askew were both indicators of his brilliant mind. He was too busy thinking to realize that his appearance had strayed from the tidy way he'd arranged it upon rising.

While she was busy comparing Hollander's form with that of a man she would be better not to contemplate, he noticed her in the doorway to the parlor and nodded to her cordially. He moved toward the kitchen.

She blocked his path. "It's frigid outside, wouldn't you say?"

Perhaps not the most brilliant conversation starter, but it delayed his departure for a moment. He even gifted her with a smile and said, "Indeed. Though I much prefer today than when the wind roars."

She nodded in sympathy. "You have to be out in the cold, on that driver's seat, for hours on end. It must be torture. At least I spend the bulk of her time in the hothouse."

"Fetching bouquets is a welcome change," he agreed.

Although he seemed warmer to her than he had with Catt earlier, this conversation wouldn't precisely ease her mind in terms of her objective. Was he Monsieur V? Maybe she should try flirting to see if that loosened his tongue a bit more.

She feathered her fingers over his sleeve, a bit wet from the flurries clinging to the wool. With a warm smile—the kind she would never give Catt—

she purred, "It sounds as though you could use someone to snuggle up to on those long journeys."

She had never in her life been so brazen. Listening to the words erupt from her mouth chased heat into her cheeks. What was she saying? She wouldn't be able to go through with the suggestion if Hollander did accept. And if he didn't...

Raising his eyebrow, he looked over her shoulder, then stepped back. The cool demeanor he'd given Catt slipped back into place and he sidestepped her form in order to arrow for the kitchen.

"Fortunately, I have a moment or two between deliveries to come and warm myself in the kitchen. If you don't mind, I'm chilled to the bone." Tipping his head to her cordially, he didn't wait for her response but escaped into the next room.

When Rocky turned around, she found Catt standing down the hall, having returned from stowing away his outerwear. His expression was impassive. Rocky's stomach turned to lead as she realized that he'd witnessed her failure to seduce the information out of Hollander.

With a scowl, she stormed down the hall toward her partner. He fell into step behind her and they entered the hothouse seconds later. When she turned to him again, the impassive expression had turned to one that looked hauntingly close to amusement.

"Did you learn anything?"

She glowered at him. "You know very well that I didn't. He only ran off because you interrupted him."

That sobered Catt's expression. "Forgive me for getting in the way." His voice had an edge to it like steel.

What was troubling *him?* He wasn't the one who had embarrassed himself trying to flirt. She'd practically asked a stranger and potential traitor to warm her bed and she'd still somehow been turned down. She didn't even want to romance Hollander, but his evasion stung nonetheless. If a man came along who she wanted…

She cleared her throat, returning to the topic at hand. "He was warmer toward me than he was toward you."

"I bet he was."

"What is that supposed to mean?"

She bristled and stepped closer to face him toe-to-toe. His back was to the hothouse door, so he had no escape unless he groped for the door handle. Catt wasn't one to back down from an argument, however. In this case, he had instigated it.

His blue eyes glittered in the wan light sifting from the windowpanes. He opened his mouth, no doubt to deliver a scathing retort.

Instead, his gaze dropped somewhere in the vicinity of her mouth. Was her chin wobbling? She firmed it, not wanting to show any sign of weakness or uncertainty over the scene that had just transpired.

Softly, he said, "I meant only that he is a man. Any man when faced with your wiles would be warmer than if he spoke to me."

Had he not seen her failed flirting attempt? She wouldn't precisely call that reception a warm one.

She batted a strand of hair away from her cheek. Glancing away, she muttered under her breath, "You might want to tell that to Hollander."

Catt caught her gaze and held it. His expression was intent. "You're a beautiful woman, Rocky. I thought you knew that."

She hadn't. At least not in any useful way. Truthfully, she'd never given much thought to her physical appeal. She wasn't out to attract a husband, so what should it matter?

Suddenly, it mattered. A warmth spread through her at the compliment, and she averted her gaze. She didn't know how to respond. It wasn't often that a man complimented her beauty. Catt never had before.

For a moment, it seemed as though he wanted to say something else. He raised his hand halfway to her shoulder, then lowered it again at his side. He flexed and released his fist. The silence stretched on between them.

She took a small step back, struggling to recall what it was they were talking about. The thick floral scent of the hothouse didn't help. It made her head a bit fuzzy.

Or maybe that was due to Catt's nearness.

He cleared his throat, drawing her attention once more. "It appears if we want to get information about Hollander, we'll have to go about it some other way. He doesn't seem likely to open up to us."

Rocky narrowed her eyes as a thought occurred to her. Why hadn't she thought of it before? "Not so fast. I have a secret weapon."

He raised his eyebrows. "You do?"

Rocky smiled. "Felicia gave it to me months ago." For a very different purpose.

Now she was finally going to get to use it.

Chapter Fourteen

Rocky gritted her teeth as she opened the door a crack. She braced herself against the frigid cold evening. The night air clawed at her as if trying to draw her out into it. Given her druthers, she'd rather be warm in bed.

Instead, she and Catt perched near the side door of the manor facing the stables as they waited for Hollander to return. What was taking him so long? This seemed like an awful late hour for Lady Belhaven to send him on an errand.

"How much later can David stay away?" Rocky muttered under her breath. She adjusted the bodice of her dress again, deliberately showing off the swell of her cleavage. It was dark enough in the corridor that she hoped Catt wouldn't notice her nervous fiddling.

What if Felicia's gift didn't work? Rocky would have nothing but her own wiles to fall back on, and the experience earlier that day had proven to her that those held little sway over her prey.

In a dry voice, Catt said, "Given the level of detail David imposed on me when describing his hopes for this evening, I doubt he'll be back any time soon."

But would Hollander? That was the question. Rocky hadn't expected him to be away this long, even if Lady Belhaven had mentioned something earlier about sending a man on an errand. Supper had long since passed. It must be ten or eleven of the evening.

When she peeked out the door for what felt like the twentieth time, she was just in time to watch the tail of a closed coach pull into the stables. She shut the door, warming herself a moment before she inevitably had to brave the cold. She didn't want to wear her pelisse and risk losing some of her allure or muffling the perfume she now dabbed onto her wrists.

"How do I look? Alluring?"

Rocky doubted that very much. She wasn't skilled enough to fashion her hair in one of the comely coiffures worn by the Graylocke women. She owned no cosmetics and her dresses were plain at best. The only advantage she held was the perfume Felicia had given her, the one that purportedly made men fall in love—or at least in lust.

She fidgeted with the line of her bodice and decided that she didn't want to know Catt's answer, after all. "Is the perfume working?"

"You look the same as you always do."

Then...no.

He fiddled with his cravat, wiggling one finger beneath to loosen it. "I don't see how a perfume is going to change anything."

Definitely no effect, then. Did she have to wave it in front of his face in order for him to catch the scent? Her cheeks heated at the thought and she was grateful for the darkness. Maybe she'd try it on Hollander and hope for the best.

"It isn't just any perfume. It's Felicia's special love perfume, the one she peddles...or used to. She assured me it works, to incite lust if nothing else."

It must work. After all, Felicia had managed to ensnare Gideon's affections when he'd remained aloof for so long. Rocky had begun to think him uninterested in love, marriage, or even women. Apparently, all he'd needed was to find the right woman to lure his attention away from his plants all the time.

Rocky spent a lot of time with plants. It was her job. Did that mean that she should start looking for the right man? Shaking her head to banish the thought, she raised her wrist to her nose and sniffed. She caught a faint whiff of musk, but it could have been her imagination. Felicia had warned her to use no more than a few drops at her pulse points. More would overpower the senses.

For a moment, Catt remained silent. He seemed stiff, but it was difficult to tell without being able to make out his expression. "I don't see how inciting Hollander to lust will help the situation."

"It will loosen his tongue." Or so she hoped.

"If you say so..."

Catt didn't sound convinced, but she didn't have time to argue with him. Not if she wanted to take advantage of the fact that Hollander was alone. She adjusted her bodice one last time, muttered, "Wish me luck," and exited into the bracing cold.

No more snowflakes fell from the still air but the chill was enough to raise gooseflesh over her exposed skin. She balled her hands in her skirt and lifted it clear of the snow as she picked her way to the stables. The lantern outside the door beckoned her forward with a pool of yellow light. She took a deep breath and slipped inside, leaving the door ajar slightly in case she needed to make a quick exit.

The inside of the stables wasn't much warmer. The icy cold wasn't quite as bone-deep, tempered by the musk of horses and hay and the bubbling warmth of a brazier in the corner. Hollander, unhitching the horses from the coach he'd parked along the back of the building next to a phaeton and curricle, glanced up as her footsteps echoed in the silence. He laid his hand on the bridle of one of the pair and led the horse into a stall. As he passed her, returning for the other, he said, "Miss Rockwood. I didn't expect to see you out here at such a late hour."

Perhaps the perfume didn't work, after all. Or maybe it only worked on women as attractive as Felicia.

Unfortunately, Felicia wasn't here to ply her wiles or Hollander would have spilled his secrets much more easily. Britain relied on Rocky, instead.

As she trailed him toward the coach and waiting horse, she tried her best to impersonate her best friend's wife. Felicia could charm the shoes off a pony.

Rocky smiled. "Please, call me..." 'Rocky' didn't exactly inspire the most feminine of images. She usually insisted on being called that simply because it was a more neutral name. In this case, she wanted to draw attention to her femininity. "Joy." She fought not to make a face. She *hated* being called by her given name. Even her sister called her by her nickname.

Hollander paused beside the tall bay and laid his hand on the horse's bridle. He glanced at Rocky, lingering a bit though he didn't say a word.

It appeared that she was going to have to do all the talking. Why hadn't she rehearsed this with Catt?

She put on her warmest smile. "You took a very long time tonight to return." She stepped closer, keeping her shoulders thrust back to draw attention to her chest. It was cold enough in the stables for her nipples to pucker.

Hollander's movements slowed as he simultaneously undid the buckles on the harness hitching the horse to the carriage and ogled Rocky's chest. Was the perfume working, after all?

Bolstered by the thought, she stepped a bit closer. When the horse snorted and stamped, she thought better of it, keeping her distance. Hopefully she could flirt with just as much effectiveness from a pace away.

He led the horse away from her to the center aisle of the stables and slid his gloved hand into the curry comb. As he rubbed circles over the horse's back, flanks, and neck, he cast sidelong glances at Rocky.

She stepped closer. The horse no longer seemed in as irritable a mood. At the very least, the beast didn't protest this time. She tried batting her eyelashes at Hollander.

"I waited ages for you to return."

He paused in his task to turn to her, a small smile tugging at his lips. His gaze dropped to her mouth. That was a good sign, right?

"You waited for me, did you, Joy?"

She held her position, trying not to flinch at the sound of her name. "I did. Why were you gone so long?"

He stiffened and moved to the other side of the horse. Blast! She would never get him to spill his secrets if he refused to remain in the same vicinity as her.

"I had to work," he said, non-committal. When she rounded the horse's rump, giving it a wide berth in case it decided to kick, he added, "I nearly have enough blunt saved to become independent." His gaze lingered on her in a meaningful way as he ogled the way her dress clung to her figure.

Rocky frowned. "How? I know how much I'm paid as a botanist and, no offense meant, but I can't imagine that you would be paid a large sum of money more than me."

He darted his gaze across the stables as if searching the area for occupants. Stepping closer, he lowered his voice and bent his head to narrow the distance between them. "I work a second job."

Although she tried to keep the dubious expression from her face, she didn't think she succeeded. Even with a second job, he couldn't make more than one hundred pounds a year at best. That was far from enough to maintain an independent lifestyle.

As she opened her mouth to contest his claim, she wondered if he was about to reveal that he worked for the French. A chill crawled down her spine and she glanced toward the door. Still ajar. If she ran, she might be able to make it before he caught her.

But she had to know, first...

"What sort of job?" Her voice was a bit squeaky. She swallowed and tried again. "I can think of nothing that might afford you that level of luxury."

Her heart beat a rapid tempo in the base of her throat. She swallowed against it and forced herself to relax and maintain her flirtatious demeanor. How was she supposed to flirt with a French spymaster?

That is precisely why you came to Belhaven manor. She was the one who had decided that Hollander would be most willing to part with his secrets if she seduced them out of him. At the moment, that seemed like a very poor idea indeed. Why hadn't she demanded that Catt accompany her?

She couldn't rely on him or anyone else. She didn't need a man to fix her problems. No matter what happened, she could handle it herself.

Even so, it would have made her feel better to know that Catt was nearby, watching in case her plan went awry.

Lowering his voice, Hollander confessed, "I take the carriages out at night for an...extracurricular jaunt."

Rocky frowned. That wasn't the sort of confession she had been expecting. Did he ferry messages to and from French spies?

Cautiously, she asked, "What kind of excursions?"

"Romantic ones."

She frowned. What?

"Not for me, of course," he babbled. He caught her gaze, holding it for a moment as if to convince her of that.

She didn't say a word.

He continued, "I offer private, romantic rides to courting couples. I have quite the vast clientele, mostly those on the fringes of High Society who can't afford carriages of their own, though I have some wealthier clients who prefer that no one knows of their association or who are trying to thwart parents who disapprove."

"That is..." She didn't know what to say. It was almost sweet, save for the fact that he was accepting money for it. A great deal of money, it seemed, if he was near to financial independence. Though perhaps that was an exaggeration.

When she glanced up again to meet his gaze, she found him even closer. Her heartbeat quickened and she took a small step back. She didn't want to provoke him to action, nor did she want to discourage him from making a full confession.

She narrowed her eyes. "Lady Belhaven doesn't know of these carriage rides."

He ogled her again, lingering on the swell of her breasts and the line of her dress across her hips. "Indeed she does not. The money I make is mine to keep, save for a small cut I give David to ensure his silence."

In other words, if Lady Belhaven knew, she would not approve. Was that Hollander's secret, the reason he was so standoffish? He came into the hothouse quite frequently for bouquets...but, during the day, he also delivered them, so there was nothing suspicious in that.

He added, "I crack the window in the coach so I can eavesdrop. The occupants seem to forget that I'm around. I'm on good terms with several of the scandal rags in London, and they're always willing to pay a good price for salacious gossip."

When he stepped closer, Rocky took a step back to find herself pinned against a stall door.

Hollander took one more small step. Not pinning her against the door, but close enough for her to feel the heat of his body as he loomed around her.

He offered her a smile, though his attention wasn't focused on her eyes. This time, it was focused on her mouth. "So, you see, I find myself soon able to purchase my own carriage and work independently. When I do, I'm sure I'll find that the only thing lacking in my life is..."

Lud, don't say a wife!

He leaned closer, seeming enthralled by her. Perhaps the perfume was doing a bit too well. Was he going to kiss her? When she'd been cornered like this in the past, it had been easy for her to refuse the man in question with a strong, firm tone. She was an independent, working woman. She didn't want or need any man's attention. But was she at liberty to deny him now? After the way she'd been flirting with him—or certainly attempting to—it would look suspicious if she turned him away, wouldn't it?

Paralyzed with indecision, Rocky struggled to breathe, to think her options through as Hollander leaned even closer. Was she going to have to kiss him?

No. She didn't *want* to kiss him. She didn't have that sizzle and wave of awareness she'd felt when she'd thought Catt was about to do the same thing.

She couldn't have Catt and she didn't want Hollander...

The door to the stable banged open. Hollander, interrupted in mid-sentence, straightened and took a hasty step back as Catt entered the premises.

Although Catt wore an easy smile, the kind he donned when he was teasing Gideon and his wife, there was some kind of an edge beneath the expression. The smile didn't reach his eyes, which were cold and flat as he pinned them on Hollander.

"Is David around? I thought we might play a game of cards."

Hollander didn't glance at Rocky. In fact, he took up the curry comb again and started to apply it to the horse's flank while he answered. "He didn't tell you? He's out for the evening."

Catt gave Rocky a pointed glance. He flicked his gaze toward the door. He couldn't have said it any plainer. He was giving her the opportunity to escape.

Without looking at Hollander, she murmured, "I'm afraid I must be going. Excuse me, gentlemen." She forced her watery legs to work as she made a beeline for the door by which Catt had entered.

As she nearly came abreast of her friend, Hollander called, "Goodnight, Joy."

She suppressed a shudder at the name as she escaped into the cold, frigid air. If Catt hadn't been there and come to her rescue...

I would have handled it myself.

Perhaps, but it had been an impossible situation. Although she would have seen it through, she didn't think she would have found such a neat solution.

She owed Catt a debt. And, given their history, she doubted she would be happy when he decided to collect on it.

***

Catt silently counted to five once Rocky had made her escape from the stables before he curtly excused his intrusion and followed her. The swarm of jealousy in him stung as he turned away from the man who had almost kissed her. The man Rocky had almost accepted a kiss from.

Hell and damnation, Catt wanted to be that man!

The blast of icy outdoor air did little to quell his frustrations, though it tempered him somewhat with the return of his common sense. Perhaps Rocky hadn't been inviting Hollander to kiss her.

Perhaps she simply hadn't refused him because she'd wanted more information.

He slammed the door to the manor shut with a touch more vigor than was necessary. The warmth of the house slowly seeped through his thin tailcoat and shirtsleeves to warm his cold bones. His anger warmed the rest of him. How could she for a second have believed that it would be necessary for her to...

Morgan wouldn't ask her to seduce potential spies for information, would he? No, that would be asking too high a cost. Rocky shouldn't be required to offer her body to suspects. Even the safety of Britain wasn't worth it if she had to live with something she didn't want to do.

Or had she wanted to kiss Hollander? Catt's head throbbed. He didn't know what to think.

The hothouse resided mere paces from the door by which he'd entered. He strode to the premises with clipped steps, hoping that Rocky hadn't hidden in her room instead. But she wasn't the type to hide, and they'd agreed to exchange information after her mad venture that she'd insisted on embarking upon alone. He'd lingered by the door to the stables and heard every word, but she didn't have to know that.

He entered the hothouse. A half-shuttered lantern burned on the corner of the empty bench where they usually laid the prepared bouquets. It cast wan light and shadows across the jungle of flowering plants. Rocky turned away from him, her arms hugged around her middle as she stared at her reflection in the glass wall. When he shut the door behind him—gently, this time—she turned.

The light reflected off the lenses of her spectacles. He couldn't glimpse her eyes behind, nor read their expression. The way she clasped her arms around her middle pulled her dress tight around her torso, leaving precious little to the imagination. And, at the same time, too much. He forced himself to keep his eyes on her face rather than succumb to temptation and dip lower.

"What in bloody hell was that about?"

Perhaps not the most tactful way to phrase what he wanted to say. Rocky's expression smoldered with indignation.

"I beg your pardon?"

He ran his hands through his hair and tried to rephrase. "Please tell me you know that you aren't required to...to..."

She raised her eyebrows as she pursed her lips. "To kiss other men?" She faced him, arms akimbo.

Other men? That implied that he considered her to owe those kisses to him. He felt his cheeks heat and shifted to put his back to the lantern.

Hopefully, without the light spilling across his face, she wouldn't be able to see his blush.

"To kiss any man at all. You don't have to do anything you don't want to do."

She advanced a step toward him. He jostled the table as he retreated. He fumbled to keep the lantern from falling. If it shattered, the effects could prove disastrous. When he turned around again, she was too close. He stood between her and the light, so there was nothing to reflect off her spectacles. The thin light of the lantern illuminated the area and even though his shadow fell across her face he was able to discern the look in her eyes.

He wished he hadn't, because he didn't want to confront the ramifications. She seemed riled, yes, belligerent and accusatory, but also somehow vulnerable. Perhaps it was the set of her mouth.

"And if I *wanted* to kiss him? Am I not feminine enough to do that?"

He didn't know how to answer that. *Lawks!* He didn't think there was a correct answer. She spent most of her time trying to appear less feminine through everything from her name to her clothing. Did she want him to agree with her? Her words and tone spoke otherwise.

"*Did* you want to kiss him?" Every muscle in Catt's body tensed as he waited for an answer. He didn't know what he'd do if she said yes.

For a long moment, she didn't say anything at all. The silence stretched on between them. He dropped his gaze to her mouth, willing her to speak the words. He didn't know which answer he wanted more to hear.

If she said no, she didn't want to kiss Hollander, then maybe he... No. It would have nothing to do with him.

But if she said yes, he would know once and for all that she wasn't interested in him. That he wasn't good enough for her, as he suspected. He was in between two worlds, not of Gideon's sphere and yet not a member of the working class, either. Aside from the projects he and Gideon embarked upon, the stipend Catt received from his uncle, and now, his ventures as a spy, Catt didn't have anything that might be considered a job. He didn't own property, didn't have a title, and his own parents had disowned him for refusing to go into the army and contribute to the war.

He wondered what they would think of him if they knew he'd become a spy. They'd probably never know, and it was better that way. He had a clean break from everyone in his family save for his uncle, who had sponsored his education.

He was a mess. Zeus, he didn't deserve a woman like Rocky. Why was he even taunting himself with the possibility?

Maybe because he couldn't help himself.

Quietly, she admitted, "No. I didn't want to kiss Hollander."

Relief rushed through him. He tried to ignore it, to ignore his feelings for her. He nodded curtly.

She narrowed her eyes. Her thick eyelashes, coupled with the shadows, veiled her expression. "You don't have to act so jealous. It's not as though you wanted to kiss me." There was a high edge to her words, as if she was asking rather than stating.

He dropped his gaze her mouth. "Actually, I do."

Her breasts lifted with the swift intake of her breath. He didn't trust himself to move. He forced himself to look her in the eye. Her eyes were wide. He couldn't read her expression, maybe because he was too busy trying to decipher is own emotions.

His chest ached. Had he really just confessed that? Why wasn't she sharpening her tongue on him for the transgression?

Her lips thinned as she pressed them together. "That's due to the perfume." Her voice was a bit hoarse. She didn't move away.

He nodded, leaning closer. "Yes, it is."

No, it wasn't. His desire to kiss her long predated her application of a bit of perfume. Not to mention, he didn't believe that the perfume had any effect at all. None, that was to say, except for making her believe it had an effect, and therefore boosting her confidence. Rocky's allure was all her own.

He bent, sliding his hand to cup her jaw. She didn't recoil from his touch. If anything, she swayed into him. Zeus, this was madness.

But he had to know. He'd been consumed with curiosity. If he kissed her, would he banish that acute, almost painful awareness he felt every time she walked into the room? Kissing her might make it worse.

He lowered his mouth to hers, anyway.

The first brush of his lips against hers was tentative and fleeting. It ignited a tingle across his lips. He pulled back to look into her eyes, but she made no protest. If anything, she leaned closer.

He kissed her again, firmer. Her lips were warm and soft. With her height, he had to bend down a little to kiss her, but as she raised on tiptoe to shorten that distance, her body fitted against his and he forgot to breathe.

She felt incredible. He slipped one arm around her waist, holding her close as he deepened their kiss. She met his demand with one of her own, battling for supremacy in this just as she did everything else. She twined her fingers in his hair, holding his head steady as she took what she wanted.

She wanted *him.* The thought consumed him, the last coherent thought in his head as he surrendered to the feel and intoxicating taste of her. He ran his hand up and down her back and sides, learning her shape, learning the way she fit against him. She felt as though she'd been meant to press against him. He didn't want to let go.

He had to. He ended this kiss, his mouth and body burning from her touch. The moment he dropped his hand from her back, she sank back onto her heels and stumbled back. Her spectacles caught the light again, obscuring the look in her eyes. She raised her hand to her lips.

Blast, what had he done?

"Forgive me." His voice sounded overly loud in the otherwise unbroken silence.

He left before she came to her senses enough to chastise him for his lapse in judgment.

No, he shouldn't lie to himself. He left because he feared that if he didn't, he would kiss her again and she would realize that it wasn't due to the perfume she wore. He wanted *her.*

And, damn it all, there was no way in Heaven or Earth that she could possibly want him in the same way.

He went to bed alone, even though he couldn't stop thinking of her.

Chapter Fifteen

One minute, Catt was kissing Rocky like she was air and he'd been underwater too long. The next, he was walking away from her in disgust. What was she to think? Unfortunately, that conundrum had plagued her all night long. Despite hours of tossing and turning, she still didn't know. She could barely decipher her own feelings, let alone his.

She knew what it felt like to kiss him now, but that didn't make the tension between them any better. If anything, it made it worse. From the moment he'd stepped into the breakfast room this morning, it was as if the rest of the world had melted away, leaving only the two of them. The chasm in her chest had widened, growing hungry for something she didn't even want to think about.

The only reason he'd kissed her had been because of the perfume. So what was her excuse? He must think her a hoyden for wrapping her arms around him and kissing him back with such ferocity. Now that morning had dawned and she'd washed away all trace of the perfume, there was nothing to draw him to her. Did he think of their kiss as a mistake?

He must, because he could barely look at her. He treated her stiffly, and they soon agreed that working in separate corners of the room would be best. This time, she took the work bench near the door. It was also nearer to the oven, making the hair at the nape of her neck damp with sweat, but she didn't mind. Better too hot than too cold.

Catt worked without looking at her, fetching bouquets to match to the orders and leaving them on the bench for her to tie and arrange for delivery. As he left another such bouquet, she reached for it with a murmured, "Thank you." Their hands brushed. A tingle swept over her skin. For a moment, they locked gazes. Then he turned away and took clipped steps across the room.

Hell and damnation! They couldn't work like this. But, given the lack of progression in their search and with the masquerade ball looming in a few short days, they had to think of something. If Monsieur V was not caught before he could pass the information on to the other spy, Rocky shuddered to think of what might happen to England. She couldn't let the Graylocke's, or her country, down.

After last night, though, they could barely look at each other, let alone communicate their ideas.

Every time Rocky met his gaze, she remembered the vulnerable way he'd looked a second before he'd brushed his mouth against hers, as if he was confused by his desire to kiss her.

And well he should be, because the only reason he'd felt that way had been because of Felicia's blasted perfume! Even if it had worked yesterday to loosen Hollander's tongue, Rocky couldn't entertain the notion of using it again during the course of the investigation. What if Catt gave in to the instincts roused by the perfume and next time they did more than kiss? It would be disastrous to their friendship.

But undoubtedly a night to remember. Rocky lowered her head, biting her lip hard to try to regain her senses. He was her friend and partner in this assignment, nothing more. After this was over, she would have a talk with the Duke of Tenwick or Gideon and tell them in no uncertain terms that she couldn't work with Catt again.

That was, if she could even survive this mission with him. Her reaction to him boggled the mind.

The door to the hothouse opened. Rocky barely gave it a thought as she laid the finished bouquet in line with the others. The servants entered so many times per day that so long as she recognized their faces and ensured that the only place they went to was the bouquets, she didn't give them a second thought. She stepped back to let whatever servant had entered choose the bouquets to deliver.

The newcomer wasn't one of the servants. Nor was it Lady Belhaven, come to check on their work for the umpteenth time this morning. Rocky had never seen this man before in her life. Who was he?

There was something familiar about him in the square cut of his jaw and the shape of his nose. He wasn't quite as tall as Catt, but had a similar lean build and dressed just as impeccably. Although the dowdy gray color of his clothes wouldn't have drawn the eye, close up Rocky noticed that the cut fit him well enough to have been tailored and the material looked better made than anything a servant would wear. His dark brown hair was clipped short in a Brutus style haircut, matched with neatly groomed sideburns.

If he noticed her standing there, he didn't show it. With clipped steps he entered the room, letting the door fall shut behind him but not checking that it was properly closed. He ran his hands over the nearest potted plant, an orchid. Then he turned to the shelves containing dozens of plants, eyeing them as if he were looking for something.

Rocky stiffened. Was he looking for a specific plant? Checking for a code? She had given the plants on this side of the hothouse a cursory inspection when she'd entered this morning. Catt had done the same on his side of the room. Neither of them had departed at the same time, the better to watch over whoever entered and exited. As far as she knew, there was no code to find.

She cleared her throat. "I beg your pardon?" Who was this stranger?

When he turned, his expression was so neutral it appeared severe. Although his eyes were brown, they seemed to pierce her with the same intensity as those of the Duke of Tenwick. "Who are you?" His tone was cold, clipped, and curt.

Instinctively, she thrust back her shoulders and raised her chin. He wasn't the first forbidding man who had taken offense at finding her in a position of authority. "I'm the lead botanist in Lady Belhaven's household. This is my domain. Who are you?"

He rounded on her. Although he clasped his hands behind his back, she felt as though she were being interrogated under threat of torture. Her back touched the worktable. She had nowhere to run.

She would be showing weakness if she tried.

"A botanist, you say?" He took a step closer. "How long have you been working here?"

"A...a little over a week."

"Lady Belhaven hired you?"

"Yes, temporarily from my former employer."

"Why did he let you leave?"

She bristled. The duke had assigned her this position as a cover for her spying assignment, but she couldn't confess that. This stranger made it sound as though she had been let go for inferior work. If that had been the case, she doubted she would have gotten the reference necessary for Lady Belhaven to have hired her.

"There was an accident in the duke's orangery and as a result it is out of commission until spring when the glass will be repaired." Until then, she had been out of work. At least, work involving plants. Over the past few months, she and Catt had been busy being formally trained as spies for the Crown.

"This duke was your former employer, then? Which duke?"

She gritted her teeth. "The Duke of Tenwick. And he is still my employer. I am only on loan to Lady Belhaven for the duration of the winter."

"How long did you work for the duke?"

"Years."

"How many years, exactly?"

Catt strolled up from the far corner of the hothouse. Although he affected an easy demeanor, there was an edge to his voice and smile as he said, "I don't see as that's any of your business, friend."

The stranger's eyebrow shot up as he turned to face Catt. "And you are?"

Catt mirrored the man's stiff stance. "Wondering who you are to come in here and harass my superior."

His superior? A small smile cracked across Rocky's lips. How much had it cost him to say that?

Some of the tension radiated away from her shoulders as the stranger answered.

"I'm Lance Belhaven, grandson to the lady of the house. And, considering that she neglected to tell me that she'd hired on extra help, I am very surprised by your presence here. Where is my grandmother this morning?"

"She keeps to her bedchamber or her favorite parlor for most of the day," Rocky answered, leaving out the fact that Lady Belhaven often entered the hothouse several times a day and Catt escorted her away again. After all, they had things well in hand. Lady Belhaven seemed to battle issues with her memory.

Nodding curtly, Mr. Belhaven strode from the room without a word. Catt followed him, shutting the hothouse door forcefully. The moment it was shut, he turned to Rocky.

"Are you all right?"

He reached for her, almost as if he intended to caress her arm or pull her into his embrace. She took a small step away and wrapped her arms around her torso. She must be imagining it. After their kiss yesterday, he could barely look at her. He would never touch her like...

Like a lover.

She bit her lower lip, trying to get herself under control. Their kiss had changed the dynamic between them, just as she'd known it would. She shouldn't have let him do it, but she hadn't been able to resist. If he tried again...

But he wouldn't. She shouldn't let herself believe something that might disappoint her later.

"I'm fine," she said, injecting her voice with steel. "He didn't touch me."

"No, but he was far from friendly."

Rocky narrowed her eyes, staring at the door. "What if he had reason to be?"

"What do you mean?" Catt stepped closer, but he didn't attempt to touch her. Instead, he leaned his hip against the work table.

She forced herself to look into his eyes. There was nothing there to alarm her. The same Catt she saw every day. "He was touching the plants, almost as though he was searching for one with a code. The duke would have told us if there was another Crown spy among the household."

Catt narrowed his eyes, but nodded slowly in agreement.

"Then, in order to know that code, he must be a French spy."

Suspicion crossed Catt's face as he also glanced toward the door, giving her his profile. Rocky took advantage of his distraction to admire the curve of his cheek and shape of his nose. When he turned back, she quickly looked away.

"Are you certain that's what he was doing?"

"No, but we certainly can't discount the possibility."

He straightened. His posture seemed stiffer than usual. "No, I suppose we can't."

Rocky frowned. "You disagree." She braced herself, waiting for the inevitable argument.

"No, I agree with you wholeheartedly."

Then why was he standing that way?

The door opened again, capturing their attention. This time it was one of the staff. Benjamin Faulker.

He nodded. "I passed master Belhaven in the hallway. I trust he found what he wanted in here."

Actually, he'd left empty-handed. "I think he was looking for Lady Belhaven."

Faulker made a face. "Indeed. I've not seen him take an interest in the hothouse in all the years I've tended to Lady Belhaven and now twice in the span of a few days." Faulker forced a smile. "Perhaps he is taking a new interest to have something in common with his grandmother. Lord knows they should all treat her better. She's a fine woman."

"That she is," Catt said.

"Well, then, I'm here for Lady Hastings' posies. Need to deliver them early today."

Rocky handed over the flowers and they watched Faulker leave.

"Well, that was interesting," Catt said.

"Maybe Lance's visits weren't so innocent."

Catt turned to face her. "You've thought through the implications, of course."

Rocky nodded. "We've been looking among the staff, but if Lady Belhaven's grandson is involved..."

"We need to investigate the possibility that Lady Belhaven is also involved."

He looked as though he'd bitten a poisonous plant. Since they'd arrived, Catt had taken a shine to Lady Belhaven, treating her as he might his own grandmother. Truthfully, Rocky didn't like the idea that she could be a traitor any more than he did.

"She might not be." She was, after all, bordering on senile with her memory loss. Not to mention that she was unsteady on her feet and unable to withstand the physical vigor that spying entailed. But even if she wasn't directly involved, she could know of the involvement of the person in her house. She might be sheltering them, funding them, encouraging them.

He beckoned to her as he stepped away from the work table. "Come here a moment. I'd like your opinion on something."

Rocky followed him as he led the way toward the hot brick oven. When there, he crouched beneath the shelving and reached in behind several pots. He pulled out a small terracotta pot. The scrawny-looking plant it contained was stripped of over half its leaves. It had only one small flower, an orange bloom.

She frowned. "Is that a poppy?" It wasn't a species she'd worked with often, but she recognized the shape of the flower and the construct of the leaves.

"I thought so, too," Catt answered as he replaced it. "I wanted a second opinion, in case I was wrong."

"Lady Belhaven has no other poppies. Why this one?"

"My guess?" He raised his eyebrows. "For the leaves."

She frowned as she tried to recall if she'd ever read a paper on the properties of the leaves. Pursing her lips, she shook her head.

He informed, "I've never tested the theory myself, but I've read that the leaves have hallucinogenic and calming properties. When brewed into a tea it can reduce anxiety and in stronger doses, relieve pain."

She rocked back on her heels and slowly straightened. "Why is it in Lady Belhaven's hothouse? It certainly isn't for the flower. Do you think that's what Lance was looking for?"

Whoever had hidden it hadn't tended it well, given its dilapidated state.

Catt stood as well. They were so close together that the heat of his body seeped into hers, even stronger than the oven at her back. Or, at the very least, more alluring. She followed him a few paces away from the hot brick wall.

"Maybe. I don't think Lady Belhaven put it there," he said, keeping his voice low. Who did he think would hear? They were across the room from the door, which was shut tight.

"Why do you say that?"

"Note the position. She wouldn't have been able to easily bend and retrieve the leaves. And, given her skills, I imagine she would have been able to tend it better."

Rocky nibbled on her thumbnail as she nodded slowly. "I agree with you."

"Maybe Lance has an opiate problem?" Catt suggested.

"Or maybe someone is using it to keep Lady Belhaven in a state of confusion."

"Or to keep her from feeling pain," Catt suggested.

"Could be either, but the question is, does it have anything to do with Monsieur V?"

Chapter Sixteen

How were Rocky and Catt supposed to maintain a working relationship when every time she looked in his direction, she relived his kiss? She'd hoped after spending a full day working with him that the bizarre awareness afflicting her would fade. It hadn't. If anything, it had grown stronger overnight. So strong, that she found it almost impossible to hide her attraction to him while they worked. She had to get away.

Grabbing the watering can, she went on a circuit of the manor's houseplants. As she reached Lady Belhaven's favorite parlor, a footman left, walking in the opposite direction. She couldn't tell who from the back of his head—most likely Stefan given the build. Rocky paused in the doorway. Lady Belhaven was in there, seated in her usual chair next to the fire. Her grandson, Stanley, lounged on the sofa next to her. He flipped through the pages of a book.

The plants in this room were thriving, thanks to the care Lady Belhaven lavished on them. Rocky didn't need to tend them. She started to take a step back, but the movement caught Stanley's eye. When he looked up, he gave her a warm smile.

"Do come in."

"Rocky," Lady Belhaven greeted. She clasped her hands in front of her middle. "Is something amiss in the hothouse?"

"No, all is well. I just came to check on the plants."

And to escape from Catt's presence for a moment. Rocky should have been searching for clues while away from Catt, but she didn't know where to start. Was Lady Belhaven aware of the French spymaster in her midst?

The old woman waved her hand toward the corner, where one of several ferns resided. "By all means, go ahead."

Rocky danced from foot to foot. "I don't want to interrupt..."

Stanley slipped his finger between the pages of the book as he closed it. He leaned against the back of the sofa, crossing his legs at the ankles. "Poppycock. You aren't interrupting anything. I would feel like a heel if I kept a pretty woman from her work."

Rocky narrowed her eyes at him, but upon earning no rebuke from Lady Belhaven, she reluctantly entered the room. She would tend the plants here quickly so she could move on. If both

Lady Belhaven and Stanley were occupied, then their rooms would be unattended. If there was anything to be learned in their private chambers, Rocky would discover it.

Just as she watered the last plant in the room, another man entered the room. He was older than Stanley, but shared features with both Belhavens in the room. Most likely, this large, imposing man was Kenneth, Lady Belhaven's son, who Catt had mentioned to her previously. Given his temperament, Rocky hastened to be away.

As she reached the doorway, the greeting between family members turned from civil to vicious. Coldly, Lady Belhaven said, "If you're here to beg for money, save your breath. My opinion on the matter hasn't changed."

Kenneth's posture changed. He seemed to loom over both seated parties like a thundercloud. Even Stanley sat straighter, wary.

"You turn away your own son without a second thought, yet keep this degenerate well inlaid? He's in ten times deeper than I am!"

Lady Belhaven turned to her grandson. "Is this true?"

Stanley raised his hands. His posture turned relaxed, lackadaisical. "I had an off night, Grandmother. I'll win it back, I'm sure."

A cloud formed over Lady Belhaven's expression. "I cannot condone gambling, Stanley. Surely you must know that nothing is certain."

Although she delivered him a lecture on the subject, her expression and tone were almost indulgent. He looked properly chastised, though Rocky suspected this was an act and he was unrepentant. The easy manner with which he held himself indicated that much.

Lady Belhaven concluded her lecture by asking, "Did you have a moment to look in on Mrs. Draper? I am confined to the house due to this blasted weather and haven't heard from her."

Kenneth, disgusted, made a disgruntled sound, swung on his heel, and stormed from the room. In the process, he knocked into a fern and toppled it. The dirt spilled onto the floor. He jostled Rocky as he stepped out of the room.

"Don't stand there gaping. Make yourself useful, wench," the big man snapped.

Rocky's spine turned to steel. She bit her tongue to keep from pushing her luck. At Tenwick Abbey, the duke would never allow anyone to treat his servants with disrespect, let alone a member of his family.

It was one more reminder that Rocky was in a different world, a dangerous world.

She crouched to right the plant and clean up what dirt she could. The rug would need to be beaten of the rest. She'd have to find one of the maids and tell them.

Behind her, Stanley answered, "She has that well in hand, Grandmother. Indeed, I did visit Mrs. Draper on your behalf. She is in good health, aside from the flaring of her gout now and again. She gave me a letter for you. Shall I read it so you don't tax your eyes? I can transcribe a response and deliver it when next I go out if you'd like."

Rocky stood, dusting off her skirts. When she straightened, she found Stanley staring at her as he unfolded a letter from his pocket. He cast her another warm smile.

Frowning, Rocky swept out of the room before she had to wonder what *that* was about. Did she still smell like Felicia's perfume?

***

Catt nestled himself in the furthest corner of the hothouse, out of view of the doorway. This drew him close to the hot brick wall as he worked, but he shucked his jacket, rolled up his sleeves, and endured the discomfort. While Rocky was away, he meant to take advantage of the solitude. Someone in the house had planted that poppy in the hothouse. If he was in luck, he might discover who it was.

Not that luck appeared to be on his side. Despite the fact that he'd jumped upon the excuse Rocky had given him—that he'd only kissed her due to the perfume's effects—the tension between them was palpable. She despised him for the liberties he'd taken. Worst of all, he couldn't bring himself to regret it. He relived that kiss every time he shut his eyes.

With a sigh, he crouched to tend to the plants situated beneath the shelving, in pots on the floor.

The hothouse door opened while Catt continued his task. He twisted to glance over his shoulder in case the person who entered was someone other than Rocky. Although he wanted to catch whoever had hidden that poppy, he didn't want to leave the hothouse unattended for Monsieur V to tamper with. Morgan still hadn't deciphered that code, last Catt had checked the exchange point, and until he did, Catt wanted to be vigilant. If he didn't know what was being said he could, at the very least, discover *who* was saying it.

With the deliveries of the morning over with, none of the footmen had any business entering the hothouse. Lady Belhaven often arrived to ask after their care of her plants. Sometimes she even inspected their work, but she had yet to find fault in it. In fact, Catt suspected that she only checked to make herself feel useful. Given the conversations he'd had with the staff, Lady Belhaven hadn't relinquished her position in the hothouse willingly. If not for her poor eyesight and the fact that she could no longer physically keep up with the demand of the orders that arrived every day, she might have never hired Catt and Rocky. Catt even suspected that Morgan had had a hand in convincing the old woman to retire. The Duke of Tenwick could be very persuasive, upon occasion.

The person who entered was neither a footman nor Lady Belhaven. It was Mr. Dowden, the cook. Catt froze, holding his breath. What business could he have in the hothouse? Ever since Rocky had caught Eliza attempting to poison everyone, none of the kitchen staff had entered save for the scullery boy fetching bouquets for Hollander to deliver. Even he entered only rarely, when everyone else was engaged in a task and couldn't be spared.

Was Rocky right in her suspicions of the seemingly jovial man? Could he be Monsieur V? Catt waited, partially hidden in the leafy foliage of the plants, as Mr. Dowden crossed the hothouse. He didn't pause to tamper with any of the plants, but made a beeline directly for the poppy. He crouched, stretching his arm out, a bit red in the face as he stripped a few leaves from the plant. He held his tongue between his teeth. When he retracted his arm, he glanced up and discovered Catt staring at him.

His expression turned hostile. Catt straightened quickly, bracing himself in case this got ugly. Part of spy training was in the dirty, underhanded fighting that took place in London's underbelly. If he needed to, he could defend himself, even against an opponent who weighed more than him.

Catt held his hands loose and ready at his sides, his feet spread. He tried to mimic Morgan's ducal stare, even though his insides were quivering. How long would Rocky be away? He would have felt better to have someone nearby to witness the altercation, especially if Mr. Dowden *had* killed his wife. At the same time, he didn't want that witness to be Rocky. She was too easily riled, too quick to jump into a fight. He didn't want to see her in danger, especially against an opponent so much bigger than she was.

He tamped down the irrational fear. They were spying partners, not lovers. She had been taught how to handle herself just as well as he had. If she knew of his protective thoughts, she would not be happy about them.

Catt took a deep breath and said, "Perhaps you'd care to explain why you're keeping an opiate in Lady Belhaven's hothouse?"

The cook's neck flushed with color. The infusion of red climbed up to fill his ears and face. Despite the color, he didn't look embarrassed or guilty. He appeared...hostile.

Bloody hell. Catt tensed, preparing for a fight. He wanted answers, not for this to come to blows!

Mr. Dowden seemed to deflate as he breathed a gusty sigh. He clenched his fist around the poppy leaves. "The opiate is my secret ingredient in Lady Belhaven's calming tea. It's the only thing keeping my job."

Catt didn't understand how those two statements could possibly be connected, but he forced himself to relax. He kept his fists balled at his sides just in case. "Perhaps you ought to explain."

"I know my daughter has been trying to oust me from my position in order to claim it for herself."

He did? Interesting.

The big man shrugged. "It's been going on for quite some time. Little mishaps or errors that seem to lead back to me, only I know I didn't make them. Lady Belhaven's grandson has even taken it upon himself to reprimand me and warn me that if the errors continue, Lady Belhaven will turn me out."

Catt narrowed his eyes. "Which of her grandsons?"

"The barrister. Lance."

Interesting. Catt would have thought him to be more distant from his grandmother, given the infrequency of his visits. After all, whereas Stanley had been in residence at the house since the moment he and Rocky arrived, and Kenneth had visited on multiple occasions, Lance had only visited once. Or at least he'd only made himself *known* once. But if he'd threatened the cook and been to the hothouse more than once this week as Faulker had insinuated, then maybe Lance was up to something.

During his visit, he'd appeared to have a greater than necessary interest in the servants staffed in the house. Rocky seemed to find him suspicious and, to be honest, so did Catt. But he couldn't discount the possibility that the man in front of him was Monsieur V. He had to be vigilant, and explore all avenues.

Mr. Dowden continued. "I've been with Lady Belhaven since she could first afford a cook. Eliza grew up in this household. I don't want to deprive my daughter of anything, but Eliza is more like her mother than like me. She's cold, calculating. And she dislikes me. If Lady Belhaven turned me out of the house, I can't count on Eliza to support me."

Catt steeled himself against a wave of sympathy. He knew what it was like to be turned away and left in the cold. If not for his uncle, the only person in his family to have nurtured Catt's scientific curiosity, Catt might have wound up a soldier instead of a spy. Somehow, he didn't think that he would have survived long past his first battle.

Oblivious to the emotions Catt battled, the cook continued. "The only reason Lady Belhaven hasn't turned me away is because I am the only person in the household able to brew her calming tea correctly. No one knows about the poppy leaves I add in. If they did, I would be expendable."

Was he asking Catt to keep his secret? Catt pinched the bridge of his nose as he thought. It was immoral. But it had nothing to do with his quest for Monsieur V.

Or did it? Simply because he had uncovered one of Mr. Dowden's secrets didn't mean that the cook wasn't hiding another. What of the matter of his dead wife? If he'd killed her...

The cook added, "I'm doing nothing wrong. My tea helps Lady Belhaven overcome her nervous spasms. And it eases the pain in her joints."

"Shouldn't she have all the facts so she can make an informed decision? She doesn't know she is being dosed with opium."

The cook's mouth firmed. A muscle in his jaw twitched. "It's helping her, not hurting her. I'm careful to only give a medicinal dose. What's the harm?"

Catt didn't know how to argue with him. He didn't even know whether he wanted to. He needed to discuss this with Rocky. Waving a hand, he said, "It's none of my concern."

Mr. Dowden looked hesitant. "You won't tell Lady Belhaven."

"I won't tell." For now.

With a curt nod and a flash of relief, the man strode briskly from the hothouse. He shut the door behind him. Catt paced, unable to concentrate on the work he should be attending in the hothouse. When he'd taken up the assignment to find Monsieur V, he hadn't expected to be confronted with so many other secrets and given the choice of whether or not to reveal them. Was it really his decision to make? He was hunting a traitor.

He craved Rocky's decisiveness. She would know what to do. What was taking her so long?

When the door to the hothouse next opened, Rocky entered. Catt had made several circuits of the room and happened to be idling in the same position as he had been when Mr. Dowden had left over half an hour ago. The moment Rocky shut the door, she frowned.

"Finally," Catt said with feeling. He beckoned her closer.

Hesitantly, she crossed to him. A small furrow formed between her eyebrows as she studied him. "Did I miss something?"

"I discovered who has been hiding the poppy."

She looked surprised. "Who?"

He told her of his confrontation with Mr. Dowden and everything the cook had confessed. When he finished, Rocky nibbled on her thumbnail. A thick lock of her hair, shorter than the rest, had fallen free of her coif to curl against her cheek.

"What should we do?" he asked.

Her frown deepened as she dropped her hand. "You truly want my opinion?"

"Of course." Why wouldn't he?

That teasing lock fell into her eyes, half-obscuring them.

Squaring her shoulders, Rocky said, "We don't need to make a decision regarding the poppy use just yet. He could still be Monsieur V. If he is, we'll have stopped this subterfuge as well."

Catt nodded. Her words made sense, as he'd known they would. He felt better going along with what she said than having to think of the right course of action himself.

That lock of hair was driving him mad. He liked to look into her eyes when he spoke to her. She didn't appear to notice it. Giving in to instinct, he reached forward and tucked the strand behind her ear. His fingers grazed her soft cheek on the way. Why did her skin have to be so smooth? It made him wonder how soft she would feel in other areas. That only made him ache for something he couldn't have.

His gaze dropped to her mouth. They were utterly alone in the hothouse. He could kiss her again, and no one need ever know.

But this time, he didn't have the excuse of the perfume to hide behind. If Rocky didn't feel the same pull toward him that he did to her...

She'd kissed him back the other day, without any influences clouding her mind such as Felicia's perfume. *Could* she feel the same attraction to him as he did to her? Was she fighting it, too?

He started to lower his head to find out when the door to the hothouse opened.

Chapter Seventeen

Rocky froze the moment she heard the door latch jangle. Her heart hammered in the base of her throat, a painful and insistent beat. Her eyes widened as she stared up at Catt. What were they doing? No one could see them like this.

They shouldn't even *be* like this. This...close. This...wanting.

Her instincts kicked in and she urged Catt back into the corner. A space between the work table where they arranged the bouquets and the shelving unit against the wall provided some cover. The leafy fronds spilling from the pots camouflaged their forms. She pressed herself into the space after him.

Her back pressed against him. His heat surrounded her, different from the warmth radiating from the brick wall next to them. This heat came with a sizzling awareness that traveled up her spine. When she squirmed, Catt snaked his arm around her and pinned her to his body.

What was he doing? She was afraid to turn and ask.

A figure entered the hothouse. A leaf obscured Rocky's view of him. She squinted, tilting her head to get a better view.

The scullery boy? Why would he be in the hothouse at this hour? The time to deliver bouquets was long past.

The adolescent scratched at his face and checked over his shoulder to ensure the door was shut. He didn't appear to notice Rocky and Catt in the corner. As he tiptoed into the room, his shoulders hunched and his expression guilty, Rocky fought an inner battle. He couldn't be involved in their hunt for the spy—he was little more than a child! If anything, he was being taken advantage of, and that notion didn't sit right with Rocky at all. Who was bullying him to help in something he didn't want to do? When she tensed, Catt caressed her a bit with the hand over her stomach. A flood of awareness drenched her. For a moment, she'd forgotten he was there.

Although she half-expected the scullery boy to produce a needle and start poking holes into the fauna, he tiptoed to a shelving unit mere feet away from Catt and Rocky's position. He crouched, pulling out the poppy plant. He stripped off more of its leaves. It was starting to look quite bare, indeed.

Rocky twisted, raising her gaze to Catt's face. He turned his face down to look at her.

With her eyes and a jerk of her chin, she asked, *Should we interrupt him?*

He looked hesitant for a moment, then nodded and dropped his hand.

Relief gushed through her that he'd understood what she was asking despite the fact that she hadn't said a word. Would anyone other than him have been able to understand her like that? But they'd spent so much time together over the past week— not to mention the years they'd known each other— that she didn't have to think about it. She knew instinctively that he would understand her.

She slipped through the gap between the shelving unit and the work table. It was a tight squeeze, requiring her to turn sideways, but she managed it without snagging her dress. She planted herself in the scullery boy's path and raised her eyebrows.

"Are you certain you should be doing that? Perhaps you ought to tell us who put you up to it."

The boy blanched, turning whiter than the lily on the shelf behind him. He thrust the poppy pot away from him. It teetered and fell as he stood. Rocky crossed her arms, waiting for an explanation.

Instead, the boy fled.

When the scullery boy, Eric, fled around the shelves lining the middle of the hothouse, Catt could have headed him off near the door. However, Rocky bunched, dropping her arms as she prepared to run after him. He stopped her, grabbing her arm before she did.

The scullery boy bolted out the hothouse door. It fell shut after him.

Rocky yanked her arm free of Catt's hold. She rounded on him. "What did you do that for?"

If he hadn't been used to the fire in her eyes and her stinging tone, he might have been offended. Ignoring her accusatory demeanor, he kept his stance and tone carefully neutral. "The boy is shy of you. It's been obvious since we arrived. Will you let me speak with him? He might open up to me more."

"Why?" Her mouth twisted. "Because you're a man."

"Yes." He knew this was a sore spot with her, so he spoke over the top of her when she opened her mouth. "This has nothing to do with your capability and everything to do with the fact that young boys relate better to their own gender. It isn't a reflection on you."

She said nothing, but her mouth flattened into an unhappy line.

"May I try to get him to talk, at the very least?"

Angrily, she waved her hand to the door. "Quickly. Before he runs too far."

Where did she think he would go? Lady Belhaven's manor wasn't so big, and even if the boy was scared, Catt didn't think he would forfeit his position in the house by running away.

Nevertheless, he didn't argue with her. He nodded curtly and strode out of the hothouse and into the corridor.

At this time of year the sun swiftly set, leaving the corridor awash in shadow despite the window at the far end. Light glimmered from the kitchen, where the cooks were hard at work preparing the night's meal. Would the scullery boy have returned there to continue his work? Catt checked, but he saw only Eliza and her father. He pulled back before either party noticed him.

So where was the boy? He would be missed soon enough if he didn't return to work. Catt could wait for him, but he sensed that the boy was in a delicate state at the moment. Not only would he be more likely to spill his secrets to someone with a gentler touch than Rocky—not that Catt would ever imply that she was inadequate in anything—but he likely could use some reassurance. Catt's stomach clenched as he combed the manor for the adolescent.

He found Eric sulking in the shadow of the servant's stair. Catt approached with slow footsteps, careful to keep his posture and demeanor nonthreatening. The boy tensed as he lowered himself onto the stair next to him.

"Don't run," Catt said, keeping his voice low. "I only want to talk."

Eric said nothing. The glow of a lamp or candle from somewhere further in the manor cast a dim light that stretched just far enough to make out the contours of his face. Whether due to the lighting or some natural pigment, the boy's face appeared waxen and drawn.

He said nothing, giving Catt time to collect his thoughts before he ventured, "We know the poppy was not planted by you."

The boy looked relieved. "I swear, I didn't even know what it was for, when I first found it. I just thought it was another of Lady Belhaven's flowers."

"I take it you never told her of it."

"No. It was in such a sorry state I was afraid she would sack me for mistreating it, so I looked it up in the library first."

The color rushed back into his cheeks in a flood. He pressed his lips together and didn't say another word.

Catt stifled a sigh. He knew not every person they cornered would be as willing to spill their secrets, but for some reason, he considered this one to be key. Could he come at it from another angle?

Keeping his posture carefully casual, he mused, "I've heard from others in the manor that Mr. Dowden killed his wife."

Catt shot a glance toward the boy in time to catch his confused expression. Eric shrugged. "I don't know if that's true. It was before my time here."

"The kind of man to bully someone into fetching from his stash would certainly be capable of killing, wouldn't you say?"

Fear crossed the boy's face. "You think Mr. Dowden...?" He pressed his lips together and shook his head. "No. Mr. Dowden isn't forcing me to do anything." The mixture of emotions on his face was all but indecipherable. Was he disappointed or afraid? Catt wouldn't tell.

Gently, he said, "You're certain? I will take you at your word. If you tell me Mr. Dowden is to blame for the existence of the poppy, I will believe you."

"Well, he is," Eric scowled. "But he doesn't know that I found it."

Interesting. Catt had been so certain...

Maybe he needed to purge all preconceptions from his brain and listen to what Eric was trying to tell him. The boy was clearly on edge, moments away from divulging the truth. If Catt pushed the wrong way, he might close up and offer nothing.

Softly, Catt promised, "I won't tell him."

That didn't seem to ease Eric's discomfort.

Catt took a deep breath, trying to think. "Did you take the leaves for yourself?"

"No!" The boy recoiled, hunching in on himself as he vehemently denied the notion with words and body language.

"For who, then? Lady Belhaven?" The boy had already confessed that he hadn't informed her of the plant's existence. Hadn't he?

Tight-lipped, Eric shook his head. He wrapped his arms around his knees and didn't say a word.

Someone was undoubtedly extorting him. Could this be connected with Catt and Rocky's assignment? For some reason, Catt didn't think so. What benefit could Monsieur V take from the use of opiates? Unless he wanted to indulge for himself, but that seemed careless and irresponsible, two things that Monsieur V had long since proven himself not to be. The French spymaster didn't make mistakes, didn't descend into a state that might loosen his tongue. He was meticulous in everything he did; if anything, opiate use might make him sloppy. Therefore, it was unlikely that Monsieur V was the man forcing Eric to steal the poppy leaves for him.

Who, then? Should Catt walk away and leave the matter as it was?

He gritted his teeth. He couldn't. For Rocky's sake, if nothing else. She had a soft spot for adolescents forced into a tight corner. He didn't know what had gone on in her past to warrant such ferocity, but he knew he couldn't let Eric walk away without at least making an attempt to learn who was truly behind this behavior.

Catt laid a hand on the boy's shoulder. "Eric, I can't help you if you don't tell me what is going on."

The boy hid his face. "You can't help me, either way. Lady Belhaven wouldn't believe you any more than she would me."

Catt took a deep breath, trying to maintain his calm, neutral tone. Snapping at the scullery boy for his reluctance would do more harm than good. Fear was not going to win him any answers; trust would.

"How do you know? I believe the lady is quite fond of me."

He did escort her back to her rooms nearly every time she visited the hothouse. Sometimes, she asked him to take tea with her there. He wasn't always at liberty to accept, depending on the day, but she certainly wouldn't offer if she abhorred him.

Eric swallowed audibly. "It involves...her family." His voice cracked.

Catt waited, but he offered nothing more. Gently, Catt said, "Who in her family? Her son? Her grandsons? All three?"

Lance had strode into the hothouse as if it was his rather than his grandmother's. Had he learned about the poppy and wanted some for himself?

To be honest, Catt couldn't picture it. Lance didn't seem the type to indulge in such a fashion. He was upright, collected, calculating. The kind of qualities Catt pictured in Monsieur V.

Stanley, on the other hand, was more self-indulgent and seemed to live for his own pleasures. The only reason Lady Belhaven seemed to treat him differently than her son was because he was more considerate. At least, as far as Catt had been able to tell.

After a long, drawn-out moment, Eric's shoulders slumped forward in defeat. He let out a gusty sigh. "A couple months back, when I was helping Lady Belhaven in the hothouse, she had a fit."

Catt frowned. "What kind of fit?"

"Dizziness. It happens from time to time. She fell, but I managed to catch her on the way down so she wasn't as hurt as may be."

Catt strongly suspected that by 'catch her' Eric indicated that he had cushioned the old lady's fall.

"Go on," he said slowly. He didn't understand what her health had to do with her family...unless one of them was trying to do away with her?

He didn't want to think of that possibility. He stowed it in the back of his mind, for consideration at another time.

"Lady Belhaven has a draught in her bedchamber that she keeps on hand to give her strength against the dizzy spells. I ran to fetch it for her while she recovered."

Catt nodded. He waited for the boy to continue. Since none of this explained the poppy in any way, he sensed there was more to the story. Silence wrapped around them, punctuated by the distant sounds of the servants going about their chores. No one lingered in this section of the manor, for the moment. That didn't mean that they would remain in privacy for long.

"You found the draught," Catt prompted.

"I found more than that." The scullery boy fiddled with his fingernails, picking at them. "I found Mr. Belhaven in her room, helping himself to the money in her purse."

"To which Mr. Belhaven are you referring?" There were three, after all. Even if, given the conversations both he and Rocky had overheard, Catt suspected he knew precisely which man Eric meant.

"Her son," the boy confirmed.

The answer didn't surprise Catt in the least. He'd known the man was a fiend from the moment they'd met.

"You didn't tell Lady Belhaven," he guessed.

Eric shook his head. "I can't. Who will she believe, a scullery boy or her own son?"

Catt would like to think that the old woman had enough sense to see the truth, but he didn't speak as much aloud. Truth be told, Eric was likely correct. If Lady Belhaven had wanted to see the truths of her son's character, she would have disowned him and barred him from the house rather than simply refusing him money.

"How does this matter relate to the poppy?"

Catt sensed he wouldn't be happy with the answer, but he had to know the full truth. Hell and damnation, how was he going to tell this to Rocky?

She would want to charge into Mr. Belhaven's home and flay him alive.

The adolescent scratched his head. "It didn't, not at first. When I caught Mr. Belhaven, he threatened that if I told his mother that I'd found him in her room, he would see me sacked. He'd see that I never found another position. He'd say *I* was the one stealing, not him."

In one paragraph, the boy expressed all the injustice of the class system. Catt had never considered himself much of a radical, though the fact that he straddled the lines of the class system and didn't truly fit into any category gave him a unique perspective. Now, however... Was this what had happened to Rocky when she was young? He suddenly appreciated the Graylockes and their liberal dispositions when it came to formality and the separations of class. Although they had copious servants, neither Lady Graylocke nor Morgan would ever stand for such an injustice to occur under their roof. They treated those who worked for them as people, as equals, as least as much as one could treat someone as an equal when that person looked after one's every need. At the very least, they one and all treated their servants with respect.

Here, Eric had caught a man in wrongdoing, which under any other circumstance might have given him an advantage against the person he caught. But no, Mr. Belhaven had twisted that with his privilege to take advantage of the scullery boy instead.

Eric continued. "I promised not to say a word, but that wasn't the end of it. He started to ask me for favors. I don't know how he came to learn about the poppy, but once he did, about a month ago, he's been making me fetch him the leaves so he can imbibe."

"My sympathies." What could Catt do? What could he say? Kenneth was, unfortunately, as far beyond his grasp to punish as Monsieur V. He and Rocky hadn't been sent here to right the world's wrongs; their only concern was with Britain and the war. Softly, he added, "If it's any consolation, should you be turned out of the house, I can see you get a good recommendation to work for the Duke of Tenwick."

"A duke?" Eric snorted. It was a sound of disbelief. His voice was laden with distrust and bitterness when he added, "What can you do? You're only a servant, like me. Them lords and ladies don't listen to the likes of us."

Catt wasn't a servant. He was a friend to the Graylockes, and he was fairly certain that Morgan would take Eric in if only Catt explained the situation. But he couldn't say either thing to the boy, or risk giving away his true purpose in the house. To Eric, Catt *was* nothing more than a servant. That was his role here, and he'd best not forget it.

He clapped the boy on the shoulder. "Well, you have my silence. And Rocky's as well. I'll see to it."

Eric looked a bit alarmed, but he bit his lower lip and nodded. Catt squeezed his shoulder and stood. He needed to tell Rocky what he'd learned. She wasn't going to like it.

The real question was whether or not he could stop her from doing something that might jeopardize their purpose in the household. He squared his shoulders and prepared for another battle of wills.

The moment he stepped into the hothouse, he found Rocky pacing. She'd lit a lantern, but that only threw her shadow against the glass wall, distorting her reflection. He couldn't catch her expression in the glass. When he shut the hothouse door, she rounded on him. Impatience bled from her pores.

"Well?"

He pressed his back against the door, barring her escape. "Eric confessed the situation to me."

She looked relieved. Had she not trusted him to get the boy to open up?

"And?" She stepped closer, a pace away where she didn't have to raise her voice.

"He's being forced into it, as you might expect."

"By whom?" Rocky's jaw was set, her eyes hard. She looked ready to do battle.

He couldn't let her.

"Kenneth." As a thundercloud darkened Rocky's expression, Catt hesitated. He knew that she wasn't going to like the explanation of the situation any more than she did the culprit. "Eric caught him stealing from Lady Belhaven and has been blackmailed into silence."

Catt knew he should have put it more delicately, given the way Rocky became riled at the mistreatment of working class adolescents. He caught her gaze with his, willing her to understand that he'd told her the bald truth because he trusted her not to do anything rash.

Her expression knit into a mask of outrage. She whirled away from him, storming the length of the hothouse before turning back. Her posture was rigid. Even across the room, he could tell she was shaking.

Blast! He should have broken the news more gently, after all. He strode away from the door and caught her as she turned back toward him. They were so close—he didn't think twice, but wrapped his arms around her and drew her close to his chest. His heart thumped hard as he waited for her to thrust him away.

She didn't. Instead, she buried her face in his shirt. "It isn't right." She grabbed fistfuls of his jacket like she plotted to wring someone's neck.

He rubbed her back, slowly feeling the tension leave her. He'd never seen her worked into this much of a lather. But, usually, if she found something to be out of sorts she was at liberty to fix it. This time, their hands were tied.

"No," he said softly. "It isn't."

She tipped her face up to his. Her gaze snapped with indignation and outrage. "We have to do something."

He'd never felt more helpless in his life than when he had to tell her, "We can't. Not yet. We're here to catch V."

The tension returned to her body. He pulled her even closer, resting his cheek on top of her head. "I'm sorry. If I could do something, I would. I told him I could get him a position with the Graylockes, but I don't think he believed me."

Rocky trembled. "Kenneth deserves to be punished."

"He does."

Catt couldn't refute that. Unfortunately, he couldn't condone it, either. They couldn't draw attention to themselves and there was every chance that if they spilled the truth to Lady Belhaven that Eric would be right and she would discount their tales in favor of her son.

That left inaction, and while it didn't sit well with Catt, he could see no other option for them. They had one mission and one mission only; if Kenneth was not Monsieur V, then he was no concern of theirs despite his heinous actions.

To his surprise, Rocky started to relax against him. She wrapped her arms around his waist and clutched him tight. A bit tighter than was comfortable, but he wasn't about to complain. Certainly not when she seemed to be calming down and returning to her usual state.

Had he...helped? He continued to rub circles over her back as emotion drenched him. He didn't know anyone able to calm Rocky when she worked herself up like this. No one except...him. At that moment, he felt strangely powerful. Important. He spent most of his life feeling superfluous—an extra body at a dinner party when needed, or company while Gideon worked through one of his brilliant breakthroughs with their research. Catt wasn't needed, not really.

At that moment, he felt needed. Like he'd made a difference. He turned his face into her hair, afraid to speak and ruin the moment.

"So what can we do?" Rocky asked after a moment, her voice soft.

He sighed and lifted his head, though he didn't release her. She didn't seem to mind that she still stood in the circle of his embrace. In fact, though she'd lessened her death grip, she still held him close. She tipped her face up to his. She looked more vulnerable than he'd ever seen her.

He hated it. He wanted the strong, confident woman he knew so well. Unfortunately, he didn't know how to bring her back, or even if that woman would still want to stand here, like this.

"I don't know," he admitted softly. "Discovering V's identity is our top priority."

She nodded, her expression resigned. "I know."

"Perhaps after we complete that task, we'll be at liberty..." He trailed off, not knowing what to say. If they exposed Kenneth's thieving ways, they would upset Lady Belhaven, who appeared to be in a delicate state of health whether or not she cared to admit it.

If they confronted Kenneth, Catt doubted that it would do a damn bit of good. With that man's temper, they might only wind up hurt.

The only good they might be able to do would be to remove Eric from the situation and install him in one of the Tenwick estates. But would that be good enough to ease Rocky's conscience?

He didn't know.

"I'm sorry," he murmured. "I wish we could do more."

She burrowed her face in his chest again. "As do I."

He didn't know how long they stood that way. He wanted to ask what had happened in her past to make her so vehement in the defense of adolescents, but he didn't want to shatter the moment. For all that he'd hugged her to offer her comfort, he found the closeness of her body to be soothing to him, as well. He'd never taken comfort from someone like this. He didn't want it to end.

So he said nothing. He steeled himself against the moment they would have to separate and return to their usual selves. The bullish Rocky who second-guessed every word out of his mouth, the tantalizing woman he wanted to kiss but couldn't. In the back of his mind, he feared what this moment would do to their fragile friendship.

Even that fear couldn't pull him away from her at that moment. He didn't want this newfound intimacy with her to end.

Chapter Eighteen

Rocky deadheaded the orchid with a bit more vigor than necessary. Throughout the night, she had been haunted by the knowledge of Kenneth's misdeeds and plagued by dreams of her past. Once she was out of that situation and settled at Tenwick Abbey, she had vowed never to stand idly by while something similar happened beneath her nose.

At Tenwick Abbey, where she'd had the power and freedom to be herself, it hadn't been an issue. The Duke of Tenwick didn't tolerate the mistreatment of his servants, young or old, by anyone. She'd become complacent, forgetting of that long-ago time when she'd been cornered into doing something she didn't want to do. The Graylockes had been her salvation, offering her a safe space to blossom into the strong, confident woman she was today. In a less hospitable environment, she might have withered instead.

She couldn't just leave Eric here to wither, though she wasn't in the same position here as she was in Tenwick Abbey. While on good terms, she wasn't personal friends with one of the Belhavens. She couldn't protect him in the same way, not without bringing him to Tenwick Abbey. And, with Monsieur V still at large, she wasn't at liberty to leave the household or play her hand. Everyone in this house believed her nothing more than the Graylockes' gardener. In a sense, she was and always would be. But they didn't know of her personal connection to the family, how they had welcomed her in and treated her like a friend simply because she and Gideon shared a calling.

She couldn't do anything to help Eric right now and it was eating her up inside.

Catt's hand covered hers. The touch was calm, soothing. She glanced up into his blue eyes. He didn't say a word, but somehow she knew that he guessed the stormy turn her thoughts had taken. She released the breath she'd been holding. The muscles in her shoulders relaxed. Just like that. With nothing more than a touch and look of shared understanding, he brought her peace. It wasn't the first time he'd calmed her this morning.

She didn't understand it. She twisted her hand to squeeze his and then returned to her work. A few last bouquets and they would be done with orders for the day. She carefully clipped off an orchid to add to the bunch, ensuring that the rest of the plant was thriving and would soon produce another flower from one of the buds tipping another stem.

Then she set the finished bouquet on the table and took up the last card to be filled. She couldn't decipher the scrawl at all. Lady Belhaven's hand had shaken too much as she'd written this one. Most of the cards were done by a servant's hand in neat script and delivered into the hothouse as the day went on, but Lady Belhaven liked to make herself useful as well when Catt and Rocky turned her away from the hothouse for fear of her overexerting herself. Rocky had come to differentiate her handwriting from the others. With a sigh, she showed the card to Catt, who couldn't puzzle out its meaning, either.

"I'll ask," Rocky grumbled under her breath.

Catt caught her by the elbow as he returned the card. "Are you all right?"

You know I'm not. She gritted her teeth and looked away. "As well as can be."

He held her gaze for a moment longer before he released her. He didn't say a word, but she felt the full weight of his warning nevertheless.

Don't do anything rash. Don't give us away.

She let out a slow breath as she tried to answer his warning the same way he delivered it—with her eyes. *You can trust me.*

"I'll return shortly. We have work to do."

He nodded, a crisp movement, as he returned to said work. Rocky turned away to hide the relief and confusion she felt that he wasn't going to make her stay. She needed to stretch her legs right about now, to exercise away some of the seething emotion at her helplessness. She departed from the hothouse without giving him the time to reconsider.

He *could* trust her. And it appeared he did. She didn't know what to make of that.

She made short work of consulting Lady Belhaven on the order. Although it took the old woman a moment to decipher the script, they sorted out the order and Rocky left to return to the hothouse. She passed Miss Towney—or was it Mrs. Abrahams now?—on the way, her arms full of linens as she sought to redress the beds.

Just as Rocky reached the stairs, a man made a disgusted noise and poked his head out of another of the parlors. Kenneth. Rocky froze with her foot on the servants' stairwell and tamped down the sudden surge of rage. She balled her fists.

"You, wench. I've been yanking the bell pull for half an hour. Where's my tea?"

I am a gardener, not a serving maid. Not that she suspected Kenneth would know the difference. He wouldn't be able to identify a plant if it grew out of his ears.

Gritting her teeth, she took a deep breath before she turned to face him. His posture was arrogant and hostile, looming in the doorway and taking up nearly all the space. His indignant expression would have scared a lesser woman than Rocky.

At that moment, it was all she could do not to storm up to him and sock him in the nose. That was, if she could reach that high.

You are a servant, she reminded herself, not that it helped. Thinking of her mission helped somewhat, however. When she felt calm enough to speak, she said tersely, "I will see you get your tea." She bit off each word.

"Get to it, then." The heinous man turned away, muttering under his breath, "Lazy sods. I should see you all sacked."

Rocky vibrated with the urge to do violence. The bite of her fingernails in her palm did little to quell the urge. She bit the inside of her cheek until she tasted blood and even that only made her want to exact the price of blood from Kenneth's hide. How could Lady Belhaven have raised such a worthless, self-indulgent, inconsiderate creature? She turned away and stormed down the stairs.

By the time she reached the ground floor, clarity returned and she wondered where Abby was. If Mrs. Abrahams was hard at work in the rooms, wasn't it Abby's job to answer the bell pull? Though Rocky understood her reluctance in this case entirely. What was Kenneth doing, idling in one of the rooms while his mother resided in another? He didn't live in the manor.

As she passed the hothouse, she paused. The hot, wicked urge for revenge mounted and she ducked into the humid room. Catt looked up from his task. The moment he spotted her expression, he stiffened.

She ignored him and stormed up to the iris plant, snatching two of its leaves.

Catt tentatively brushed her shoulder. "Rocky? Are you all right?"

If he was asking, he already knew the answer to that question. She wasn't all right. She hadn't been since last night, when he'd revealed the true depth of the depravity going on in this house. Ever since, she'd been in a constant state of unsettledness, soothed only now and again by his fleeting touches and unflappable demeanor. If he could face this, so could she. She knew, at heart, that Catt was as dismayed at being unable to fix the situation as she was, though perhaps it wasn't as personal to him.

"What are you doing?" he asked, his voice gentle.

She fumed and turned away from the shelf of plants. "Kenneth mistook me for a maid again. He wants me to bring him some tea."

It would be the last time he would ever make such a request from her.

Catt didn't try to stop her as she stormed out of the hothouse. He didn't try to tell her that, however abhorrent the man was, seeking revenge would solve nothing and only sink her to his level. Deep down, Rocky knew that. She was going to do it anyway. And he was going to let her.

In the kitchen, she directed Eliza to boil the kettle. As the teapot was being readied, Rocky slipped the iris leaves into the pot alongside the tea leaves. Steeped, they probably wouldn't have as nauseating an effect as they might if consumed raw or whole, but Rocky hoped they would upset Kenneth in some small way. He deserved much more. He deserved to be strung up by his heels for taking advantage of a young man who had done no wrong at all. Eric had been in the wrong place at the wrong time. That was his only crime. But because he was a servant, Kenneth saw him as little better than property and treated him with the same lack of respect.

Rocky tried to breathe deep, to keep from confessing her or Kenneth's sins to Eliza as the hawkish woman looked almost sympathetic. Although the cook's assistant tried to probe to discover what ailed Rocky, she hid behind the fact that Kenneth had mistaken her for a maid. That seemed to answer Eliza's question to satisfaction, because she wrinkled her nose and nodded. She poured the boiling water into the pot and set it on a tray with a single cup, a bowl of sugar lumps, and a creamer.

Just as she arranged all the items on the tray for easy delivery, a sharp gust of wind from outdoors skirted through the doorway to the hall, followed by Abby's rosy-cheeked form. Her hair was mussed, a piece of straw sticking up from her strands. Rocky bit her tongue to keep from voicing her disgruntlement.

The mystery of who David's ladylove is has been solved, at least.

Thrusting the tray into Abby's hands, Rocky said, "Mr. Kenneth Belhaven would like his tea served in the upstairs green parlor."

Without waiting to ensure that Abby would comply, Rocky strode past her and returned to the hothouse. When she entered, Catt was tying off the second-to-last bouquet—the last was the one she had sought clarification on. He paused, raising his eyebrows at her in question.

That look spoke volumes. *Did you go through with it?*

When she smirked in answer—*I did*—Catt mirrored the expression. For a moment, they shared a secret smile. It was foolhardy and petty to exact revenge against Kenneth by giving him an upset stomach, but Rocky did feel a bit better for having done so. Catt seemed to share the sentiment.

It felt surprisingly good to know that she wasn't bearing this burden alone.

Chapter Nineteen

The cold bit through Catt's greatcoat, chilling him to the bone. He turned up his collar to shield his neck and stuffed his gloved hands as far into his pockets as he could. The snow crunched underfoot as he navigated the all-but-deserted street just outside of Mayfair. The air was still and silent. With the bitter cold, everyone with sense was indoors, keeping warm by the fire. Curtains rustled as he passed, a testament that the tall, squashed houses on either side of the street were occupied by people with more sense than he. While Rocky enjoyed work in a balmy hothouse, he had volunteered to go out to the drop point and retrieve any correspondence Morgan might have left him.

The task wasn't as straightforward as it sounded. Because they were on an assignment for the Crown, he had to be assured that he hadn't been followed. This meant a roundabout route, a stop at the pub without David this time, pausing to purchase something trivial at a local shop. By the time he reached his destination, more than an hour had passed for what might have been a fifteen-minute walk at most. By that time, Catt's cheeks were numbed and he'd begun to wish he'd sent Rocky instead.

Although he'd kept an eye peeled while he walked for signs that he had been followed, he checked once more before he stepped up to the side of the building. The third brick from the corner at level with his clavicle came loose once he dug his fingers into the crevice. He carefully removed it and retrieved the packet of papers nestled behind. After replacing the brick, he paused to thumb through them.

Although the top message was one from Morgan—Catt recognized the handwriting—the letter beneath caught his attention. Was that his uncle's handwriting? Morgan or Tristan must have forwarded it to him. Catt stuffed the missives from Morgan into his pocket and unfolded the one from his uncle.

It contained one single line: *They're the subject of centuries of inbreeding. You're worth ten of them.*

Catt frowned. What?

In true form with his uncle's absent-mindedness, the letter didn't contain any other helpful clues. If not crosshatched over a letter Catt had written to him, he might have thought it was for another intended recipient.

But, upon re-reading the letter he'd sent to his uncle last May, the response suddenly made more sense. From time to time, Catt sent his uncle a letter that he assumed would be left unanswered. Truthfully, he would have doubted that his uncle even read them, if not for the fact that the man possessed an acute memory during their infrequent visits and often addressed every point that Catt had written him in the convening year. His uncle, a scholar, spent too much time lost in his research to properly answer the letters and Catt had taken to writing him during times of frustration, when he needed to confess things he could say to no one else.

In this case, the letter had been sent on the heels of the Graylockes' last annual house party. Catt had confessed to feeling inferior to the Graylockes, nothing more than a number to fill out their ranks. He didn't even have the drive and purpose that Rocky did.

At least, he hadn't—not before he'd been inducted into the ranks of the Crown spies. Now he had purpose aplenty, not that he could confess as much to his uncle.

And his uncle's response to Catt's feeling of inferiority was to call the Graylockes the product of inbreeding. Catt chuckled as he shook his head.

What would Giddy say if he knew he'd been thus insulted?

Catt would never tell him, of course, but it was amusing to imagine his expression.

Stuffing the missive in the opposite pocket, he tugged out the letter from Morgan. As suspected, it was written in code. Catt had brought a graphite pencil with him and worked diligently over the next few minutes to render the message sensible.

When he did, his heart flipped. *He's done it.* He read the message twice, to be sure.

Morgan Graylocke had decoded the cipher of the plant leaves. The packet he had sent contained an explanation of the cipher. The next time Catt and Rocky intercepted a message, they would be able to decode it. Not only that but Morgan had given another clue. He was sure Monsieur V had been away from Lady Belhaven's house the first night Rocky and Catt arrived and he would likely be going out for another clandestine meeting within a fortnight.

Catt grinned as relief poured through him. For the first time since he and Rocky had arrived at the Belhaven residence, Monsieur V would no longer be a step ahead of them. They would be able to catch him, to complete their mission.

He returned the packet and letter to his pocket and hurried back to Lady Belhaven's townhouse, where Rocky awaited him. He couldn't wait to tell her the good news.

***

Rocky finished her cursory inspection of the hothouse, satisfied that Monsieur V hadn't slipped in any coded plants while she wasn't looking. As she straightened, the hothouse door opened. She turned, eager to hear if the Duke of Tenwick had left them anything at the drop point.

Instead of Catt, Lady Belhaven's grandson Lance stepped into the humid room. His face and form were just as tidy and composed as they had been upon their first meeting.

And just as forbidding.

Without so much as a greeting, Lance stormed toward her with ice in her expression. She took an instinctive step back before she realized she was cornered against the shelves.

"Mr. Belhaven."

Rocky fought the urge to curtsey. Even if she was in the position of servant to his family, she refused to cower in front of him. She locked her knees instead and met his gaze boldly.

Where was Catt?

She shoved aside that wayward thought. She didn't need any man to fight her battles, not even Catt. The question was, why did she suddenly feel as though she'd stumbled onto a battlefield? She hadn't seen nor heard from Lance since the last time he'd entered the hothouse.

"Where is my grandmother?"

He'd get a better answer if he asked one of the other servants, not her. She was shut in the hothouse all day and rarely left, save to relieve herself or fetch a bite to eat or a cup of tea from the kitchen.

She squared her shoulders. "Have you checked her favorite parlor or her bedchamber?" If not abed for a nap, she could usually be found in the parlor.

"When was the last time she came down here?"

Rocky frowned as she thought. "This morning?" She couldn't recall the time for certain, but today, like every day, Lady Belhaven had taken a moment before Catt had escorted her away. He hadn't gone far down the corridor before she'd doffed his arm and insisted on walking the rest of the way on her own. He'd returned in mere moments.

In a brusque, cutting tone, Lance asked, "How often does she come down?"

"Daily."

Sometimes more than once a day, especially if her memory failed her and she forgot that she'd already checked on their progress once. As irritating as it was to have their work thus constantly interrupted, Catt never lost his patience with the old woman.

"Does she ever stay to work?"

"Of course not." Rocky infused her spine with steel. "She hired us to manage the hothouse and that is precisely what we do."

"Then why does she come here?" His expression was cutting and his tone was accusatory.

She gritted her teeth. "She likes to check our progress in the mornings." And the afternoons. And sometimes even in the evenings, when they should be done their work but often were still checking the plants for signs of a code.

Despite their vigilance, they hadn't intercepted another message since the last. Though, given the hectic state of the hothouse in the mornings, it was impossible to be certain that none had gone out.

"Why not deliver a report to her yourself and save her the trouble of navigating the stairs?"

Clearly, Lance had never entered the hothouse during its busiest hours. Catt and Rocky scarcely found the time to breathe, let alone leave the enclosure to seek out their employer. With the onset of the Season, the orders had been snowballing ever since she and Catt had arrived to take on their new position.

Tightly, Rocky answered, "We do so every morning once the orders have been filled."

If he suggested she ignore her work in order to seek out Lady Belhaven and thus slow the progress overall...

"And the plants? How often to do you check on them?"

She frowned. "Constantly." Was he trying to find out when the hothouse would be empty? She and Catt remained in the hothouse, either separately or together, from breakfast until supper.

"The plants outside the hothouse?" Lance raised an eyebrow in an arch, intimidating expression.

Reluctantly, she admitted, "Every second day. They don't require as much tending as the ones inside the hothouse."

"Because my grandmother has been tending them herself."

So she suspected. But she couldn't do anything about that. Lady Belhaven would continue to fiddle with plants until the day she died. Her grandson would have to come to terms with that.

"Perhaps."

The door opened and Catt stepped into the tense situation. A rush of relief surged through

Rocky as Lance stepped back, out of her personal space. Without a word, he turned on his heel and exited the room.

Catt stared after him, his shoulders around his ears. When he turned back to Rocky, concern was etched across his face. "Are you all right?"

She nodded, mute.

He stepped closer nevertheless. When he raised his hand to her cheek, she yelped. His hands were cold.

"Forgive me." He dropped his hand and took a step back.

She glared at him. "You're cold as ice."

He smirked. "I was just outdoors." His smile faded as he glanced toward the shut door once more. "What was that about?"

"I don't know," she admitted. She hugged herself. "He asked about the plants."

Suspicion entered Catt's face, a sharp edge. "Why?"

She shrugged, helpless. Whatever the reason, she doubted it was good. Why would he be asking about their regime with the plants? "Did you get a message?"

Catt nodded stepping closer. "He's cracked the code."

"That's wonderful. We can decipher the next message!" Rocky tried to keep her voice low and her excitement in check.

Catt nodded. "And something else. He said that V was not here in the house the first night we came and the he will be traveling for a meeting within a fortnight."

Rocky chewed her bottom lip. "Who wasn't here that first night? Most everyone was here. Was the cook here? I remember Stefan and Lewis at breakfast the next morning. Stanley was, but not Lance. But he's not really of the household. Could he be V?"

"I don't know, but I remember that first night thinking that the house was very quiet after supper. Everyone seemed to go to bed very early. V could have slipped out and met with their contact then come back before sunup."

"True. But you say they have another rendezvous soon?"

"Yes. Well, that was his plan as of when Morgan sent the message. But if V knows we are onto him or if our presence makes him alter his plans, that meeting may be called off."

Had they foiled Monsieur V's plans with their vigilance in checking the plants? Was that why Lance had come to the hothouse and was he now searching for an alternate way to send his messages, maybe through Lady Belhaven's houseplants instead?

Rocky knew for certain that Lance was not in the house their first night. She'd never even seen him here until recently.

If his earlier interrogation meant their presence had foiled his plans, then Lance was either in league with Monsieur V...or he was the man they were looking for.

Chapter Twenty

Rocky was haunted by the phantom touch of Catt caressing her cheek. Only this time, his hands weren't as cold as ice, they were so hot they set her aflame. And he didn't stop with a touch—he kissed her again, too.

She'd spent years without thinking, wondering what Catt's kiss would be like. Years at odds with him, their personalities grating on one another. But they didn't fight as much since they'd kissed, did they? If she kissed him again, would she undo all the good that first kiss had done?

She couldn't sleep. Tangled in the sheets, she thrashed until she freed herself. She fumbled for her spectacles on the nightstand. She couldn't find her house slippers, so she tugged on her boots instead and donned a wrapper over her nightgown. At this hour, everyone was abed, asleep. Exhausted from the day, as she should be. No one would see her in her wrapper if she left her room.

Catt wasn't the only thing on her mind—she'd spent at least an hour in bed mulling over the pieces to the puzzle that was Monsieur V—but he was by far the most prominent thing on her mind whenever she closed her eyes. She would be a beast in the morning if she couldn't find a way to fall asleep, preferably without thoughts of him swirling in her mind.

She didn't know how to do the second, but a glass of warm milk usually helped her to fall asleep on troublesome nights. Slipping out of her room, she moved quietly through the manor to the kitchen.

The light of a lantern glowed from the front closet. Not wanting to encounter anyone, Rocky pressed against the wall and peeked from the corridor. The light silhouetted the form of a large man as he pulled on his outer wear. Her breath caught. Was that Mr. Dowden? Why was he leaving the manor at this hour? He clutched a bouquet in his hand.

The message from Morgan echoed in her mind. Monsieur V would likely leave for a rendezvous within a fortnight. Maybe tonight.

Rocky had to get Catt. As silently as she could, she jogged down the corridor toward the men's quarters. Thankfully, those were closer to the front door than the women's quarters. If Mr. Dowden had been pulling on his greatcoat, she didn't have much time to rouse Catt.

She counted the doors as she passed and didn't bother to knock on his when she found it. The latch opened easily—it was unlocked. She slipped into the room, squinting so she didn't bang into any furniture as she crept toward the bed. Although there was no light, the shades of darker gray silhouetted the bed and the lump in it.

She shook that lump, praying that she had the right room. "Catt."

He caught her wrist, his grip like iron. After a heartbeat, he said, "Rocky?" His voice was gravelly. It shivered through her like a physical touch.

"Wake up."

He released her and sat up, clutching the blankets to his waist. She danced from foot to foot, impatient. He wore a nightshirt—that much she'd been able to tell from shaking him—so he had no need to be modest. Even if he'd been unclothed, it wasn't as though she was able to see anything.

"Why? What time is it?"

"Late," she whispered back. "We don't have time. We have to go. Get up and get dressed."

Hesitantly, he swung his legs over the side of the bed. "Why?"

"Mr. Dowden is about to leave the house."

If Catt asked her why one more time, she would drag him from the bed and shove him out of doors regardless of if he cared to dress or not.

He didn't ask why, but he made no move to stand. "Would you mind waiting in the corridor? I'm not wearing any breeches."

Of course he wasn't. It would be odd for him to wear breeches to bed. Though, now that he'd pointed it out, her gaze dropped to his lap as she pictured it.

Heat blossomed in her cheeks and she thanked her luck that the darkness covered her blush. She backed toward the door, stumbling over his boots in the middle of the floor. "Hurry," she said. "I'll get our things from the front closet."

She would have to wait until Mr. Dowden had departed in order to do so, but hopefully they wouldn't be too far delayed by the action. As he dressed, she slipped along the hall, pausing to listen to Mr. Dowden swear as he struggled to tie his boots. Finally, he gave up and stuffed the laces into the boot tops before he opened the door.

As it started to swing shut behind him, Rocky bolted for the front closet. The cook had taken the lantern with him as he departed, forcing Rocky to find her and Catt's coats by feel. If she was wrong, hopefully they would return before the owners of the vestments realized they were missing. As she shut the closet door with her hip, Catt appeared at her side. She stuffed his coat into his hand and bolted out the door before donning hers. She shrugged it on as she descended the stairs, her boots crunching in a freshly-frozen inch of snow. Catt followed after, pulling the door shut behind him quietly.

The bitter cold wrapped around her, numbing her as she struggled to do up the coat's buttons. The air was completely silent and still, the sky an inky black. Light came from two directions down the street—a streetlamp on a nearby corner and a bobbing light. Although she hadn't been pleased that Mr. Dowden had taken the lantern earlier, now she was. If not for that bobbing light, she didn't know if she would have been able to pinpoint what direction he'd taken.

Before the light faded entirely, she grabbed Catt by the hand and towed him in that direction. He came willingly, matching and then exceeding her speed as they raced along the icy street. When her footing wobbled, he steadied her and they continued. He slowed only when they drew near enough to the light source to make out the shape of the figure holding it.

Mr. Dowden led them down a maze of alleys in the neighborhood. They held back, waiting for him to vacate each one before they continued after him. Rocky's ears burned from cold, but she didn't say a word. She drew her coat up over her nose despite the way it made her spectacles fog. She followed after Catt's indistinct form, shoving her hands into her pockets as she walked. It was a bit warmer that way, but not by much. She should have paused to find their scarves, gloves, and hats, but she might have lost Mr. Dowden if she had. Hopefully, he didn't lead her too far.

Before long, Mr. Dowden opened a waist-high iron gate and strode into a cemetery. Rocky balked. When she would have turned back, Catt slid his bare hand onto her elbow and guided her onto the premises. The moment she tugged her coat down from around her mouth to speak, her spectacles began to clear of fog. As she passed him, he caught her gaze. He shook his head, his mouth a grim line. The light from Mr. Dowden's lantern stretched tendrils over Catt's face, darkening the color of his eyes. His breath fogged in front of his face.

With no more than a look, Catt reminded her of why they were tailing the cook. He might have killed his wife. He might be Monsieur V. She couldn't turn away simply because she felt as though she were intruding on a private moment.

He might only be using the cemetery as a screen to pass through onto his real destination. She squared her shoulders and nodded to Catt. They continued on, stepping in Mr. Dowden's large footprints to keep from making too much noise.

Catt approached first, with Rocky trailing after him.

The cook meandered along the tombstones until he reached the far corner. When he set down the lantern, the light suddenly grew dimmer as it was partially blocked by the slabs of granite. Rocky took one more step, brushing the back of Catt's coat as he hung back to watch Mr. Dowden. The big man knelt to wipe the snow from the tombstone in front of him before he left flowers on the grave. Whose grave—his wife's? Rocky couldn't read the chiseled lettering from here.

If he'd killed her, why would he leave flowers on her grave? Perhaps he suffered from remorse.

But that didn't sound like the kind of behavior a traitor might exhibit.

Rocky waited, shivering in the bitter cold, as Mr. Dowden murmured in front of the gravestone. His voice was too soft to carry. She warmed her hands with her breath, then tucked them as far up the sleeves of her jacket as possible. The chill tightened around her, seeping through the thick wool and into her bones. Her wrapper and nightgown beneath were little barrier. The cold air gusted underneath, chilling her legs.

After a time, Mr. Dowden straightened. He rubbed his eyes and gathered up his lantern. He didn't turn around, but continued to stare at the grave, his posture defeated.

Softly, he murmured, "Eliza looks just like her, you know."

Rocky jumped. Was he talking to them?

With a gusty sigh, the cook turned around. Rocky took a hasty step back, her foot crunching in the snow and announcing her presence. Catt didn't budge. He didn't seem overly worried that Mr. Dowden had caught them spying.

The yellow glow of the lantern played over Mr. Dowden's face, making his eyes look bloodshot. Or had he been crying? Rocky's gut pinched. She shifted from foot to foot. Why were they out here? She shouldn't have entered the cemetery.

When she groped for the back of Catt's greatcoat, silently begging for them to leave the cook in peace, Catt caught her hand in his. His fingers were cold, but still warmer than her own. He held her tightly, but didn't look at her.

Mr. Dowden confessed, "It's the anniversary of her death tomorrow. Or is it today already? I'm not sure of the time."

Rocky didn't own a pocket watch, let alone carry one with her, so she could neither confirm nor deny that.

"Did you kill her?" Catt asked, his voice as hard and cold as diamond.

Rocky squeezed his hand. Was the direct route the way to go? They didn't have the truth serum that Gideon and his wife had made for the Crown. They wouldn't be able to confirm whether or not anything the man told them was true.

Mr. Dowden hung his head. Softly—so softly, Rocky didn't at first know whether or not she'd heard correctly—he confessed, "I might as well have."

What was that supposed to mean? Rocky squeezed Catt's hand. He returned the gesture, a reassuring tightening of his grip rather than the vice she had him in.

In the same calm, unflappable tone, Catt said, "Why don't you tell us what happened?"

It didn't take much prodding for the bigger man to confess his sins and sorrows. Soon, he began to babble, telling them of the way life in Lady Belhaven's house used to be, before her business grew to the point where she could afford multiple servants and carriages.

In the beginning, there had been only Mr. Dowden, his wife Rosemary, and Lewis.

"We were like a family. Lady Belhaven, her son and daughter were grown, both moved out of the house though her daughter never married. Her son would bring his two boys, barely knee-high, over every week for Lady Belhaven to watch. But the lady, she was busy in the garden most of the time, so the boys would be underfoot in the house. Eliza minded them, though she's but a handful of years older than Lance."

The man shuddered. He swiped a hand over his face as he collected his thoughts.

Rocky shivered. Her ears burned with cold along with the tip of her nose. Her cheeks were numb. "Maybe you'd prefer to have this conversation where it's warm."

Catt looked sharply at her, his eyebrows knit together. What, was he afraid the cook would have a change of heart in the ten minutes it would take to walk home? Rocky tugged her hand free and slipped it into her pocket. She was frozen to the core. If they remained out here much longer, they might catch a chill or worse.

Mr. Dowden didn't appear to hear her. When he dropped his hand, he continued his tale.

"I suspected her affair with Lewis long before I learned the truth of it. I shouldn't have been so shocked, but the moment I had it confirmed, I—" His voice broke.

Rocky exchanged a glance with Catt, suddenly more alert. Mrs. Dowden had had an affair with Lewis? Grimly, they both turned their gazes to the cook. Catt coaxed out more information.

"You were angry."

The big man nodded his head. "I lost my temper."

Had he killed his wife, after all?

"We got into a fight. Eliza wasn't far and Rosemary begged me to keep my voice down so our daughter wouldn't hear, but I was too far gone. She snapped. She left the house, racing into the cold without even taking her coat."

When he fell silent, the night air wrapped around them like a shroud. Was that the truth of the story? Mrs. Dowden left the house, never to be heard from again? If so, Rocky couldn't understand why Lewis had been so adamant that she was dead, killed by her husband. He had no proof.

Though, he had confessed at the time that he didn't have proof. Only a suspicion.

But his suspicion, if indeed he'd had one, had been born from the fact that he had once been lovers with the deceased woman. Had he killed Mrs. Dowden and simply wanted to throw the suspicion onto her husband?

"What happened next?" Catt asked. His voice was soft and gentle, the same voice he'd used on Lady Belhaven and on Eric, the scullery boy. Catt had a gift for calming people, getting them to open up.

Hunching her shoulders against the cold, Rocky tried her best not to be noticed as she waited for the story to unfold.

Mr. Dowden's shoulders trembled. He covered his face in his hands and slowly collected himself. His voice was thick with grief when he continued. "She came back hours later, but the damage was done. Pneumonia, the physician said. By the time she was sick enough to warrant calling a leech about a mere servant, it was too late. He could do nothing to help her."

Mr. Dowden wept openly. Rocky winced, afraid the tears would freeze on his face.

Catt stepped forward, patting the man on the shoulder by way of comfort and murmuring something too soft for Rocky to catch the words. She stepped aside as the men passed. Falling into step behind them, she mulled over the information.

The troublesome part of the story was that Mr. Dowden seemed genuine, at least to her. If what he was telling her was true, then he didn't kill his wife. No one had. She had died from a terrible, unfortunate illness. Perhaps he had, as he seemed to think, driven her to it and been its cause peripherally, but she hadn't been forced out into the cold. She could have taken the time to collect her coat. In fact, there was no proof that was the day she had contracted pneumonia. She might have already had it and no one known.

At Lady Belhaven's manor Mr. Dowden paused in the entryway. He seemed a little less sad now that he'd unburdened himself. He looked at Catt and Rocky questioningly.

"But what were *you* doing out in the cemetery in the middle of the night dressed like that?" he asked.

Rocky's heart skipped. What would they tell him?

But Catt was a quick thinker. "We have relatives buried there, too."

Mr. Dowden nodded apparently satisfied with the lie. Then he turned and walked toward the servants rooms.

Shoot! Rocky didn't like the bent of her thoughts at all, because she was inclined to remove Mr. Dowden as a suspect. They still hadn't decided what to do about his poppy plant, short of throwing it out or barring his use. But if it helped Lady Belhaven with her nerves—or worse, if she was addicted to the opiate without realizing it—that course of action could do more harm than good.

She and Catt had a decision to make on that front. One more decision, piled on so many others.

As Catt accepted her coat, he murmured, "Do you believe him?"

She sighed, defeated. "I do. Do you?"

He hung the outerwear in the closet and shut the door. Mr. Dowden had left the lantern on the table next to the closet, and it continued to emit a yellow circle of light, enough to read Catt's expression. He looked harried.

"I do as well."

Turning back to her, he blew on his hands, then took hers and rubbed them between his to encourage warmth. She tipped her face up to his, battling the urge to sink against him and feel the entire warm length of him against her. It was silly—they were dressed in nothing more than their nightclothes with the addition of his breeches and his nightshirt haphazardly tucked into them, but at that moment she'd never found him more handsome.

Maybe it was the absent, brilliant air he cultivated while he thought. Once he warmed her hands, he stopped rubbing them, but continued to cup them between their bodies.

"If he's telling the truth, then Lewis—"

She tensed. "I know. He misled me."

Obviously, Lewis would have known that his affair with Mrs. Dowden had played a role in her death. He had deliberately withheld that information and pointed the finger solely at Mr.

Dowden. Had he truly believed they wouldn't be able to find out?

"Do you think he pointed me in the wrong direction to mask what he is?"

"A traitor, you mean?" Catt mused. He ran his tongue slowly along his lower lip as he thought. "It's a possibility, if he guessed your game."

Rocky, along with Catt, had been given extensive training by the Crown on how to remain inconspicuous. However, the day Lewis had caught her and confessed his suspicions about the cook's sins, Rocky had been trailing Stefan to learn more about his habits. She hadn't noticed Lewis's presence until too late, and by then he might have puzzled out that she was in search of something different than a liaison.

"I don't know if he knows that we're searching for V."

Catt's hands tightened on hers for a moment before he released her. "Neither do I, but we'll have to be vigilant."

"Whether he guessed or not, it's clear he's hiding something."

Catt offered her a smirk, but it seemed weary. "Whatever he is hiding, we will learn of it," he assured her. "That's what we do."

Chapter Twenty-One

Catt had been battling his attraction to Rocky for too long. If he were honest with himself, probably longer than their forced proximity due to this assignment. The night before, when she'd roused him from bed, he'd been afraid he was dreaming.

No, not afraid. Because his dreams would undoubtedly have included something more pleasurable than freezing his arse off in a snow-covered cemetery. The fantasy had gripped him when he'd finally fallen asleep. He'd woken to the illusion that he felt her nearby again.

Rocky seemed no less tense and sleep-deprived than he did this morning. She vibrated with contained energy, her shoulders hunched up under her ears as they completed their last circuit of the hothouse for the day, searching for any signs of the code Monsieur V had employed. So far, Catt had turned up nothing. Granted, he was a bit distracted with Rocky, even if she was across the room from him.

He wasn't worthy of her. At least, he'd never considered himself to be. How was the disowned son of a soldier supposed to compare to a woman with as much drive and zest as Rocky? She was always so confident, so capable and independent. She didn't need anyone, not a man and certainly not a man like Catt. And, if she didn't need him, why would she want him?

She didn't, of course. He should stop thinking about how it felt to kiss her, stop imagining what it might be like to wake up with her nestled in his arms. Once this assignment was done, maybe his head would clear a bit. He'd ask Morgan for an assignment away from Tenwick Abbey. Away from Rocky.

Helpless, he glanced to her again. If anything, she looked even more tense. She was working herself into a lather again. Sooner or later, she would snap from the strain.

Without thinking, he moved closer and rubbed her back. The muscles in her shoulders were as hard as rock. She jumped at his touch, tilting her face up to his.

Kiss her.

He couldn't do that. He dropped his hand. "Maybe you should head to bed early tonight. We're nearly done. I can finish the inspection."

The hostility he knew so well lined her expression. By now, he recognized it as cover for a deeper insecurity. He couldn't fathom what; Rocky was the most strong and capable woman he knew.

"I am perfectly capable—"

"Yes," he interrupted. "You are. You should know me well enough by now to know that I'm not trying to insinuate otherwise." He ran his fingers through his hair, not caring if it stuck up on end a bit.

Rocky's posture relaxed, but her chin was still set in a mulish expression.

"You're mulling over what we know. I can see it in your posture. Why don't you let me tend to this part of our job, since you won't be able to ignore that part of it? Take a bath. Go to bed. Whatever relaxes you."

He swallowed thickly, hoping that his desire to help with that relaxation didn't show on his face. They were friends, for Heaven's sake! If she knew how much he desired her...

She nodded slowly, her hostile expression fading. It left something vulnerable behind, the soft part of her that she tried to hide with her prickliness.

"Thank you." Her voice was soft. It raised gooseflesh over his skin. He fought not to fidget.

Instead, he stepped aside, indicating the path to the door. She held his gaze for a moment longer before she nodded and left the room. He fought to remain in place, reminding himself that he still had work to finish.

And that he wasn't worthy of her.

As he resumed checking the last patch of plants in the room for signs of tampering, he tried to focus on that fact, perhaps the only thing keeping him from running after her and...

What? Kissing her? She might slap him. Or sharpen her tongue on him.

Or kiss him back...

He didn't know what frightened him most.

You're worth ten of them. His uncle's words. A silly, typical response from the old scholar, but Catt didn't doubt for a second that he meant the words. His uncle didn't say things that he didn't mean.

Catt didn't need to be worth ten of one of London's peers. He only needed to be worthy of one woman. Was he? He doubted she would have relinquished her work to anyone else. She didn't trust others to do as thorough a job as she did.

Except, it seemed, she trusted Catt.

Could he be worthy of her, after all?

He swore under his breath as he finished the inspection and came up empty-handed. He stared at the door to the hothouse, willing himself to rein in his emotions. He couldn't follow after her. It would be madness.

But what if it isn't?

Maybe he'd rather be mad, anyway.

Shoving aside his misgivings and all the imagined what-ifs that might occur if she didn't hope to see him as much as he did her, he strode from the hothouse and meandered toward the servants' quarters. Had she already reached her room? He hadn't taken long to finish the inspection. They'd been nearly finished as it was.

As he turned into another corridor, he froze in place. He found Rocky pinned against the wall, barred from escape by Stanley's larger form. He braced one hand on the wall by her head, hemming her in with his body on the other side. And, although his stance and expression were lecherous, it was clear to Catt that Rocky did not feel the same.

A hot, murderous feeling filled his chest as he fought to catch his breath. He couldn't stand idly by, even if it might raise suspicion in Stanley's eyes as to their true identities and purpose in the household. If Rocky wouldn't stop him, Catt would.

***

Lost in thought, Rocky ambled to the servants' quarters by rote. She was consumed with thoughts of the mission, the tangled web of secrets in the

Belhaven household, and who was left on the suspect list. Unfortunately, that last number was still larger than she would like. Although she and Catt had uncovered a frightening number of secrets and suspected still more, they hadn't truly ruled out many people.

Stefan and David likely didn't have the time to command a network of spies, given that they were so engrossed with their ladies. Likewise, Hollander spent his free time amassing a fortune beneath Lady Belhaven's nose. But however unlikely it was that they found additional time to keep in touch with French spies, recruit new ones, and sift through the information presented to them by such spies, it wasn't impossible.

Eric was too young to be Monsieur V, and Eliza was of the wrong gender, but that didn't mean that neither of them knew of the true culprit or aided him. Mr. Dowden might be consumed by guilt over his wife's death, but that didn't mean that he wasn't working for the French. Lady Belhaven's son and even her grandson Stanley seemed too self-indulgent to be mentally capable of the level of cleverness Monsieur V employed at every turn. But there was still the question of Lewis, Lance, Lady Belhaven herself and even Faulker. Did Lady Belhaven know a French spymaster operated beneath her roof? Was she aiding him? Rocky liked the old woman too well to want to consider such a thing, but she had to push her feelings aside and look at the facts. The fact remained that one of the possible suspects whose secret she hadn't yet divined was related to Lady Belhaven; the others had been a servant for decades. If either were the French spymaster she sought, how could Lady Belhaven have no inkling?

So wrapped up in her troublesome thoughts was she that Rocky didn't notice that she was no longer alone in the dimly lit corridor until a shadow moved. She jumped. When she squinted, trying to discern more than the figure's silhouette by the light of a lamp in a bracket at the far end of the hall, her heartbeat sped. Who was there? The other servants, save for whomever was due to remain awake to help Lady Belhaven should the need arise, were all abed, leaving the floor utterly quiet. Had Monsieur V deduced Rocky's purpose in the house and decided to confront her? The lamp flame wavered, close to sputtering out. She battled a sudden wish that she'd never left Catt.

The man stumbled closer. The light slanted across his face, illuminating his identity. Stanley Belhaven. His disheveled hair stuck out over his forehead, half-falling into his eyes. He stank of whiskey.

"There you are, love."

Her skin crawled. *Please tell me he did not come looking for me.* Aside from a few unreturned warm smiles, which she'd assumed he'd given all of the female staff, he hadn't paid her a whit of attention. If he had, she would have rebuffed him long ago. Or, at the very least, gone out of her way to avoid him. She injected steel into her spine as she prepared to face him.

At Tenwick Abbey, she'd come across a scattered few intoxicated guests who liked to have their way with maidservants. A sharp refusal and the occasional knee to a tender area swiftly made uncomfortable situations disappear. But at Tenwick Abbey, she didn't fear a rebuke. In fact, the one time a guest had complained of her reaction to the duke, he'd ejected the man from his home.

Her life hadn't always been that way. In the first household she'd worked for, she hadn't had a choice whether or not to accept a man's advances. The question was: did she have the choice now? She didn't rely on Lady Belhaven to keep her employed, but she needed to stay in the household long enough to complete the assignment the Crown had set her. Britain might not be able to insinuate another pair of spies into the house if she found herself ejected.

Her situation was dangerous, precarious, and her throat tightened. She struggled to breathe evenly, not to let him know that his advances affected her in any way. Some men confused fear for arousal; others still preferred the fear. She held herself stiffly, making her refusal clear in her posture.

Her voice, she kept to a more neutral tone. "Are you turned around, Mr. Belhaven? These are the servants' quarters."

He grinned, his smile a bit lopsided. His eyes caught the light, looking glazed. Just how much had he had to drink?

"Where else would I go for a spot of fun?"

Anywhere else. Rocky clenched her fists, fighting the inferno of anger that woke at his words. He was the son of her employer. She couldn't use her spy training to beat him to a bloody pulp. Had he tried to take advantage of any of the other female servants in the house?

Worse, had he succeeded?

When he staggered closer to her, Rocky took an instinctive step back. She needed to think of a way to rebuff him, a way to convince him she wasn't worth it or desirable. Unfortunately, Rocky didn't know a way to do that. With men of his class, sex was as much an exertion of power as it was of desire. Her mind whirled so fast, she couldn't catch any of the thoughts long enough to examine them.

Her back struck the solid wall. Stanley followed her, planting a hand by her head. The rest of his body blocked her escape, his arm crossing the air in front of her chest. She fought back a retch at the stench of liquor and cologne. She had to find a way to deter him from this path, or at the very least distract him enough for him to relax his stance so she could slip beneath his arm and run to her room. If she tried while he was still on alert, he would catch her.

How could she make herself less desirable to him? Did he even care that she was here instead of one of the other servants? If Catt had been there in Stanley's place...

No. That was a ridiculous thought. Catt would never corner a woman on her way to bed. He was more honorable than that.

Rocky blurted the first thought that entered her mind. "I'm engaged to someone else."

Wait. *Where* had that come from? She didn't want to get married. Did she?

Stanley leaned closer. "I don't see a ring on your finger."

"We can't afford one."

The man made a low, grating sound that was probably meant to be seductive. It just made Rocky want to shake him like a rattle until he stopped.

"Sounds to me like you need to look for a man who knows how to take care of you."

Sounds to me like you need a swift kick in the—

No. Violence had to be a last resort. *Think!* What would make him back off short of blistering his manhood?

Or perhaps she only needed to buy herself time. He swayed a bit, leaning heavy against the wall. Had he consumed an entire whiskey bottle? From the smell, she would guess so. If that was the case, it wouldn't take much more alcohol to render him oblivious and unconscious.

"Perhaps you'd care to share a drink with me instead," she said, trying to imitate a seductive purr. Given the rigidity in her shoulders and the tightness in her throat, she didn't think she succeeded.

Lud, she didn't *want* to share a drink with him. Or take him to bed. The only man she wanted to do those things with was...

No one. She wanted no one. All she craved was a good night's rest and the ability to finish this assignment before it was too late.

Stanley started to lower his head as if hoping to steal a kiss. Grimacing, Rocky turned her face to the side. If he touched her, she might gag. That, or snap and turn her fists on him.

Movement blurred at the corner of her eye. As she glanced up, she locked gazes with Catt as he stormed around the corner. His posture mirrored hers, the fury evident in the stiff set of his shoulders and his balled fists at his side. His mouth was set in a tight line. Without saying a word, he stormed up to Stanley, wrenched the man away from Rocky, and laid him bare.

Rocky gasped and pressed against the wall as Catt's punch landed. He, like she, had been taught the dirty, underhanded fighting tactics of London's criminal class, but she hadn't expected him to use them. He was a lanky botanist, devoted to study, not to strong-arming others. He didn't rouse to violence, not even when she attacked him viciously with her words during one of their many spats.

Apparently, finding her with a man provoked him to violence. As Stanley staggered and lost his footing, Catt's pugnacious stance didn't waver. Never mind that Stanley was almost as tall and had at least two stone on Catt. Catt looked prepared to face down an army if he must.

Her heart jumped at the tremendous thump that echoed along the corridor. She cringed. Who would wake up and investigate? Her heart thundered in her ears as she waited for someone to find them.

A door opened along the hall, easing nearly shut as the inhabitant caught sight of who was out there. Rocky squinted, catching movement that might have been a figment of her imagination or might have been other people peeking from their doors. Whatever the case, those roomed along this corridor opted not to interfere. Given that their employer's grandson was currently groaning and clutching his face, they were likely afraid of the repercussions falling on them.

Rocky didn't blame them. How could Catt... What had he been thinking?

Stanley staggered to his feet. At first, they didn't seem like they wanted to hold him up. His legs wobbled like he was made of jelly and he lunged toward Catt before he straightened and managed to stay upright. Rocky would have taken a step back to get out of the way, but Catt held his ground. He didn't budge, not even when Stanley snarled at him.

The intoxicated man let out a stream of insults better suited to a dockside tavern than a house near Mayfair. He jabbed his finger through the air at Catt. "I'll have your job for touching me."

Catt glared. "I'd say I'll have yours for touching her, but let's face it, you're good for nothing."

Rocky sucked in a breath. What was he saying? This was the grandson of their employer, albeit a temporary employer. Stanley was of a higher class than they were.

Then again, until this assignment, Catt had been of that class as well. He hadn't had to work for a living, surviving off a stipend instead. His family had connections to the peerage, if technically only on the very fringes themselves. Catt didn't know what it was like to work for a living, to be treated as lesser even though you put in more effort. Rocky did. Those of the working class avoided quarrels with the upper echelon. They didn't instigate them, not for any reason.

Considering that his brother was a barrister and his grandmother cultivated the goodwill of half the *ton* in London, Stanley might be able to do more than take away Catt's job. Panic rose inside her until she tamped it down.

Don't be ridiculous. Catt was Gideon's personal friend. The Duke of Tenwick would never allow a friend of the family to be punished. Not to mention, they worked for the Crown now. Her lot in life wasn't what it once was, even if she did have to pretend otherwise for the sake of her anonymity.

"Leave." Catt bit off the word, his voice as frosty as the window glass. "You aren't welcome in this section of the house."

Stanley opened his mouth, but Catt took a step toward him, balling his fists. His eyes were as cold as ice as he stared the intoxicated man down. The only time Rocky had ever seen a stare that intense and commanding was on the Duke of Tenwick.

Although Rocky expected Stanley to argue, what little sense he possessed took claim of his brain and he staggered out the hall in the direction of the family quarters. Would he tell his grandmother what had passed? Would she see Catt and Rocky ejected from the manor? She was prodigiously fond of her grandson.

Rocky wrapped her arms around herself, afraid to move as her mind whirled. Catt held his position until Stanley was safely out of sight. The moment the other man reached the staircase and disappeared from view, Catt turned to Rocky.

His posture changed immediately—from intimidating to concerned. He reached for her. She slid out of his grasp, taking a step back along the corridor and dropping her arms from around her.

"What were you thinking?" She battled to keep her voice quiet. She shook like a flag in the wind.

His eyebrows snapped together. "I was thinking that he was taking advantage of you and had to be stopped." Unlike her, he made no effort to keep his voice down. His words were clipped.

Outrage unfurled within her, and she welcomed the familiar burn. "I can take care of myself."

"Then why didn't you? Don't tell me you wanted..." He didn't finish his sentence. His expression contorted with distaste.

"No," she said quickly. Perhaps too quickly.

"Then why?"

"He's the grandson of our employer."

Catt's mouth flattened into a grim line again. "All the more reason why I had to step in. That doesn't give him the license to touch you."

She crossed her arms, shielding herself from the fierce look in his eye. She'd never seen him so riled. "You shouldn't have come to my rescue. I'm not some damsel in distress."

He threw his hands in the air. "Will you stop taking everything I do as a personal attack? I'm not trying to undermine you or belittle you. I stepped in because I couldn't fathom doing anything else when the woman I love is in danger."

The words rippled in the air between them. Panic crossed his expression as he heard them for himself. He winced, but he didn't step away. He didn't try to deny it.

Rocky couldn't breathe. "The woman you *what?*"

His expression turned serious, without a trace of the easygoing amusement she usually loved. "I love you, Rocky. I have for some time."

He pressed his lips together, not saying another word more. Even if he had, she wouldn't have been able to hear it. Her ears rang. He...he *loved* her? When? How?

She didn't know what to say. She couldn't think properly. It was as though her mind had gone blank the moment he'd spoken the words.

He passed his hand across his face. After he heaved a deep breath, he met her with composure. She couldn't tell what he was thinking behind those sky-blue eyes.

"Rocky..."

She took a step back, then another.

"Rocky, wait—" He reached out as he took a step forward.

She didn't wait to hear what he had to say. She spun on her heel and fled, her mind filled with questions. She needed quiet and...and time to think.

What had just happened?

Chapter Twenty-Two

Rocky wandered the manor aimlessly. Her neck ached from constantly looking over her shoulder to check if Catt had followed her. She didn't know whether she hoped or feared more that he had. She wanted time to herself, time to think.

But...he *loved* her?

As she reached the kitchen, she met Lady Belhaven in the hall.

"Ah, Rocky, dear. Would you be able to help me a moment? I'm a bit dizzy. I don't want to drop this."

Reflexively, Rocky took the tray from her, the teacup rattling in its saucer as she slipped into the kitchen and set it on the nearest flat surface. She turned to help Lady Belhaven onto a stool, keeping her hold on the old woman's arm until the fit passed. It took mere moments.

"Thank you. I'm sorry to be such a burden. I only wanted a glass of milk and a bit of cake before bed."

"It's no burden," Rocky answered. She frowned as she took in the old woman's lack of color. She looked almost yellow. Was she ill? "Where is Abby?

I thought she was to tend you tonight. She could have gotten this."

"What?" Lady Belhaven looked confused. "No, Abigail isn't tending me tonight."

"I can carry this up for you when you're ready to walk," Rocky said.

"Thank you. You're an angel."

Rocky didn't know if she would go that far.

Lady Belhaven narrowed her eyes. "Is something troubling you? Why don't you fetch yourself a glass of milk? We'll have the seedcake here. It's too bothersome to have to bring the dishes all the way back down the stairs, in any case."

Again, what Abby was for. How she had let Lady Belhaven slip past her, Rocky didn't know. With all the extra-curricular activity going on in the house, maybe Abby had been otherwise occupied.

Although Rocky didn't much care to talk about what Catt had just confessed in the corridor—had he meant it? Had he blurted it meaning something different? Maybe he loved her as a sister or a friend—she had already promised to escort Lady Belhaven to bed. So long as the woman wanted to remain in the kitchen, Rocky had to do so as well. Stifling a sigh, she fetched herself a glass of milk and a slice of seedcake, not wanting to eat any of the slab Lady Belhaven had cut for herself.

When she settled onto a stool opposite the old woman, who seemed to have a bit more color in her cheeks now and at the very least was able to sit upright without swaying, Lady Belhaven studied Rocky. Fighting a grimace, Rocky endured the prolonged stare, hoping her employer wouldn't pry.

"What's troubling you, dear?"

It had been too much to hope for, Rocky supposed.

She gave the old woman a tight smile. "Catt and I had a fight." It seemed the least personal thing to confess. Given the stubborn set of Lady Belhaven's chin, she wasn't about to take 'nothing' for an answer. And, even if he was a degenerate, Rocky didn't know whether she should inform her employer of Stanley's appalling behavior. If he tried to force himself on the other women in the house...

Mentioning something could lose her the lead botanist position. She and Catt had to remain in the household until the Masquerade party. After that, she might be able to confess the truth to Lady Belhaven.

Perhaps Stanley would mention the encounter to his grandmother to attempt to roust Catt from the house for striking him and the truth would come out. That outcome posed an equal danger to their continued presence in the house, but at least it would take the decision out of her hands.

"Fights are always difficult, between...friends."

Rocky sipped from her glass to buy herself a moment to think. Lady Belhaven hesitated over the word 'friend.' Did she suspect that Catt and Rocky were more than mere friends? Rocky brushed a lock of hair away from her hot cheek.

They weren't more than friends. They'd shared a single kiss, and that during the throes of Felicia's perfume. Perhaps a time or two since then, she'd wondered if he might kiss her, but he hadn't. She'd thought he didn't feel that way about her.

Then why had he said that he loved her? It seemed impossible. They fought. They hated each other...didn't they? Well, she didn't hate him. And, over the past week, they'd grown more and more cohesive working together. They didn't argue nearly as much.

She rubbed her forehead. *Could* he love her?

Her stomach quivered at the thought. She was afraid. Afraid he did love her...afraid he didn't. Why had he said it?

After she finished chewing her bite of seed cake, Lady Belhaven asked, "What was the fight about? Perhaps it was merely an overreaction on both your parts."

Rocky tamped down a bubble of nervous laughter. That, she couldn't possibly answer. After a moment, she said tentatively, "It was personal, not professional." She offered no more information. Lady Belhaven wasn't a friend, she was an employer.

Fortunately, she seemed to sense that Rocky would give her no more detail than that. She took a sip of milk to wash down her next bite of cake. "I've found there are two kinds of men in this world. Those who look down on women no matter how hard we work, and those who seek to build us up. If your Mr. Catterson is of the first persuasion, there may be no reasoning with him."

"He isn't." The words slipped from between Rocky's lips before she considered them.

The impact coursed through her like a shiver. Catt *wasn't* one of those men to try to tear down the women around him. He always treated her with consideration and respect, even when they were at odds. In fact, despite provoking him several times, he'd never once told her that he considered himself her better.

Then there were the moments when they weren't arguing. When she made herself ill with tension and couldn't eat, but he managed to diffuse it with a smile and a flippant joke. Or when he held her, just held her until she regained control of her emotions and could continue working. He didn't think less of her in those moments. If anything, he helped her to accomplish more. He knew precisely what she was capable of, and when the stress was starting to get to be too much. Like tonight, when he'd sent her to bed ahead of him despite the fact that they could have accomplished in five minutes what it had likely taken him ten minutes to do. He knew her, knew when her quick mind was getting the best of her...sometimes before she did.

In that moment, she couldn't fathom what her life might be without him. Oh, Lud... She thought she loved him, too. She pressed her hand against her mouth, trying to seal in the words, the realization. She'd reacted abominably when he'd confessed his feelings. What if she couldn't make amends?

Gently, Lady Belhaven patted the hand Rocky had clenched on the table. Her hand was soft, her skin almost delicate and fragile. "If he builds you up, then why are you fighting him? There are many more men of the first class than of the second."

Rocky frowned. Was the old woman encouraging her to pursue Catt romantically? No, she couldn't be. "Isn't there a rule against romantic entanglements in the household?" Her cheeks heated as the question slipped out. What if she'd misinterpreted the woman's words? She'd given away that she had considered Catt in that light.

Lady Belhaven frowned. A swarm of bees erupted in Rocky's stomach as she waited for a response. Could she take the question back?

"There is no such rule here. Why would you think that?"

There wasn't? But Lewis had been explicit... Rocky fought not to frown. Why would Lewis have lied about that? "Forgive me. I must have misunderstood. But..."

The old woman waited for her to continue.

"If there isn't such a rule, there are two people in your house who would very much like to announce their marriage."

"Oh?" Lady Belhaven's eyes lit up. "Are you referring to yourself?"

Heat scalded Rocky's cheeks. "No. Miss Towney and Mr. Abrahams have been married for a couple weeks, but they feared being turned out of the house if you knew."

"What nonsense! I'll have to speak with them tomorrow. Why would I bar them from happiness? If anything, I encourage it." The woman finished off the last of her milk and smiled. A white film clung to her upper lip before she licked it off. "For now, I think I should retire for the evening."

Grateful to no longer be the focus of the conversation, Rocky stood and helped the old woman to bed. The climb up the stairs was slow and wearisome, but she tried not to show it. As they traveled down the upstairs hall, Rocky noticed a small library, the glow of the moon splashing in from tall windows and illuminating the room.

"One of my favorite rooms," Lady Belhaven's voice was sad. "Though it doesn't get much use from my family. They seem to prefer less literate pursuits."

When they reached Lady Belhaven's chambers, Rocky couldn't find Abby anywhere. She dressed her employer for bed herself and saw her settled before she left.

The moment she was alone again, her heartbeat quickened and her head spun. She wiped her clammy palms on the wool over her hips. She'd bungled the moment earlier. If she knocked on Catt's door, would she be able to make amends? Tell him that she felt the same for him, kiss him. And then what? She was too afraid to contemplate after that, not when she didn't even know if he could forgive her.

This wasn't the right time to pursue romance. They were in the middle of an assignment! But if not now, when? Her heart hammered as she slowly made her way toward the servants' quarters.

She paused in front of Catt's door, battling the urge to tremble like an earthquake. Her heart lodged in her throat, throbbing out a swift, painful beat. It matched the hot knot of sensation beneath her ribs as she thought about turning around and continuing to her room. Although it sounded simpler to give into the fear clawing at her throat, it wasn't. She had to know if she could fix this, if he still loved her despite the way she'd reacted. She couldn't bear to lose him. Taking a deep breath, she raised her fist and rapped on the door.

Her decisiveness buckled beneath the onslaught of nerves the moment her knuckles met the wood. What if he turned her away? It was too late to back down.

Maybe—

He opened the door. His cravat and jacket were gone, his shirt unlaced to show the shadowed hollow of his throat. His red-blond hair stuck up at odd angles, as if he'd run his hand through it a time or twelve. He licked his lips, then opened his mouth to say something. For an instant, Rocky saw a flash of the same uncertainty written across his face that gripped her.

She opened her mouth, but she didn't know what to say.

"Rocky, I—"

I love you, too. She opened her mouth, but her throat tightened. She couldn't do it. She couldn't say the words.

She stepped forward, snaked her hands around his neck, and kissed him instead.

***

Catt couldn't breathe as Rocky pressed her mouth to his. Was this real or was he dreaming? She hadn't seemed pleased when he'd confessed his feelings for her. If anything, she'd seemed appalled.

That memory, more than anything else, convinced him to savor this moment. He didn't know if it would still be there when he opened his eyes. He wrapped his arms around her, holding her close. The soft curves of her body molded to his, impeded only by their clothes. She felt incredible. Better than incredible. He kissed her like he was finishing what he'd started outside in the hall. She clutched him like she'd never let go. But he couldn't keep kissing her, as much as he wanted.

Aching in more ways than one, he lifted his head. When he straightened, still supporting her against his body until she regained her balance, she gulped for breath. She opened her eyes slowly, her thick eyelashes fluttering across her desire-darkened eyes as she looked up at him. He'd dreamed of that look. Far too often, of late.

His throat worked as he struggled to find words. He was usually more eloquent than this. "Why?" His stomach tumbled like it contained an acrobatic team as he waited for her answer.

Those thick eyelashes veiled her eyes. Her arms unhooked from around his neck and she dropped down from the balls of her feet.

"Just kiss me."

For one impossibly long moment, he continued to stare as he tried to absorb the moment. She was really there. She wanted him to kiss her. But earlier in the corridor...

He shook his head. He shouldn't examine it too closely. If he did, he might not like what he found. So, instead of thinking, he bent to kiss her again. As his mouth descended on hers, the tense muscles in her body relaxed. He surrendered to the feel of her, the taste of her. He couldn't get enough. Zeus, but he loved her. Did she feel the same?

After an altogether too brief kiss, he separated their mouths again. He opened his mouth, but didn't speak. What if she didn't love him? What if, like any other women he'd met who had expressed interest in him, she only wanted him for a night? He licked his lips.

She sank her teeth into her lower lip and lowered her gaze to his chest. "Are you going to invite me into your room?" Her voice sounded hoarse.

His knees weakened. Was she asking…? He swallowed hard as he struggled to rein in the flare of desire. Instead of speaking, he stepped to the side, clearing a path into his room.

She straightened her shoulders and stepped inside. Without looking behind her, she shut the door. Her gaze caught his, the candlelight on his nightstand reflecting off her spectacles. He couldn't read the expression in her eyes.

By Jove, he wanted to. When he stepped closer, she tilted her face up to meet his. Her lips parted as if she anticipated his kiss. She made no protest when he slid her spectacles away, though she looked a bit disappointed when he took a step back to set them next to the candle. She didn't move from the door. Given the way she leaned on it, she might not be able to. Was she just as nervous about this as he was? He still didn't know why she'd come. Usually verbose, this time, she hadn't rubbed two words together.

Needing an answer, even if it wasn't the one he hoped, he stepped closer and slid his palm over her jaw, cupping her face. He searched her gaze.

"Why are you here, Rocky?"

Damn him, but he hadn't meant to confess his love for her. He hadn't even realized he'd felt it, not that strongly, until he'd seen her with Stanley. This upset the tenuous balance between them. Did she hate him? Love him? He didn't damn well know, and her expression gave away none of the answers he sought.

She licked her lips. Softly, she admitted, "I want you."

Three simple words, but they made him burn. He swallowed hard, not sure if she meant what he thought she did. But then her gaze slipped past him to the bed, the desire evident in her face.

The urge to kiss her crested over him, but somehow he managed to hold himself still. He ached to press her against his body, to become as close with her as he could possibly get, but he had to be certain she was telling the truth. If she was only saying she did because... He didn't know why. Some last-ditch attempt to salvage their friendship by turning it into something else. He didn't think she would do that, but she hadn't explained herself, hadn't...

She hadn't said she loved him, only that she wanted him.

It would have to be good enough, because he didn't know if he had the strength to turn her away. It was taking all his willpower not to succumb to her right here, right now.

"Are you sure? There's no...undoing this." He didn't know if she was a virgin, and frankly didn't care. Who she chose to share her body with was her business, but he hoped it would be no one but him from this moment on.

She nodded, speechless for once in her life.

Tentatively, he lowered his head enough to lay a hesitant kiss across her lips. A brief touch before he pulled back again. He needed more than a nod. He needed her to convince him. Why him, if she didn't love him? Why now?

She licked her lips. The slow slide of her tongue was torture. Although she tried to look away, his hand on her cheek prevented it. He needed to see her eyes.

"I'm not afraid of this."

He was. He was afraid she was doing this for the wrong reasons. He loved her too much to surrender if he knew she'd regret it come the morning.

"I want you," she repeated, her voice firmer.

Heaven help him, but she must. It couldn't be near the feverish need he felt to claim her, but it was close enough.

"If I'd never said…"

Lud, he was an idiot. He couldn't even force out the words, afraid that she might tell him she didn't love him back. Better he not know one way or another. At least that way, he could pretend.

"I'd still want you." She lowered her gaze to his lips. "But I might not have admitted it."

Zeus. That was the battle he had with himself every day. Surely she felt the same for him as he did for her. *Please let her feel the same…*

He laid another tentative kiss on her mouth. This time, when he parted, he returned again. He couldn't help himself. His lips parted this time, but he retreated as she snaked out her tongue to meet his.

The third time he returned, he'd made his decision. He loved her. She wanted him. He craved her like he'd never craved anyone or anything.

He melded his mouth to hers, devouring her. He deepened the kiss, his tongue tangling with hers in a hot, fervent dance. Whereas with his previous kisses he'd kept his hands on her back, now he touched her in all the ways he'd wanted to for weeks. He slid one hand around to the back of her head, his fingers tangling in her hair as he held her steady. His other hand circled her hip as he rounded to her bottom and pulled her closer to him. He ran his hand down her leg, urging it up around his hip. The tight skirts hampered the movement, making him growl with frustration as he pulled them up over her knee before trying again.

Zeus, yes. She lost her balance and leaned heavily against the door. He pinned her there, their bodies pressing against each other in the most intimate way. He rubbed his growing erection against her, driving them both mad as he kissed her senseless. She clutched at his shoulders and the back of his head as he moved against her. He palmed the globe of her bottom as he lifted her against him. When she slid her hand down his back to his rear, he slid his tongue into her mouth, the thrust a bit desperate. He needed her.

She released his rear to bring both hands to his chest and the ties on his shirt. She kissed him as she worked the ties free to the point where they stopped at mid chest.

He kissed his way along her jaw to her throat. He loved the sound that she made as he found a sensitive spot. She melted against him and he was only too happy to hold her up. He reveled in the feel of her

"Speechless?" he asked with a grin, his voice rough.

"Stop talking and take off your shirt."

When he released her, she leaned heavily against the door. Taking a step back, he pulled the shirt over his head and let it drop to the floor. Her gaze devoured the sight of his bare chest, as brazen and unapologetic as she was about everything else in life. As she swept her gaze lower, to the fall of his breeches, he unconsciously drifted his hands in that direction as well. He paused.

Licking his lips, he stepped closer again and claimed a kiss. As he tilted her back over one arm, he fumbled at the buttons of her dress with his free hand. They loosened, the halves parting to show her gauzy chemise beneath. She sank her fingers into his shoulders, clutching him fiercely as they kissed. It was a heady combination.

When he straightened, he traced the edge of her chemise as it gaped low across her chest. She sucked in a breath, swelling her breasts. His gaze rapt on her body, he peeled away the dress. Her dusky nipples peaked against her shift, the color hinting at the tantalizing flesh beneath. He traced her areola with the pad of his thumb. She bit her lower lip as she arched into his touch. Lud, she was so responsive. He couldn't wait to make her writhe in pleasure.

He didn't take her invitation, but chased her dress down over her hips. It took some persuasion to get the fabric to leave her body, but once over her hips, it pooled at the floor by her feet.

He dropped his hand as one last doubt claimed him. He could still walk away, postpone this until a better time. But if he did, he might lose her forever. The dilemma paralyzed him.

She took the decision out of his hands by toeing off her shoes and climbing onto the bed. She sat on her heels, facing him as she waited for him to join her.

His hands hovered over the buttons on his breeches. As she shimmied back into the middle of the bed, she gathered the hem of her chemise in her hand and rose onto her knees. When he undid one button, she raised her shift higher, to mid-thigh. He ogled the bare strip of flesh between her chemise and her stockings. He worked another button free. She hiked up her shift by another inch.

The rest of his buttons came undone in a flurry. With each, she lifted her chemise higher, baring more of her body. By the time he was done, the material bunched around her waist and he couldn't look away. He wanted to see more of her. He shucked his breeches. A shiver coursed through him at the appreciative look in her eye as she licked her lips.

His cheeks burned with color. As he joined her on the bed, he helped to strip away her chemise. He tossed it somewhere in the vicinity of his breeches as he laid her back on the coverlet. His gaze was rapt on her body, her round breasts giving way to the curve of her waist, her wide hips, and the graceful column of her legs. He opened his mouth, but nothing came out.

"It looks as though it's your turn to be speechless."

He licked his lips. "Rocky, you're beautiful." Reverently, he traced the curve of her breast.

She squirmed. As he flicked his fingers across her erect nipples, she gasped in a breath. And that was before he lowered his mouth. The flick of his tongue and the suction of his mouth made her writhe.

"Oh..."

He grinned as he lifted his head. "Like that, do you?" He didn't give her the opportunity to reply, but lowered his head again. This time, he grazed her nipple with his teeth. She arched off the bed with an incoherent cry.

He shifted closer as he ran his hand over her stomach and dipped between her legs. She opened her legs a bit wider to him as he delved between her folds. His fingers slipped between her hot, wet heat.

His Adam's apple bobbed as he swallowed. "You're wet. You want this."

"I wouldn't be here other—whoa!"

He slipped his middle finger through the moisture and into her intimate flesh. He slid as deep as he could reach before he pulled out and added a second finger.

She gripped his hair. "Oh my. That feels…" She moaned. "Incredible."

He shifted position, moving lower on her body with a wicked smile. "It gets better."

"Oh, good." Her breathless voice sent shivers coursing down his spine.

When he leaned down, she met him halfway and he kissed her long and deep. He positioned himself between her legs, lowering himself onto her body. His tip brushed her slick folds and he groaned. The sensation was too potent. He trembled with need. As he broke the kiss to take some of his weight on one elbow, he guided himself into her core.

They both moaned at the slow slide of his skin against hers. At that moment, there was no question in his mind that they had been made to do this. He thrust deep, savoring the feel of her. The slow pace was maddening, but he wanted this moment to last. He never wanted to be parted from her. If she only wanted him for tonight…

She curled her fingers into his shoulders. "Can you go faster? Not that I want this to end sooner but—"

He kissed her. "I know what you mean." His voice was every bit as breathless as hers. He changed position, rising onto his hands and knees as he quickened his stroke. She wrapped her legs around his hips, lifting herself to meet his thrusts. Each time he sheathed himself fully in her, the slap of skin was almost overpowered by the sound of his groans, coming thicker and thicker together.

He moaned her name with each stroke, leaving no doubt that he was completely focused on her, here, in this moment. She reached bliss as he cried out. Her body convulsed around him, trying to keep him close, but he pulled out and spurted his hot seed onto her stomach. He shuddered, his arms shaking as he struggled to hold himself upright. Satisfaction radiated through him, making his limbs weak. He wanted nothing more than to collapse onto the bed next to her.

Not yet. He rolled off the bed, scooping up the first cloth that met his fingers—her chemise. He folded it over before gently wiping his semen from her skin. He dropped the chemise back on the floor as he met her gaze.

I love you.

He didn't dare speak the words again, not after her reaction last time. Instead, he leaned forward and kissed her. The nervous flutter in his chest disappeared as she responded to the languorous kiss. When he parted from her, she smiled. He tucked a strand of her hair away from her face before he straightened.

He blew out the candle next to the bed, dousing them in darkness. The bed dipped as he rejoined her. He tucked her beneath the coverlet, enfolding her body with his. As he threaded his fingers through hers, she let out a blissful sigh and snuggled closer.

His chest ached. He loved her so much in that moment, squeezed onto the narrow bed and forced to press against one another lest they fall off, that he didn't know how he would let her go come the morning.

What would happen now? If he asked her to marry him, would she say yes or would she take it as an insult to her independence? He hugged her closer, burying his face in her thick hair.

"I love you." The words were muffled by the tendrils.

She didn't respond, not even with a hitch of breath. She was already asleep.

He traced the length of her arm and whispered, "Please don't leave."

Chapter Twenty-Three

Catt expected the next morning to feel different. More profound or maybe even awkward. Instead, he and Rocky rose and went to work as usual. He was no less aware of her presence in the hothouse as they hurried to fill orders. If anything, he found his attention wandering to her more. The only difference was that instead of battling it, whenever they crossed paths he indulged the urge to touch her. Small touches to her arm or cheek, to remind himself that she was still there. They didn't have time for anything lingering.

Aside from the usual orders they had to fill, they had the plants that would decorate the house for the masquerade ball to consider. It was a delicate balance. Some blooms could be clipped for delivery, but each plant had to have at least one other, depending on the species, in order to be used as decoration during the masquerade. This meant that, once the orders had been filled, Catt and Rocky ensconced themselves in the hothouse to take a tally of the plants in bloom and inform Lady Belhaven how many more orders they would be able to fill without impacting the decorations for her ball. The number was likely smaller than she hoped.

In fact, she didn't seem to believe the sheer numbers of orders that had gone through these past couple weeks and insisted on taking a tour of the hothouse herself. Catt offered his arm and escorted her while Rocky babbled about the health of the plants. By the end of the tour, the old woman clutched Catt's arm tighter than ever, but she stubbornly refused to sit.

"Is there anything you can do to coax those buds to bloom faster?"

In less than a week? Unlikely. Catt exchanged a glance with Rocky, who shrugged.

"I have a solution I feed the plants at Tenwick Abbey during dry summers. We could try that, but I can't guarantee it will take effect in time."

"We must try." The lines in Lady Belhaven's face seemed to deepen the longer she remained standing. Her complexion turned waxen, sweat beading on her upper lip. Catt tensed, preparing to catch her should she lose her footing.

"Are you certain you wouldn't like to sit down? Perhaps I can get you something. A tonic or a finger of spirits?" It was early in the afternoon, but alcohol might help to fortify her.

"If you'll escort me up to my parlor, I'll be fine. Faulker can fetch me a libation."

Catt did as she asked. When the parlor proved empty of footmen or even her grandson—a fact for which Catt was grateful—he found and sent Stefan to her on his return to the hothouse. When he got there, Rocky was busy mixing the solution she intended to give the plants.

He set to work helping her without question. She'd never shared her recipe with him before, so he waited for her direction. They worked in silence save for her instructions. When a lock of her hair battled free of her coif, he couldn't resist the urge to tuck it behind her ear. She leaned her cheek into his hand as she worked.

"I spoke with Lady Belhaven last night."

"Oh?" He dropped his hand.

Finished with her preparation, Rocky divided it between two watering cans. "She told me that she never implemented a rule against marriage or romance beneath her roof."

He frowned. "But the Abrahams were so certain..."

"Indeed. And Lewis informed me of the rule shortly after my arrival."

"Why would he, if there isn't one?"

She set aside the empty bowl and turned to him. He stood close enough that her skirts brushed against him. He wanted to kiss her, but that would have to wait for their work to be done. This was a serious conversation.

Rocky's gaze glittered behind her spectacles as she said, "Why don't we find Lewis and ask him?"

She slipped her hand into his and tugged him toward the door. In the corridor, she dropped it again, but his palm still tingled from the contact. He ignored it for the moment and followed her in search of the butler.

They found him in the unlit sitting room next to the front door. He lounged in a chair pulled up to the window, frosted over with ice crystals but still letting in some of the gray daylight. His expression was vacant. He nursed a tumbler in his hand. On the sideboard, a decanter with amber liquid had the crystal top on askew.

Catt followed Rocky into the room. Sensing that Lewis was in a troubled state to be drinking in the middle of the day, he shut the door behind him. Privacy might win them more of a confession, if Rocky didn't bungle the opportunity with a lack of diplomacy.

With a sigh, Lewis swallowed the rest of the libation and got to his feet. He was a little unsteady.

Rocky frowned. "Are you certain you should be drinking that?"

Catt bit his tongue. That was precisely the sort of thing he'd feared she'd say. Lewis was relaxed enough to say things he might not normally, but if they put up his guard, he might think twice.

With a shrug, the older man tottered toward the sideboard. "Lady Belhaven doesn't notice, so long as there's always enough to fortify her when she needs it. Her worthless son and that one grandson drink it like water." He lifted the half-full decanter. "Would you like one?"

Catt rested his palm in the small of Rocky's back, trying to caution her with a touch not to say anything brash. He answered for them both. "Thank you, no."

"You lied to me, Lewis." Rocky's posture stiffened and she crossed her arms.

The butler glanced to them, his eyes bloodshot. He splashed more alcohol into his glass and returned to the chair. Rocky crossed the room to stand in front of him, so he had no choice except to look at her. Stifling a sigh, Catt followed.

Still indignant, Rocky said, "You told me there is a rule against marriage in the household. There is no such rule. Lady Belhaven denied it personally."

The man grimaced. "There should be. Marriage and affairs among the staff are bad for work."

Frowning, Rocky turned to look over her shoulder at Catt. He feathered his hand over her back, reassuring her. If anything, their liaison had helped to bring them together. It wasn't distracting or in the way—in fact, he'd been more distracted by her when he'd been fighting his attraction to her. Now, free to touch her as he pleased, the tension between them having softened, they worked as one to complete what they needed to. They trusted each other.

"How so?" Catt asked, his voice hushed.

The man rolled the tumbler between his palms before he took another gulp. "I loved her, you know."

Rocky stiffened. "Who?"

"Rosemary. Mrs...."

He didn't complete the name, but he didn't have to. Catt and Rocky had heard all about Lewis's alleged affair with Mrs. Dowden prior to her death. Apparently, it was true.

The butler lifted his head. His bleary eyes looked watery and red. "He didn't deserve her. He has a temper, you know. She got caught in the middle and blamed..." He sighed. "I loved her deeply. If not for me, she might still be alive..." He shook his head, the lines around his eyes etching deeper as he finished his glass. "That is why it is disastrous for couples to engage in the household. I couldn't let something like that happen again. So I've warned every new man and woman who come in. No one's dared to ask Lady Belhaven about the rule directly." He raised his gaze, glaring at Rocky. "Except for you."

Catt stepped closer. The man seemed unstable. He didn't want Rocky to be hurt in any way, physically or verbally. Softly, he said, "That was a terrible tragedy, but it isn't indicative of what might happen."

The man could have tried not to engage with another man's wife. Even if it seemed that her marriage was less than happy. That deceit was what had led to her death, that and her own foolishness in leaving the house in the dead of winter without proper clothing. Whatever had happened, it was in the past.

Though it seemed that neither man involved had ever recovered from it.

Lewis shook his head and leaned back in the chair. He seemed to be enveloped in the past. "You're young. You'll learn." His voice broke. Tears leaked from the corners of his eyes as he stared out the window and whispered the name of the woman he still loved, over a decade later.

***

Rocky let Catt usher her away from the intoxicated, grieving butler. She couldn't imagine being so in love with a person as to be affected so deeply by her loss more than ten years later.

If Catt suddenly died—

She shoved the thought viciously away and led the way back to the hothouse. She and Catt were now Crown spies. This wouldn't be their only assignment. Chances were, the next would be even more dangerous. There was every possibility that he might die...or she would. It didn't seem fair, not now that they'd finally found their place together. But she couldn't fathom turning her back on Britain and knowing Catt, neither would he. The only thing they could do was trust in each other and look out for one another.

She didn't even know what their life would look like beyond this assignment. For now, with her stomach twisted in knots, she couldn't bear to think of it. She stepped into the warm, humid hothouse, letting the heat wrap around her like a hug. Then she turned to Catt. She wasn't sure what to say about them or their future, so she focused on work again.

"Do you think he could be V?"

Catt followed her as she crossed to the work bench to claim one of the watering cans. She passed him the second one.

He looked dubious as he said, "It depends how often he drinks."

Lewis had seemed confident that Lady Belhaven wouldn't discover his imbibing. How could he know for sure unless he'd done it before? Many times.

She sighed. "It's not likely he would be. That leaves...who?"

Someone with plenty of access to the hothouse. Lance Belhaven. Maybe Lady Belhaven, since she came in so often to check on her plants and the orders. The possibility for the culprit being anyone else sank lower and lower with each staff secret they revealed.

Catt set down his watering can and cupped her cheek. "We'll find him. We're close."

Empty words, considering he couldn't be any more certain than she was over their suspects or lack thereof. But the look in his eyes was encouraging. He believed that they would complete this assignment.

Hopefully sooner, rather than later. They'd been here for weeks.

Nodding, she pulled away to tend to the plants. She didn't know whether the solution she'd created would encourage the plants to grow enough to make a difference by the time of the masquerade party at the end of the week. Perhaps if she'd fed the plants this solution upon her arrival, but a few days was far too short a time. There were a few plants that were mostly bud and no blooms; with luck, those buds would open by Friday, but it wasn't guaranteed. She spotted more cards stacked on the front work bench, a testament that Lady Belhaven hadn't heeded her warning at all. If they filled the orders, how many plants would they have left in good enough shape to display the pots around the house and ballroom?

As she poured the last of her solution into a potted geranium, she noticed markings on the leaves of the lily next to it. "Catt?"

He rounded the table immediately. By the time he reached her, she was busy running her fingers over the plant. The holes were man-made, just like the last. Damn and blast! They hadn't left the hothouse unattended for very long, fifteen minutes at most.

The moment he noticed where her attention was directed, Catt's eyes widened. "I'll get the package Morgan sent." He beat a hasty retreat from the hothouse as Rocky found a pair of forceps. When she peered into the lily's throat, she found a rolled-up slip of paper there. Delicately, she extracted the paper and unrolled it.

As expected, the message was in code. She waited for Catt to return, anticipation clawing at her insides. Fortunately, she didn't have long to wait. He returned within minutes with the sheaf of papers the Duke of Tenwick had sent.

They started by deciphering the leaves first. The code was complicated, but given the explanation the duke had sent with the cipher, he believed the leaves to signify numbers only. The slip of paper contained the accompanying instructions. If the Duke of Tenwick was right—and, given the confidence every spy she had met had bestowed upon his brilliance in decoding messages, Rocky had every reason to believe he was—then the leaves they decoded with difficulty appeared to be some kind of date or time. Or both.

"This Friday at midnight," Catt murmured under his breath.

She concurred. "The night of the masquerade."

They set to work on the second part of the message, scrawled in an entirely different kind of code, albeit still a brief one given the minute size of the paper. This one was even more brief.

It read: *Henry VIII*.

Rocky's heart beat quicker as she raised her gaze to meet Catt's. He looked just as excited as she was. If they were right about the date and time, then Monsieur V intended to attend Lady Belhaven's masquerade dressed as King Henry VIII.

"Do we send it?" Catt spoke in a hush, his voice tight.

"Yes." In order to lure Monsieur V out into the open, they would have to ensure that his recipient got the message as planned. She rolled the paper back up and used the forceps to carefully insert it into the throat of the lily once more. "Can you check the cards? Where will the lilies be delivered?"

Catt strode to the front of the room to find out while she worked at her delicate task.

When he returned, his eyes held an excited gleam. He held only two cards. "I'll send a message to Morgan with these names and addresses and the content of the message that will be delivered." When he met her gaze, he grinned. "We've got him, Rocky."

Chapter Twenty-Four

Rocky fidgeted with the strap on her dress. She was dressed almost identical to a dozen other Cleopatras at the masquerade tonight, the better to blend in. She would rather have worn breeches than this flimsy piece of fabric.

Next to her, Catt was dressed as a domino. The hood of the burgundy cloak covered his telltale blond hair and the accompanying black half-mask hid his features. Unfortunately, Rocky had no mask to complete her anonymity; she had to hope that her years among the servant class had taught her well enough on how to blend in and be forgettable.

Normally as servants, they wouldn't be attending a masquerade but Morgan's instructions had been clear. They needed to attend to catch Monsieur V. Hopefully, no one of the household would recognize them in costume. Of course, if Monsieur V really was one of Lady Belhaven's servants, there would be another of them in costume who wasn't supposed to be.

Rocky tensed at the thought. They'd failed in their task to identify the spy and now they risked

Monsieur V being able to pass the secret information to his contact at the party. She could not let that happen.

"We'll get him," Catt whispered, leaning down so his voice didn't carry. His voice was firm and confident.

As he found her hand and squeezed it, some of her nervousness melted away. She took a deep breath and nodded, scanning the throng for anyone dressed as King Henry VIII.

For all that she wasn't technically a peer, Lady Belhaven's masquerade was a crush. Every downstairs parlor and withdrawing room was decorated with one or more of the plants from the hothouse. The rest had been scattered here, in this lofty ballroom. The room, nearly three times the side of the hothouse, was only one story high, but no less magnificent for the low ceiling. A quartet set up in the only corner devoid of flowers. Along the perimeter of the room, chairs were nestled in pairs between more potted plants. A narrow arch led to a buffet room with food and drink constantly replenished by servants. Lady Belhaven had hired a handful of temporary staff members to help set up, tend to the guests, and clean up after the masquerade. Although the Duke of Tenwick hadn't confirmed as much, Rocky suspected that one or two of those temporary servants were Crown spies.

The duke himself was in attendance, dressed to mirror Catt and a number of the other guests in a black domino. His very pregnant wife was dressed as a harlequin—a common enough outfit, though with her protruding belly she did not at all go unremarked. The pair, along with Lord Tristan Graylocke and his wife, Frederica, were guarding a voluptuous woman dressed as Venus who appeared to have trouble sitting, given the way she grimaced. According to the missive the Duke of Tenwick had sent Catt and Rocky before the event began, this woman was their informant, the French spy they had captured and convinced to sing for them—the only person the Crown had at hand who would be able to confirm Monsieur V's identity should they come face to face.

In comparison with the round Duchess of Tenwick, who looked as impish as her costume suggested, Tristan and Frederica looked tame. The lady was dressed as a moon maiden in a silver dress with moons and stars in her hair. They went well with the moon-eyes she and her husband exchanged when they thought no one was looking. He was also in silver, though with the way his doublet and shirt billowed out, coupled with his mask, Rocky guessed that he was meant to be a knight. His ancestral suit of armor must not have afforded him enough range or silence of movement to suit his spying needs.

Gideon and Felicia were also there, both in Grecian costumes—Gideon dressed as Pan and his wife as a Greek goddess or maiden. The pair stuck fast to the other two young women who must have come to make the heavy Graylocke presence at the event seem like a family affair. Miss Charlotte Vale, Frederica's younger sister, looked like a rosy-cheeked Bo Peep with her blonde hair dressed in ringlets. Lucy Graylocke, with her hair in a similar style, played Red Riding Hood.

Although the red drew the eye, even Lucy and Charlie's costumes blended in with the colorful crowd. There were harlequins and columbines, Cinderellas and even a wolf or two, Greek and Roman gods, cross-dressing women, skirts that fell no lower than the knees, historical costumes, sultans, fortune tellers, cupids, Scottish, Chinese, and Egyptian clothing, and even some in formal ball attire with the inclusion of a mask. The room, which might comfortably have fit two hundred people, certainly fit more than that.

How were they ever supposed to find a man dressed as King Henry VIII in this? Since at this raucous gathering it drew less attention to be in pairs than to be alone, when Catt offered Rocky his arm, she took it without question and they strolled the perimeter of the room in search for their man. The party, well under way, had thus far yielded no results, though guests continued to arrive, mingle, and depart in a dizzying whirl of bodies.

Catt and Rocky chatted of inconsequential things like the weather as they walked, in case someone listened in on their conversation. Rocky only attended to the conversation with half a mind as she searched the crowd for anyone dressed in Tudor clothing. Her breath caught as she spotted someone, a man. Was that...Lance Belhaven?

"There. By the door. He just entered."

Rocky jumped at his soft voice and glanced at the door. *Fiddlesticks!* There were two of them!

"I found one, too." She pretended to brush a strand of her hair away from her cheek, using the movement to gesture to the man standing next to his brother and grandmother.

"Bloody hell."

Rocky agreed with him wholeheartedly.

"It's nearly midnight. How are we to know which is our man?" He muttered the question under his breath, but she still heard.

"Let's make our way back to the Graylockes. We'll follow Lance, they can follow the other fellow."

Catt turned their trajectory and swore. "Confound it, there's a third!"

Three King Henry VIIIs. Three possible suspects for Monsieur V. Had the slippery spymaster planned it that way?

"Forget the other two. V must be Lance." She didn't recognize the other two, not at this distance.

His jaw clenched as he scanned the crowd and lowered his voice some more. He leaned closer, whispering into her ear as he trailed his finger along her arm like they were lovers.

Which they were. But, in this case, they didn't discuss anything romantic or illicit. They discussed treason and how best to thwart it.

"What proof do you have? We can't discount the other two on a hunch, not when we're so close to capturing him."

"V had access to the hothouse. He must be someone we've crossed paths with," she said, her voice little louder than a hiss.

"Unless he's had someone else place the codes for him."

Her mouth thinned. It was a possibility, and one they'd entertained on more than one occasion with the suspects who didn't fit the description. "We'll find out which it is at midnight, won't we? Once the grandfather clock chimes, one of the three will attempt to leave the ballroom."

All they had to do was follow the right man.

The crush was so tight that they barely made it halfway across the ballroom toward the Graylockes in the corner when the chime of the grandfather clock sounded. *Bong, bong...* It was nearly overpowered by the music as it came to the energized end of the song. Applause followed from the guests, masking the grandfather clock.

Rocky whirled to check on her suspect. "Lance is moving toward the exit."

"So are the others."

She dropped her hand from his sleeve and whirled to check for herself. They were. "Hell and damnation! We have to follow."

He nodded. "I'll take Lance—"

"No, I'll take Lance. He's my suspect."

Catt let out a short sigh, but didn't argue. "Fine. I'll take the one by the door. What about the third?"

She turned. "Where are the Graylockes?"

His mouth thinned as he searched the crowd for an ally as well. No one. Not a single person they could confirm to be a spy in the mash of bodies.

A flash of red caught Rocky's eye. "Go after your man before he escapes the party," she told Catt. "I see someone and will relay the message."

He nodded but didn't argue further, parting ways from her instead.

That flash of red belonged to Lucy Graylocke. The Duke of Tenwick's youngest sibling wasn't a spy for Britain—in fact, Rocky had been instructed to keep the family's hand in spying a secret from Lucy and her mother—but Rocky had no choice. All she had to do was get Lucy to keep close to the last man and prevent him from leaving the ballroom. She never needed to know why.

Ahead, a flash of a pink dress and blonde curls alerted Rocky to the fact that Miss Vale's attention had been claimed by her next dance partner. A strike of good fortune, for it meant that Lucy was alone. When Rocky clasped her by the elbow, she gasped.

"Rocky? Don't startle me like that!"

"I need your help." Rocky's voice was strained with urgency.

The playful air around Lucy vanished immediately. "How?"

"There's a man, King Henry over there—" Rocky pointed. "—who I need to keep in the ballroom."

Lucy narrowed her eyes. As a budding fiction writer, she smelled a story even when there wasn't one to be found. Though of course, in this case, there was.

"Why?"

"He said something untoward and I intend to confront him."

"So why don't you?"

Blast! Rocky hadn't thought through her story before she'd approached. Her heart hammered as she saw Lance slip closer to the door. He was nearly away!

Out of desperation, she pointed to him. "I lost the man in question in the crowd and I can't be sure which he is. I think that one, but I can't follow both at once. Will you keep the other man in the ballroom just in case?"

Warily, Lucy asked, "Why do you need to talk to him so badly? What did he say?"

Lud, why did she have to be so curious on the matter? Rocky grappled to concoct a suitable explanation. She settled on the first answer she thought Lucy wouldn't question, given her personality.

"He told me that women shouldn't have lead botanist positions because we've got nothing between our ears."

Lucy's expression darkened. "That fiend! I'll—"

"Just keep him in the ballroom. I'd rather have at him, myself."

Lucy nodded, her chin set and her eyes glittering like chips of ice. She squared her shoulders like she was about to enter a room filled with the most vicious matrons in the *ton*. Lucy was much stronger than her overprotective brothers gave her credit for. She could probably handle the truth. In fact, she would probably be an asset to the Crown.

But Rocky didn't have time to enlighten her, let alone seek a second opinion on the matter before she blurted something that might get her sacked. She had to go.

"Thank you."

She bolted toward the door just as Lance slipped along the hallway. Truthfully, she felt sorry for whomever happened to have worn a Tudor costume tonight. That poor man might soon get the tongue-lashing of his life by Lucy. Rocky didn't for a second believe that he might be Monsieur V.

She was on the trail of the French spymaster. *She* would be the one to confirm his identity and take him into custody. Whereas the Duke of Tenwick's previous orders had been to watch and wait, now that they might have a chance to nab the traitor, he had given his full permission to take advantage and arrest the blackguard if it looked as though he had uncovered Rocky and Catt's purpose in the house. It was why the Graylockes were here en masse; to provide backup if needed, as well as escorting their infamous prisoner for her to confirm Monsieur V's identity.

The throng impeded her path. Luckily, she was small enough that she was able to squeeze between most people. The fact that she was female for once worked to her advantage as the polite men in attendance melted out of her path and tipped their hats to her.

By the time she reached the entryway to the darkened corridor that led to the kitchen, her heart pounded in her throat and she had trouble remembering to breathe in her excitement. The resultant shortness of breath left her annoyed and slowed her progress farther as she leaned against the wall.

As Eliza passed, a full covered tray of food in her hand, Rocky asked, "Have you seen Lance?"

"He went out the back way toward the terrace. Why?"

"His grandmother sent me to look for him."

With a nod, Eliza resumed her duties.

Rocky bolted down the corridor. This one led in a straight path past the hothouse and kitchen to the door closest to the stables. But Eliza had mentioned the back terrace, which meant that Rocky had to slip through a small parlor toward another short corridor that led into the back of the estate. Had it been summer, the doors of the ballroom would have been open to allow guests to mingle on that terrace. However, those doors were now shut and the frigid open air was the perfect cover to exchange sensitive information about the realm. No one would interrupt them.

Except Rocky. Afraid she would run out of time and miss the meeting, she dashed through the door and stumbled onto the terrace. The cold immediately wrapped around her, raising gooseflesh over her bare arms and upper chest. Her flimsy indoor slippers crunched in the snow. She gritted her teeth as the cold powder fell inside, an icy awakening.

At the sound of the door and her footsteps, Lance turned with a smile. "Darli..." The word died on his lips as the smile turned into a frown. "What are *you* doing here?"

Damn and blast! She should have stopped before barreling out onto the terrace. She didn't have a ready reason. Glaring, she drew herself up, thinking to distract him. "What are you doing here?"

Confound it, she should have offered the same excuse she'd given to Eliza. Too late for that now.

His frown dipped into a scowl. "If you must know, I'm waiting for...someone else."

"A conspirator?"

Her foot slipped on a patch of ice and she scrambled to remain upright. If it came down to a fight, she wouldn't be able to arrest him out here. She'd fall flat on her face. Why had she and Catt decided to split up? His presence would have been welcome right about now.

Not to mention, he probably would have kept a cool head and stopped her from barreling out of the house.

"Have you lost your bloody mind? What are you talking about?"

She crossed her arms, refusing to break his gaze. He was hiding something. She'd found Monsieur V after all, but she hadn't expected him to be so...obvious. Wasn't the man supposed to be a chameleon, able to slip in and out of a room and use his charm and words to misdirect people into forgetting key details about him? Lance wasn't doing that at all. From the way he acted, it was crystal clear to Rocky that he was hiding something from her.

Something like the fact that he had betrayed his family and his country to the French.

"If you're not meeting a conspirator, who are you meeting?"

His face flushed, but she couldn't tell whether it was because of anger or mortification at being caught. "A...lover."

A likely tale. He probably said as much to avoid further questions. Rocky wasn't about to fall for that.

"Who?" she demanded.

The snow crunched behind her, signaling the arrival of someone else. His informant, maybe? A prickle of foreboding pierced the back of her neck. If another French spy had happened upon them, she was outnumbered. She should have thought this through.

"What is *she* doing here?"

Rocky turned to see Abby. The woman had a look of derision on her face as she looked from Rocky to Lance. Unlike them, Abby was dressed warmly in a fur-lined pelisse over her work clothes. The maid glared at Lance.

"If you think to introduce someone else into our bed play—"

That was enough to convince Rocky that he was telling the truth. She raised her hands, stepping away. "Certainly not. Forgive me, I chose the wrong place to find a breath of fresh air."

She skirted back, leaving Abby and Lance to their lover's quarrel. Only once she was safely inside the warm manor again, her hands and toes beginning to thaw, did she pause. Wasn't Abby conducting an affair with David? She glanced over her shoulder, through the frosty panes of the French door to the terrace. Lance must have convinced Abby of the misunderstanding because they were now kissing quite passionately.

Rocky rubbed at her chest to banish a twinge of guilt. Clearly, Lance didn't have a clue that Abby wasn't faithful to him. She didn't have time to enlighten him. Besides, it wasn't the worst secret in this house that she'd been forced to keep to herself.

If Lance wasn't Monsieur V, that meant one of the other two men in the ballroom was. Rocky had to find Catt. He might be in danger. Danger *she* had caused by insisting they take separate targets.

She had to return to the party posthaste.

Chapter Twenty-Five

Catt slipped into the brightly-lit corridor after his mark. Along this hallway resided the parlors where card tables had been set up, as well as the withdrawing rooms. If he followed it long enough, he would come to the intersection leading to the front door.

A man and woman ducked into a room. Sharp cheroot smoke curled into the air from a room near the far end of the corridor. Catt squared his shoulders, following his mark. The moment the couple whisked out of sight, Catt quickened his step to catch up. At the sound of Catt's clipped footsteps, the man glanced over his shoulder.

Catt didn't recognize him. Blast! Maybe Rocky had been right. If so, she was right now with a dangerous criminal.

The thought made his heart beat quicken and his palms sweaty. He nearly pivoted and chased after her and Lance. He gritted his teeth. On the off chance this stranger *was* Monsieur V, he couldn't let him leave. Not even to help Rocky. He had to trust that, with their training, she would be fine. That she wouldn't do anything rash.

Bugger Morgan's directive to watch unless his identity was compromised. He couldn't let Rocky remain in jeopardy for a second longer than was necessary. He would collect this fellow and turn him over to the Graylockes for questioning.

Stepping abreast of the man, Catt slung his arm around the fellow's shoulders and slipped a pistol from his pocket. In case someone happened by, he used the man's body to hide the weapon. He dug the mouth into the stranger's back.

"Here's what you're going to do. You'll come with me quietly and have a little chat with my friend. If he likes your answers, you'll be allowed to return home unharmed."

Catt kept his voice icy, not allowing himself to thaw toward the man even when he started to quiver beneath Catt's arm. It could be an act. Catt steered him back the way they'd come, to the ballroom.

After two steps, the man started to babble. "Forgive me. Please, I'll get the money to you. Tomorrow, even, if only you'll let me go."

Why did it seem as though every man remotely connected to the *ton* was in debt up to his eyeballs? Barring the Graylockes, of course. Catt hid his annoyance, thankful that in this case the *ton*'s predilection toward extravagance and gambling worked in his favor to deliver an excuse for his behavior. Unfortunately, Catt did not recognize the voice. The man was not part of Lady Belhaven's household. He wasn't Monsieur V. But Catt couldn't very well just let him go now; he'd have to play through.

As they neared the ballroom, he tucked the pistol out of sight, but didn't loosen his grip on the man. Walking into the crush, he scanned the throng for any of the Graylockes.

He found Tristan first and hailed him. They met on the edge of the ballroom, next to a line of empty chairs. Tristan came alone, his wife remaining by the duke and duchess.

"Where's your partner?" Tristan asked.

"There were three. We had to split up." Since Tristan was there, Rocky must have found Gideon to follow the third man. Giddy had months more experience as a spy than Catt, though not quite as much as his two older brothers. Nevertheless, Catt rested easy knowing that his best friend—aside from Rocky—was handling the third.

He shoved the man he'd caught into Tristan's grasp. "He seems harmless enough but I'll leave him to you. I have to find Ro—my partner."

The moment Tristan nodded and slung his arm around the man's shoulders, Catt turned his back.

As he walked away, he heard Tristan murmur, "You and I will have a talk. Let's get to know each other better."

The stranger started babbling about his debts again.

Catt turned to the ballroom. If his mark had gone down the brightly-lit corridor en route to the ballroom, that left only two other exits for Lance to have chosen. A narrow, closed door nestled behind the orchestra which would be difficult to reach and led to a steep staircase that ended on the floor to the family wing—and the corridor leading to the hothouse, kitchen, and exit to the stables. On a hunch, Catt headed in the second direction.

He fought the throng of bodies, every one of which seemed determined to stand in his way. His heart pounded and he tried not to picture what might happen if Rocky was discovered by Monsieur V to be a spy. If she was hurt... He would never forgive himself. However capable he knew her to be, he couldn't help the raw feeling that surged through him at the thought of her being in danger. Two heads were better than one against a man as slippery as Monsieur V.

At the mouth to the kitchen, he collided with another body. He started to apologize reflexively before he realized the person was Rocky. He hauled her into his arms, heedless of the impropriety.

None of the guests paid much attention to the servant wing, in any case.

"Thank Jove. Are you all right?"

"Yes." She fought his embrace enough to look up at him. A worried crease formed between her eyebrows. "Lance isn't V. Your mark...?"

He shook his head. "Handed him to Tristan to be sure."

Rocky paled as she peered around him, trying to search the ballroom. Reluctantly, he let his arms drop and took a step to the side.

"Can you see Lucy?"

Gideon's younger sister? He frowned as he searched the crowd. She was usually with her friend Charlie, but the blonde Bo Peep was currently talking to her sister Freddie near the rest of the Graylocke family.

Slowly, he shook his head. "No. Why?"

Panic flashed over Rocky's face. "I asked her to watch the third man for me and ensure he didn't leave the ballroom."

Catt swore under his breath.

"I couldn't find anyone else, and I was so sure Lance was V..."

She met his gaze, her face filled with guilt and fear. His blood chilled as he made the same connection he did. If Lucy wasn't in the ballroom, she must have followed the third man in an attempt to keep him from going too far.

She was at the mercy of Monsieur V, and she wasn't a trained spy.

Chapter Twenty-Six

How could Rocky have been so dimwitted? She'd been so focused on Lance being the culprit that she hadn't for a second thought that Lucy might be unable to keep the third suspect in the ballroom. She hadn't considered that if the man slipped her grasp, Lucy might follow.

Morgan's gaze had cut through her with the news. He'd marshaled the other members of the family, sending everyone but himself and his wife out to search the mansion for his sister. Even then, with Catt and Rocky, that left only three pairs of searchers. No one was to separate, this time.

Rocky squared her shoulders as she turned away from the group. Guilt consumed her. Lucy was her friend, and she might have put the girl in danger. Although Rocky didn't underestimate her the way her brothers did, the fact of the matter was that she had unwittingly sent Lucy on the trail of a French spymaster. Even trained spies hadn't been able to catch him. Lives hung in the balance, due to Rocky's blunder.

Catt cupped her shoulders in his warm palms. "I know you're angry with yourself, but we need you right now. We're grasping at mist. Help me think. V must be someone we know, someone in the house, right?"

She nodded. "There is a chance he had help inside the house, but we combed through the lives and secrets of everyone. We didn't find anything that pointed to one of them being an accomplice."

"We didn't find V either," he reminded her. "We must have missed something."

She bit her lower lip hard. *She* had missed something. But what? "If he's a member of the staff or family, he'll know the layout of the house."

Catt nodded his agreement. "He'll know which areas are off-limits to guests, and which will be unlikely to be occupied even by family."

"The family wing." Rocky slipped her hand into Catt's and towed him toward the orchestra. The music drowned out all hope of conversation or explanation, but she quickly slipped through the door and up the steps, dropping his hand. When he shut the door behind him and followed her up the dark, narrow staircase, the music was muffled somewhat.

Near the top, she explained. "The library. Lady Belhaven doesn't go in there, neither does her son, Lance is occupied, and at this hour Stanley is more interested in liquor, gambling, or women than books. It's the perfect, secluded place."

"Then lead on."

They slipped quietly down the darkened corridor. Light glimmered from select doorways in case the Belhavens returned above stairs—Stanley and Lady Belhaven's rooms, her favorite parlor. As Rocky approached the far corner of the manse, she saw the hint of candlelight seeping from beneath the door to the library as well. Her breath caught. She'd been right.

Balling her fists, she started toward that door, but Catt caught her. He spun her toward him, his hands bracketing her shoulders. She couldn't see his face well enough to make out his expression.

"Think, Rocky. If we burst in, we might startle him into hurting Lucy. We have to approach this smartly."

"How?"

"I'll fetch Morgan and the others. Keep watch on the door and don't go inside until we have backup."

Gritting her teeth, she nodded. She didn't like to remain inactive, but she had to, for Lucy's sake. As Catt slipped away again, she retreated to a darkened doorway and waited in shadow.

A faint gasp emanated from inside the room. "No, don't—"

That was Lucy's voice!

Forgive me, Catt. Rocky couldn't stand immobile. She had to try to do something.

She dashed to the door. Finding it unlocked, she threw open the latch and stepped inside. Every muscle in her body was tense, expecting to find the room splattered with red blood or a man forcing Lucy to his whims.

The only red was that of Lucy's costume as she leaned out the open window and peered at the snow beneath. She was alone. The moment she heard Rocky's footfalls, she turned. Her face was pale, her expression bewildered.

"He...he went out the window."

Rocky dashed to the window. Drat, it was two stories up! He must have shimmied down a pole that ran up the side. She stared at the footprints in the snow. Could she shimmy down there in her costume? She started to put one leg out the window when a hand grasped her arm.

"No! It's too high, you'll be hurt!" Lucy pulled her back and Rocky realized she was right. Besides Monsieur V was long gone and her first duty was to make sure Lucy was unharmed.

"Did he hurt you?" Rocky scoured Lucy with her gaze, wanting to lift her red pelisse and check beneath but she didn't dare.

The younger girl frowned. "What? No, of course not. It was all a big misunderstanding."

Rocky frowned. "It was."

"Yes." Lucy smiled. "He said you misinterpreted his words, that he never meant to imply you weren't capable because of your gender. You tend to do that, Rocky." She looked bemused. "Oh! And he wanted me to give you this, as an apology." She passed Rocky a single purple lily.

Rocky froze. She couldn't breathe as she accepted the flower. She ran her trembling fingertips over the leaf. Pin holes.

Men darkened the doorway. Catt in the lead, but the Duke of Tenwick was hot on his heels, with Gideon and his wife behind. They looked frantic.

"Lucy," the duke exclaimed. "Thank Heavens. When we couldn't find you…"

The girl crossed her arms and lifted her chin. Her ebony curls bounced. "I'm not a child, Morgan. I'm perfectly capable of looking after myself."

"You left with a man." Morgan's face clouded. "And where is he?"

Lucy pointed toward the window. "He went out there."

Morgan dashed to the window. "Gods teeth! He's getting away!" He vaulted out the window with Gideon and Catt close behind.

"Well, that's unusual," Lucy narrowed her eyes at the other women. "Just what in the world is going on?"

Somehow Rocky, Felicia and Phil managed to dance around the truth until the men came back red faced and huffing.

"He got away." Morgan narrowed his gaze on Lucy. "Just what were you thinking coming up here alone with a man?"

She looked appalled. "Nothing happened. I was looking to speak with him on Rocky's behalf. Surely you don't think..."

The duke's expression was stony. Giddy looked relieved. He wrapped his arm around Felicia's shoulders and tucked her into his side.

His eyes gleaming with questions, Catt approached Rocky and herded her into the corner, slightly out of earshot. She used his body to cover her movements as she tried to reach into the mouth of the lily to discover whether or not there was another note in the throat. Not that she would be able to decode that or the leaf without the cipher.

Catt stopped her. He took the lily from her and passed it behind him, to the duke. Tenwick also ran his fingers over the leaf, frowning. He gave an almost imperceptible shake of the head. Rocky took that to mean that it wasn't the same code she and Catt had uncovered previously, for all that it was delivered in the same manner.

Rocky balled her fists. This was *her* fault. Monsieur V had escaped because of her blind insistence on sticking to a theory rather than considering all options. Not to mention, he was now on to the fact that she'd been spying on him.

She tried to move past Catt, to give the Graylockes free rein of the room as Lucy convinced her brothers that her virtue was the same that it had been down in the ballroom.

Catt barred her path.

She gritted her teeth and raised her gaze to meet his. "We have work to do."

He stepped closer and lowered his voice. Normally, she would take comfort in the strong heat of his body, but not today. "He's gone, Rocky. Do you really think he'll return now that he knows we're on to him?"

No. Blast it all, she'd lost their only lead and she still had no idea who it was!

"That doesn't mean he doesn't still need to be caught." And she would do it, no matter what the cost. She'd let down the duke after he'd given her such a chance at a better life, and even entrusted her with this. She wrapped her arms around her torso.

Catt, seeming to notice that she was a hundred miles away, cupped both her cheeks and forced her to look at him. "He does, but you don't have to do it alone. You don't have to do anything alone. You have me now."

He looked into her eyes, swore, and ran his fingers through his hair. At his outburst, the others in the room quieted.

He didn't pay them any mind.

"Rocky, you have my support for life, if you'll have me."

Her mouth dropped open. "What?" She blinked several times, wondering if she'd imagined the words. "Are you..." She couldn't say the words. What if she was wrong? Yes, they'd taken to sharing a bed, but otherwise, their relationship was the same as ever. A deep friendship, with the strong ties of love between them.

"I am. Rocky, you mean the world to me. I love you. Will you marry me?"

Her throat tightened. She couldn't imagine spending a day without him. His support and love carried her through times when she'd be liable to tear herself apart with worry. He truly did lift her higher, not tear her down.

And she loved him, too.

She blinked away tears. "Yes. I love you, too. Yes."

Catt swept her into a tight embrace as Lucy whooped.

"Finally! Yours was the longest courtship in history."

Frowning, Catt released Rocky, though he tucked her into his side to mirror Giddy and Felicia's embrace. He faced Lucy. "What do you mean?"

The young woman rolled her eyes. "Oh, please. Don't play coy. Everyone knew you loved each other but the two of you."

Rocky exchanged an incredulous look with Catt. They had?

Across the room, Felicia chuckled. She tipped her face up to Gideon's. "Told you so."

Well, perhaps everyone but Gideon. Shaking her head, Rocky tucked her face into Catt's chest. She'd definitely found herself the better man.

Epilogue

Morgan's office in the house he shared with his wife wasn't as large as the one he once had at the ancestral Tenwick townhouse where the rest of his family resided. In fact, it barely fit all the members of the spy ring he'd called for a meeting. He'd already sent a message to Strickland, Lord Commander of Spies, though he wasn't in attendance.

Morgan stood behind his desk chair, which he'd insisted his wife take. Although Phil was several months away from delivering their first child, her feet were constantly sore and swollen and he wasn't about to let her stand on them any longer than necessary. She did enough of that while she worked on her inventions. He rested his hand on her shoulder, taking solace from her presence.

His brothers looked worried. At the back of the room, Gideon stood with his arm wrapped around his wife. His green eyes were hard. Likely he'd already pieced together what Morgan had gathered them here to say. Felicia looked no less grim and determined. If Monsieur V had been standing among them, she might have ripped him to shreds.

There was no doubt in his mind that she had a spine of steel, as she'd proven when she'd insisted on staying on as a Crown spy after she and his brother had completed the serum that he'd contracted her to make.

Jared, Phil's brother and a pivotal double agent in the French ranks, stood next to the couple, his expression serious. Tristan lounged against the wall next to the desk. He hadn't brought his wife—Freddie, though she knew of the spy network and Tristan's part in it, hadn't joined their ranks after her brush with espionage. Her mother, on the other hand, was present. Mrs. Vale perched in the sole chair across from the desk, her face composed as she clasped her hands in her lap. Although she hadn't been used for any missions since her last—keeping an eye on the French spymaster previous to Monsieur V—had concluded, she spent much of her time with her two daughters, a circle which also included his mother and sister.

Neither his mother nor his sister knew of the family's involvement in the British spy network, and to save them both the grief of worrying, Morgan hoped to keep it that way. After this business with Monsieur V, he didn't know how he would be able to do that.

His gaze rested on the last two people in the room, standing side by side with their backs to the closed door. Catt squirmed beneath the force of Morgan's stare, but Rocky met him boldly, her chin set. They'd been tasked with the impossible, and in a way they had succeeded. They'd uncovered Monsieur V's identity.

As the spy network had unmasked, Monsieur V—or Benjamin Faulker, as he'd gone by in Lady Belhaven's household, an identity which he'd likely abandoned by now—was as slippery in his daily life as he had been in his traitorous efforts. Lady Belhaven, whose memory was failing, was the only person in the household who truly interacted with him. He took his meals with her rather than the staff, and attended to her needs when others weren't about, even keeping a room on the family wing rather than among the other servants.

Rocky and Catt both agonized over the fact that they'd discounted him. During the private chat Morgan had had with both of them, Rocky confessed that she'd even encountered Benjamin once or twice in the hothouse, though he had used the same slippery methods on her to avoid her suspicions. He'd even lied to her to try to sway her toward thinking Lance was Monsieur V. Whether Faulker had known who she and Catt were all along or was simply covering all his bases remained a mystery.

Monsieur V was a master at manipulation. He used his words to paint a picture of himself in the eyes of whomever he spoke with. Oddly enough most that had come in contact with him could provide only a vague description of what he looked like. It was as if he had used some sort of mind control. Morgan didn't understand it, but Rocky was far from unintelligent. If she had been caught in the spymaster's web of words and led to discount him, it was no wonder that no one else in the network had been able to find him. They'd come so close...

Morgan was disappointed they hadn't been able to capture the slippery spymaster, but at least they had run him off before he could impart the information that would be so devastating to England. He couldn't very well blame Catt and Rocky for something he hadn't been able to accomplish, either. Although he'd lessened their fears on that part and insisted they remain in the network, he couldn't bring himself to forgive Rocky for involving his sister.

Given the single-mindedness with which she'd taken to the streets to attempt to uncover where Monsieur V had gone to ground, she didn't forgive herself, either. Fortunately, she had Catt to temper her. They made a formidable team. And, since their romantic relationship didn't seem to be interfering with their work, he allowed them to remain as such. He'd always known the two of them would be a force to be reckoned with, should they learn to put aside their differences and work together. It was gratifying to see that he'd been right.

Tightening his hold on his wife's shoulder, Morgan straightened his spine. Phil lifted her hand to rest it over his, a comfort.

"Monsieur V has vanished into smoke," he announced.

No one contradicted him. From their grim expressions, they'd expected as much, even those who hadn't been tasked to try to track him down.

"He was using Lady Montrose's matchmaking service to pass along the message to fake couples. Lady Montrose is not involved. Our eyes inside the French network—" He nodded to Jared. "—have informed me that the network is without direction. No one, as far as we can tell, has been given any instructions since the night of the masquerade. It's possible Monsieur V has been run out of London, or even England, but I cannot count on it." With a sigh, he fingered the streak of white by his temple. "I deciphered the code he gave to my sister. It said nothing of consequence and was merely a taunt letting us know that he's onto our game. He's toying with us. He knew that we installed spies in the hothouse, and he either knew or suspected that we'd cracked his initial code."

Silence reigned in the office for a moment before Mrs. Vale asked, "Do you think he has an informant inside our network?"

Her head turned only slightly toward the back of the room before she stopped herself and held still, but Phil noticed. Her hand tightened on Morgan's.

He squeezed her shoulder, offering his support.

"Everyone in this room is loyal to the Crown. As for the others in the network...we're looking into the possibility." He looked to each of them in turn. "We have to keep our eyes and ears peeled for signs of his return, or if someone else takes over the network in his absence. Right now they seem to be in chaos, and we can use that to our advantage. Without direction, some agents are having a change of heart. Others might seek power for themselves and give themselves away. We're mapping our every corner of the French's network here in London as much as we can, and insinuating spies close to them to keep an eye out." He nodded to Mrs. Vale, who had once performed such a service in Britain's name.

She returned the gesture, though she looked nervous, as though he might ask her to do it again. He wouldn't. She'd made it clear nearly a year ago that she'd only separated from her husband and put herself in such a position in order to provide for her children. They were her priority.

His gaze dropped to the swell of Phil's belly. He understood Mrs. Vale's protective instincts too well. He squeezed his wife's shoulder, keeping his worry contained for the moment. At least insofar as their child was concerned.

"Faulker made it a point to steer clear of the staff at Lady Belhaven's. Catt and Rocky barely saw him. I'm not sure any of them can rightly identify him. But my sister saw his face and seems to be one of the few people who can profile a clear description. We think he exerts a form of mesmerism over those he talks to that clouds their memory of his facial features. Lucy seems to have been immune to it and with Lady Belhaven's failing memory, Lucy might be the only person aside from Lady Whitewood, the traitor we've caught, who can identify him. There is every possibility that he might perceive her as a threat." Morgan swallowed. He rested his gaze on Jared. "I don't know if he knows of the extent of the Graylocke involvement in the British spy network. Given his parting message, I assume he does. We'll need to know the second any of his spies become active."

Jared nodded.

Morgan turned his attention to Mrs. Vale. "You're often with my sister. I'll need you to protect her as much as you can. Find excuses to spend time with her, so she's never out of the sight of a member inside this room." He looked to them all, begging them with his gaze. "We can't let him get to her. For our family, we must be vigilant."

Nods bobbed around the room, everyone's expressions mirroring his. The Graylocke family, with all its extensions, prepared for war.

And his sister was in the middle of it.

Also By Leighann Dobbs

Regency Romance

***

Scandals and Spies:

Kissing The Enemy

Deceiving The Duke

Tempting The Rival

The Unexpected Series:

An Unexpected Proposal

An Unexpected Passion

Dobbs Fancytales:

Dobbs Fancytales Boxed Set Collection

———

Western Historical Romance

***

Goldwater Creek Mail Order Brides:

Faith

American Mail Order Brides Series:

Chevonne: Bride of Oklahoma

Contemporary Romance

***

Reluctant Romance

Sweetrock Cowboy Romance Series:

Some Like It Hot (Book 1)

Too Close For Comfort (Book 2)

Witches of Hawthorne Grove Series:

Something Magical (Book 1)

About Leighann Dobbs

USA Today Bestselling author Leighann Dobbs has had a passion for reading since she was old enough to hold a book, but she didn't put pen to paper until much later in life. After a twenty-year career as a software engineer with a few side trips into selling antiques and making jewelry, she realized you can't make a living reading books, so she tried her hand at writing them and discovered she had a passion for that, too! She lives in New Hampshire with her husband, Bruce, their trusty Chihuahua mix, Mojo, and beautiful rescue cat, Kitty.

Find out about her latest books and how to get discounts on them by signing up at:

http://www.leighanndobbs.com/newsletter-historical-romances

Connect with Leighann on Facebook:

https://www.facebook.com/leighanndobbshistoricalromance/

Bio:

Although Harmony Williams has always had a fascination with plants, her lack of a green thumb put a swift end to any hope of becoming a botanist herself. That hasn't stopped her from writing about them, though! Between the *Scandals and Spies* series and the *Ladies of Passion* series, she's written over six botanists into her books. Learn more about Harmony and her books at *www.harmonywilliams.com.*